IN YOUR HANDS

A Joy Universe Novel

LOUISA MASTERS

In Your Hands

Copyright © 2020 by Louisa Masters

Cover Designer: Reese Dante www.reesedante.com

Editor: Hot Tree Editing

All rights reserved.

No part of this book may be reproduced in any form or by any means without the prior written consent of the author, excepting brief quotes used in reviews.

This is a work of fiction. Names, characters, places, events and incidents either are the product of the author's imagination or are used fictitiously, and any resemblance to persons, living or dead, business establishments, events or locales is entirely coincidental.

To the extent that the image or images on the cover of this book depict a person or persons, such person or persons are merely models and are not intended to portray any character or characters featured in the book.

Paperback ISBN 978-0-6483374-8-5

In Your Hands

When Grant Davis stepped into the job of assistant director at Joy Universe, he knew he was taking on a challenge. The AD before him left a mess nobody thought could be cleaned up—but Grant loves nothing more than beating the odds. Over a year later, he's convinced there's something hinky going on. The solution: an independent audit. What he doesn't expect is that the head of the audit team will be his old college crush.

Luke Durrant's come a long way since he last saw Grant, the man he had a steamy night with back in college. He's been married, divorced, has a successful career, and is now a parent. But one look at Grant brings all the old feelings crashing back.

With Grant's job in Luke's hands, two insecure kids, and a host of nosy coworkers, it seems like professionalism is the only option… but who wants that? Grant and Luke are willing to take the shot for a second chance at happily ever after.

And then Luke's ex turns up….

ONE

Grant
———

March

This is the moment I've been waiting for.

Sounds dramatic, doesn't it? Like something extraordinary is going to happen. Well, it is, but probably not like you're thinking. I'm about to go into a meeting with the big bosses, where they almost certainly plan to rake me over the coals. Rightfully so—my district is performing woefully. But I have a plan.

To be honest, it's really not *that* woeful. We're still doing better than one of the other districts, and on par with a third. Plus, my predecessor ran the place into the ground, so I've had a lot of cleanup to do. But that doesn't change the fact that things should be better, and I'm responsible. I'm in charge, so I'm the one who takes credit for the wins and needs to rectify the losses. When things go wrong, it's my job to come up with a plan to fix them.

Which is why I scheduled this meeting.

I knock on the door to the conference room Malcolm and Seth are using as an office while they're here.

Wait. Am I going too fast? Time for a quick recap?

My name's Grant Davis, and I'm an assistant director at Joy Universe. If you've been living under a rock, JU is the second-largest theme park complex in the world. We have four theme parks in the complex, about twenty hotels, a few campgrounds, and a world-renowned shopping and entertainment complex, including the nascent but already critically acclaimed Joy Village Theater Company. Which is why Malcolm and Seth—Malcolm Joy and Seth Holder, CEO and CFO respectively of the parent company, Joy Incorporated—are here. And now is a great time to talk to them, because the opening weekend for the new theater company was a monster success.

A muffled voice calls for me to enter, so I do. Seth is over at the mini fridge tucked into the sideboard, rummaging for bottled water, but Malcolm is kicked back in a chair with his feet on the conference table. He puts them down and stands as I enter and close the door.

"Afternoon, Grant," he says, coming around the table and offering his hand. I shake it, then Seth's.

"Thanks for seeing me. I know you're busy," I begin as we all settle around the table. They exchange glances. I know what that means—they'd intended to meet with me anyway. I just preempted them.

Good. That means I have the upper hand.

"I want an audit."

The blunt words have almost the same effect as if I'd thrown a brick through the window. Both men jerk upright, shock written all over their faces. For a second, I wonder if I've gone too far—they're both in their early seventies, after all, and I definitely don't want to be known as the guy who gave the big bosses heart attacks. But they seem healthy enough, just surprised.

"An audit?" Seth finally asks.

I nod. "I'm not happy with how things are, and I want to get everything out in the open. I want a management consultant to go through my district with a fine-tooth comb and identify where all the problems are so they can be fixed."

Malcolm studies me with narrowed eyes. "Okay," he says slowly. "I believe this is where I'm supposed to say, 'But Grant, identifying the problems is part of your job.'"

I smile.

Seth sighs. "How bad is it?"

Pasting on my most innocent look, I spread my hands. "We won't know until after the audit."

"That bad, huh?" Malcolm picks up a pen and begins tapping it on the table, staring into the distance while he mulls it over. "Does this audit need to cover the whole company, or just your district?"

I pretend to consider it. "I suppose auditing the whole company couldn't hurt. Plus, it would make the people in my district feel less anxious."

"Less anxious, or more secure?" Seth asks sharply.

I shrug again. "Aren't they the same?"

Malcolm puts his pen down. "I have just one question. Why didn't you ask Ken for this audit?"

Ken's the director of JU and my direct boss. Technically, he runs things around here. In reality, he plays a mean round of golf and pisses a lot of people off.

Unless you're family.

And therein lies the crux of my issue.

But I can't prove there's even a "real" problem without hours and hours spent compiling evidence, some of which I don't have a good reason for poking my nose into. There aren't many things in the company that I don't have clearance to see, but if you look in unusual places often enough, people start to wonder why.

Hence the reason I need this audit. A team of people whose job it is to poke into every file, every nook and cranny, ask intrusive questions and observe employee interactions.

"Ken's a really busy man," I say. "And for an audit of this scale, you'd need to know, anyway. So… I thought I'd cut out the middleman, so to speak." I try not to be obvious about the fact that I'm holding my breath. I'm taking a huge chance here—I basically just accused the director of Joy Universe, who they trust to run this huge arm of their dead uncle's company, of negligence and incompetence—at the very least.

Malcolm stands and paces over to the window. Seth looks at his cousin's back, then at me.

"As you say, this is a huge undertaking," he says gravely. "The cost alone will be prohibitive. Plus, it will take at least a year, likely more, and cause massive upheaval here at JU…. Are you certain this is necessary, Grant?"

Malcolm turns around, and they both look at me. The first trickle of sweat wends its way down my spine. This is it. The moment I've been waiting for.

"Do my district first. If it's evident that the only problems there are of my making, or lack of decent management on my part, you can fire me. I'll go without protest."

Seth studies me, but Malcolm nods.

"Then we're having an audit."

TWO

Luke
———

I stare with trepidation at the door leading from the garage into the house. If—*when* I walk through that door, I'll have to deal with a moody teenage girl and a hyperactive preteen boy. That's okay. I'm used to that. I actually *love* that—love them. But tonight I'm going to tell them that we're moving across the country, away from everything they've ever known, and I am *not* looking forward to that.

This is the best decision for all of us. This is a good thing. I firmly believe that. Things have been really hard for the kids the last five years—first their parents dying, coming to live with me and Matt, getting settled, then Matt leaving. They've both been in therapy the whole time—that wasn't the plan, but things kept happening and it was never a good time for them to stop—and it was actually Ginger's, their therapist, idea that we try a fresh start.

"You have no family here, and from what the kids have said, a lot of your 'family friends' chose Matt's side in the divorce," she explained to me when I went in for our monthly debrief. She doesn't tell me what the kids confide in her, but she gives me a general idea of their emotional health and sometimes steers me in the right direction. "Neither of the kids have very close friends. They drift between friendship groups—Mila especially. And now it seems that Jordy wants to avoid restaurants where you went to eat with Matt. A clean slate might be a good idea, especially if you can find somewhere with a strong sense of community."

"Like a small town?" I asked, pained. "I'm a business consultant. How will I find work in a small town?"

She shrugged. "It might mean a commute for you. I don't love that idea, because it'll cut back on the time you can spend with them, but it's worth looking into. Just think about it."

So I did. I'd do anything for my kids, if for no other reason than I owe it to their mother, who I loved like a sister. I thought about it for weeks, even went as far as getting online and checking out the job market—first sticking to California, though outside the greater LA area, of course, then gradually widening the circle. There were some good jobs going, even some that metaphorically made my mouth water, but they were all in big cities, and when I looked into satellite towns and bedroom communities within commuter distance, there was nothing appealing.

I was actually on the verge of looking into a career change when I went to work this morning and a golden opportunity dropped in my lap. Seriously. If I believed in a god, I would say they were watching over me.

It started about five minutes after I sat at my desk. My phone rang with a call from on high: Malcolm Joy, the CEO of Joy Incorporated. That's not unusual, by the way —most of my special assignments come direct from his office. My everyday job is to keep the company policies at best-practice level and make sure they're being implemented correctly, but occasionally a situation will flare up somewhere and I'll go haring off to that department to investigate and smooth things out.

A special assignment always gets the adrenaline flowing. As great as it is to keep things running smoothly in a company as huge and complex as Joy Incorporated, it's solving problems that's the most exciting.

So I took myself off to Mal's office with a barely leashed sense of anticipation. His cousin, Seth, our CFO, was with him, and they both wore somber expressions that made me think there was something awesome in store for me.

And there was.

"We want you to do a full audit of Joy Universe."

I blinked. A full audit? Of Joy Universe? That place is huge. It would take months—probably closer to a year and a half, depending on what kind of team I had. But more… it would mean relocating. Joy Universe is in Georgia.

As my brain raced to process what that meant, Seth held up a hand. "I know this is a lot to ask. You've got the kids, you're raising them alone, and uprooting them and moving across the country is no easy feat. We're prepared to cover all your relocation costs, plus we'll provide accommodation in Joyville. A house with a yard in a good neighborhood close to good schools."

Schools. Crap. What was the school system like in Joyville, Georgia, population… hell, what even *is* the population?

"We'll also pay for a housekeeper to take the kids to and from school and supervise them until you get home at night," Mal promised.

Wow. They were really pulling out all the stops. I don't even have that kind of system here—Mila is responsible for collecting her brother from school and walking him home. Luckily, both schools are close to the house and there are a ton of people around, but we still run into issues when either of them has after-school activities. Fortunately, I have a lot of flexibility in my hours and can work from home occasionally.

"Tell me about the issue," I said slowly, and Mal grimaced.

"We don't know," he admitted. "One of the ADs has requested an audit of his division and hinted heavily that it's necessary across the whole company. He's put his job on the line pending the results, so we're inclined to take him seriously. He's also one of the execs we've had an eye on for future advancement, so…" Mal spread his hands.

"Our gut feeling is that if he says it's needed, it's probably needed," Seth summed up. I leaned forward in my chair.

"I don't need to tell you what this will cost," I warned, and they both nodded.

"We know," Seth said. "It keeps me up at night, thinking about it. But better to find problems now while they can hopefully still be fixed."

I sat back. "What kind of team would I have?"

"What do you need?" Mal countered, and I scanned my mental file on JU.

"Three consultants, at least. An accountant. A lawyer. And five support staff, minimum. And none of them can be existing employees of JU."

"We know that," Seth snapped, but it was likely at the thought of how much that would cost rather than anything else. "Fine. Do you have anyone in mind?"

"Yes." I considered it. "There are a couple of people in my department here, and I know some people on the East

Coast who might be interested in a project like this. How do you want to handle things here while I'm gone?"

"So you'll go?" Malcolm looked hopeful, some of the stress lines on his face easing.

I shrugged. "I need to make sure the kids are on board, but tentatively yes."

Which brings me to this moment, staring at the door. I had a phone conference with the kids' therapist during our respective lunch breaks, and she was very enthusiastic about the idea. So all I have to do now is convince Mila and Jordy.

Swallowing hard, I reach out and open the door.

Jordy looks up from the kitchen table, where he's eating… a Pop-Tart? Not a healthy snack. And not good this close to dinner. Maybe a housekeeper to supervise the kids is just what we need.

"Hey, Uncle Luke. What's for dinner?"

"Pasta," I say absently, noting the number of silver wrappers on the counter. How many of those things has he had? "Are you going to be hungry?" I need to stop letting him and Mila convince me to buy that crap if he's going to eat a boxful in one sitting.

"Sure. I love pasta."

Does that mean he wouldn't be hungry if it was something he didn't like? I've been doing this parenting thing for five years now, and I was a hands-on uncle before that, but I'm still stymied by the way kids think.

I decide to let it go. "Where's your sister?" Probably in her room.

"In her room."

Yep. That would worry me less if she was on the phone with friends all the time, or even—shudder—sneaking someone in to make out with, but she's just reading or on YouTube or some other solitary pastime. I remind myself all the time that teens can be moody, and when I was her age, I would have killed for some solitary time in a space all my own. She's doing okay in therapy and the school is happy with her, so I can't ask for more.

"Go get her, will you, pal, while I change." I don't usually have to wear actual suits to work, but dress pants and a shirt are bad enough. Jordy obediently gets up and races off to Mila's room while I dump my laptop bag in the tiny room I use as an office and go change into shorts and a T-shirt. By the time I get back to the kitchen, Jordy's back at the table, about to rip into *another* silver foil package, and Mila is leaning against the counter, arms crossed, looking impatient. I grab the packet from Jordy as I pass.

"Uncle Luke!"

"You won't have room for dinner," I chide. "Besides, you've had enough of this crap." I sweep up the pile of other wrappers and crumple them into a ball, which I then lob at his head. His delighted shout is worth anything in the world.

Grinning, I turn to wash my hands and study Mila's petulant face from the corner of my eye. What I would give to see that kind of happiness from her again. She took it really hard when Matt left, and her laughter has been way too rare since.

I turn off the tap, dry my hands, and start rummaging for what I'll need to make dinner. "So, I need to talk to you guys about something. It's pretty cool." I deliberately avoid using the word "important," just like I avoid sitting them down for this conversation. Better to make this casual. "Jordy, can you set the table, please?" I hand Mila a saucepan and move out of the way so she can fill it with water.

"Are we going on vacation again?" Jordy asks, opening the drawer for the placemats. I took them to Aspen over

Christmas, wanting to avoid the dumpster fire we'd had the previous Christmas, which was the first after Matt left and a total disaster. Mila seemed to be okay with celebrating the day as long as we were away from the at-home traditions we'd had before. It was a great break for us all, anyway, and the kids took to skiing like they'd been born doing it. Jordy loved having a white Christmas.

"Not exactly, but kind of," I prevaricate, and Mila snorts.

"That makes no sense, Uncle Luke," she mutters. "Whatever it is, just say it."

"I've got to do some work at Joy Universe, and you're coming with me." There. That's the literal truth, but not quite as blunt as "we're moving across the country." I'm easing them in.

"For *real*?" Jordy shouts, and I look at him, surprised. They've been to JU before—I get a huge discount on park passes and the hotels, so Matt and I bought them family trips there twice when Mandy and Bill were still alive, and we took them once ourselves—coincidentally, only a month before Matt left. So I wouldn't have expected him to be so excited.

"Do we get to take time off school?"

Oh.

Yeah, now I get it.

"Maybe a bit," I hedge, because there probably will be a couple weeks while we move and settle.

"How long for?" Mila asks, and I can tell from her voice and the way she's looking at me that she knows this is not just for a week or a month. I meet her gaze steadily.

"A year at least. Probably closer to two." And if they're doing better there than they ever were here, I'll move heaven and earth to keep us where they're happy. Or if they want to go somewhere else, we can do that too.

Mila nods slowly, while Jordy scrapes his jaw up off the floor. "A year?" he whispers. "We're going to live at JU for a *year*?"

Um. Better clear that up. "Actually, we'll be living just outside JU, in Joyville. And you'll be going to school there." Just in case he's got any ideas about spending his days on roller coasters.

The joy in his expression dims, but only a little. "But we can still go to JU on weekends and stuff, right?"

"Yes," I say firmly, and his grin comes back. I turn to Mila. "What do you think?"

She shrugs. "School here, school there. Who cares?"

Uh-oh.

"Is there a problem at school, Mila?" Do I need to ride my white charger in to save the day? Because I will. I was the fifth person ever to hold her when she was a baby. I changed her diapers more often than I care to remember. I will wade through rivers of blood to protect her, even if it's from some snot-nosed high school bully.

"No," she says, looking me right in the eye. "But… I guess there's nothing special about it, either. Somewhere new won't be a big deal."

"Maybe it will be," I counter. "Joyville will for sure be different from LA, anyway."

She seems to think it over. "I guess."

"So I can tell my boss we're going?"

"Yes!" Jordy pumps his fist and dances around the kitchen table. Mila smiles, a little reluctantly, at the sight.

"Sure. Let's move to Georgia."

Two weeks later

Have you ever packed up two kids and moved across the country in ten days? No? I don't recommend it. And we had help—Joy Inc. paid for a packing and moving company to take care of the big jobs. The kids and I just had to pack up our most personal stuff. A house was organized for us in Joyville—we were sent pictures and video of three that a realtor deemed suitable, and we picked the one we liked best. It's a little bigger than our house here—which I've arranged to have rented while we're away—plus it has an amazing backyard, complete with entertaining area and pool. The pool sold Jordy, and although he's a good swimmer, I'm going to have to strongly remind him that there will be no pool use without an adult present.

Kiara, the director of human resources at JU, sent me some information on the schools in town, for which I want to bow down and worship her. The schools closest to our house seem to be pretty good, so I've arranged for the kids to start there next week—I want to give them time to settle into the house first, and we have to hire a housekeeper. Again, Kiara stepped up there and prescreened a half-dozen or so candidates for me. We just have to meet with them and decide who we like best. I've gotta say, if Kiara turns out to be part of the issue that necessitated this audit, I'll be devastated, because she's saved my bacon with this move.

So today is interview day. I decided to let the kids be part of the process, since they're the ones who'll see this person the most, and they've each prepared some questions they'd like to ask. I vetted the questions, of course, which was probably just as well, since Jordy wanted to ask one about stinky farts. I know I must have liked fart jokes when I was a ten-year-old, because I remember laughing at them so hard I nearly peed myself, but they just don't seem to be that funny anymore.

Growing up is a terrifying thing.

The interviews go pretty well, overall. Number one is a middle-aged mother of three whose kids are in high school and don't need her at home as much. I like that she's got current experience with teenagers, but when she suggested it might even be a good idea for the kids to all hang out together after school, part of me worried that her focus would be too torn. That's a dick attitude, I know, and completely selfish, but it seems like she's looking for a way to make extra cash while still being home with her kids, and I want someone who's completely focused on my kids while they're working. Plus, what if Mila and Jordy don't like her kids? Or vice versa? Mila and Jordy both decline to ask her questions, which tells me more than any words could what their opinion is.

Number two is a woman in her late twenties or early thirties with a lot of energy. All three of us like her, though there is a moment toward the end where it seems like she's flirting with me. I brush it off as me being so hard-up for any kind of romantic or sex life that I imagined it, but after she leaves, Mila says, "Uncle Luke, we can't hire anyone who wants to get in your pants."

Annnnd number two goes into the "maybe" pile with number one.

Number three is a guy in his sixties, just retired from his insurance adjuster job and looking to keep busy. None of us has any problem with him, and he even laughs when Jordy sneaks in his fart question, so I put him in the "seriously consider" pile.

Number four calls to apologize and explain that she's taken a job elsewhere. I take her résumé off the stack and am a little puzzled when I realize there are two more, but only one more interview scheduled. Has Kiara messed up? Or did I?

Turns out, it's neither. Numbers five and six turn up together. They're twins in their early twenties, looking to job share.

"Do you mind me asking why?" I can hear the dubious note in my voice.

Justin and Jasmine both smile, but it's Justin who answers. "We're both artists—I paint, and Jas works with glass. Ultimately, we plan to pay the bills with our art, but we need some help in the meantime. We were both looking for part-time work but thought job-sharing something like this might be ideal."

"We're both early risers," Jasmine says, picking up from her brother. "One of us can easily be here to sort breakfast and get the kids to school, then get started on the housework and errands. At some point during the day, the other will take over, then pick the kids up and run them to activities or supervise homework. And between the two of us, it's likely one will be available if you need extra help on weekends or at night."

I'm warming to the idea. I also like the fact that they're so young—while they'll still be authority figures, it would be in a much-older-sibling way, which might be good for Mila, especially.

"I try to be here for breakfast," I comment, more to see what they say than anything else. Justin shrugs, and Jasmine smiles again.

"That's fine, we can just come for the school run, then," Justin says. "Or if you do have to go in to work early, you can call. Like Jas said, we're early risers. I know Mila's old enough to watch Jordy for an hour in the morning, but she'd probably rather be doing something else."

Mila beams. I was actually surprised by how accepting

she was of having a housekeeper-slash-babysitter. I thought she'd have argued about being old enough to not need anyone, but now I think about it, she's probably relieved not to have to be responsible for Jordy. I know she loves him, but that doesn't mean she wants to "mother" him.

Guilt bites me in the ass. I should have thought of this sooner. Mila has enough on her plate just being a teenager, not to mention her parents' deaths and the divorce. She doesn't need me expecting her to grow up before her time, too.

We talk a while longer, but I'm pretty sure I know how the kids are going to vote, and I agree. Jus and Jas, as they insist we call them (and I manage it without cringing, for which I deserve a medal), are basically perfect for us.

They've barely left before Jordy declares, "We need to hire them. They're super cool. Jus said he used to play baseball. Can I play baseball?"

"Of course," I say immediately, because it's the first time since Matt left that either of them has *wanted* to take part in an extracurricular activity, and I'm encouraging the shit out of that. Jordy could ask to take up snipe hunting and I'd be all for it. "We'll find a Little League team for you, and I'll arrange my work schedule so I can come to your games. Jus or Jas will need to take you to practice, though."

His face lights up. This move is already the best thing I've ever done for my kids.

I look at Mila. "What do you think?"

She shrugs, but she's smiling a little. "I like them."

I nod. "Me too. Okay, let me check their references again, and if everything's good, we'll tell them they can start whenever they like. We could probably use some help with unpacking these boxes."

THREE

Grant
───────

"Does anyone know what this audit is all about?" Dimi asks, beer bottle in one hand, scooping up chips with the other. "I mean, I doubt it will affect us that much, since JVTC is so new. But are you likely to need me for stuff?" He's asking Derek, who he used to work for. I can see why he would be worried—running the Joy Village Theater Company is a hell of a job, especially since he's pushing to expand as fast as he can, and if he needs to take time out to help Derek, it would be a real pain in the ass.

Derek shrugs. "I doubt it. You left everything so organized, there won't be any problem with them finding what they need. The trouble will be with all the records for the past six months—none of my assistants have been worth crap since you left."

"You're just comparing them to Dimi and being too hard on them," Trav chides, handing Jason a glass of wine and then coming to perch on Derek's lap. We're on the back deck at Derek and Trav's place. Derek grabbed me as I was leaving the office and told me he'd decided on an impromptu Thursday night cookout, since that's the only night Trav and the others have off from the theater, and I was elected to help him do the grocery run.

Thursday night chillaxing with friends while someone else grills steaks? Who can argue with that?

"That's true," Dimi says. "Not everyone can be as awesome as me."

Derek throws a chip at him.

"Before you get too far off topic," Jason intervenes, "someone tell me about this audit."

Dimi shrugs. "A memo went out to all department heads a couple days ago. Starting next week, there's going to be a business process and efficiency audit of all districts and departments. The audit team will have access to everything, and we're to make ourselves available to answer questions at their convenience. That's all I know."

"That's pretty much all any of us knows," Derek adds. He's also an assistant director at JU, and a fucking brilliant one. His district is the most profitable and usually the best in the customer feedback rankings. My goal is to give him a run for his money—I'll get there, too, as soon as this audit helps me solve my problems. "But I did hear that they're starting with Grant's district."

All heads turn in my direction.

I shrug. "I got a memo telling me that, and that I'll have a nine o'clock meeting with the audit team on Monday. Other than that, I know nothing." Except that I'm the reason this is happening.

Trav and Dimi make commiserating noises, but Derek looks at me searchingly. Damn it, have I given myself away somehow? I return his gaze as innocently as I can manage, and finally he looks away.

Later, after dinner's been eaten, I'm making my way back outside from a trip to the bathroom when he corners me in the kitchen. Well—I have to walk through the kitchen and he's in there pulling a cake out of a bakery box and says, "What haven't you told me?"

I could probably have pretended not to hear him and kept going, but that would only make things worse. Instead, I go to the cupboard and pull out some plates for the cake. "I expressed some concerns when Malcolm and Seth were here," I say carefully. "It's possible they took that seriously and that's why we're having an audit."

I set the plates beside the cake on the bench and reach for the cutlery drawer, but Derek grabs my arm.

"Is there a problem I should know about?" His face and voice are dead serious.

I shake my head. "I can't say. Honestly, I can't," I rush on when he opens his mouth. "I just know that I've run into some issues that get worse the more I dig. I think…" I hesitate. I trust Derek absolutely, but if he thinks something is screwing with his district, there's no way he'll wait to let the audit ferret it out, and chances are he'll send any evidence we can use deep into hiding. "I think that you and Dimi had such a tight grip on the reins that it's unlikely you have anything to worry about." That's the truth. Derek has his finger on the pulse of everything in his district, and all his people know they can have his ear if they need it. It's what I've been trying to work toward. It's unlikely anything major would be able to sneak past him—especially when he had Dimi as his right arm. Now, though…

"How bad have your new assistants been?" I ask, and his mouth sets grimly. It's an unusual look for him—normally he's all smiles.

"Bad. I know you all think I'm just spoiled by Dimi, but there's been some definite incompetence that just shouldn't happen with experienced employees. I really thought hiring from within JU would minimize the learning curve, but…" He shakes his head.

"Between you and me, if you needed to hire another assistant, I'd look outside of JU. But other than that, I really don't think you need to worry."

He nods and picks up the cake. "Can you bring the plates and forks?"

"Of course." I'm not dumb enough to think he's going to leave it at that, but hopefully he'll let the audit do the heavy lifting.

I don't really know what to expect from the audit. I've worked in teams that have been audited before, at other companies, but never when I've been in charge, and never on this scale. I'm not surprised when I get a message over the weekend that Ken, the director of JU and my boss, wants to have a management meeting first thing Monday morning. I respond to tell him that I'm meeting the audit team at nine, and he immediately changes the management meeting to seven thirty. I wince. That's not going to make him—or me—popular.

Sure enough, there are a lot of grumpy faces in the boardroom at seven twenty-five on Monday morning. Some of that may be due to the audit—nobody's going to be happy to have all their files and records dug through and their people interviewed. Except me, of course.

It's a full management meeting, so all five assistant directors are here, plus Dimi, who kind of sits outside the usual business structure—something Derek sweet-talked Malcolm and Seth into—and all the heads of cross-business functions, like HR, marketing, events, accounting, entertainment... you get the idea. Ken's the last to arrive, which is not unusual, and he looks the grumpiest of all.

"You all know we're being audited. I don't know what's been fucked up or which of you did it or how corporate found out, but it'd better be the last damn problem they find. You're to cooperate fully with the audit team, even though they're going to completely disrupt things here for fuck knows how long, and be warned, if they find serious problems, you'll wish you never came to work here."

I sneak a glance at Derek beside me and see him glancing back. Ken's a dick, always has been, but he's never sworn during a meeting—or ever at work that I know about—and he's never threatened company employees before.

Around the table, there's general shifting and a low murmur—of agreement? Dissatisfaction? I can't tell.

"Grant," Ken barks, and I turn my attention back to him.

"Yes?"

"Your district is first. What have you been told?"

"That my district is first and that I have a meeting with the audit team at nine," I say calmly.

"Nothing else?" His gaze bores into me, as though he suspects I know more.

"Nothing else." I do know more, but not because it was told to me in a memo. And I'm not sharing it.

He grunts. "The audit team has been allocated the second-floor conference room for the duration of their stay, and one of the storerooms adjacent to it has been cleared out for them to conduct interviews in or use as an office or whatever they decide. Make certain all your people know to stay away unless invited. I won't have any allegations made that we're trying to interfere with the audit. The head of the audit team has been out here before—he's in charge of the business consulting team at corporate. Some of you will have met him. He knows how things run here, so hopefully he won't interfere too much with our day-to-day."

For the next hour, Ken goes through a list of commonsense dos and don'ts, often repeating himself, and basically just bores the pants off us all. What's the point of this meeting? He hasn't told us anything we might actually need to know—just threatened our jobs and treated us like interns on the first day.

By the time we finally get to leave the conference room, I'm desperate for coffee. I check my watch—if it were anything but Monday morning, I'd have time to hit the coffee cart in the lobby, but there's not a chance of that right now. The line will be out of control.

"Coffee?" Derek asks, seemingly reading my mind, but I shake my head.

"I don't have time." There's an edge to my voice that says how much I want it, and he pulls a face.

"We could grab the crap from the break room."

I consider that carefully. It's entirely likely that drinking that sludge will make me feel sick for the rest of the morning, but on the other hand, it's caffeine.

"Let's go."

Ten minutes later, kicked back in Derek's office, we're both already regretting it.

"How can it be this bad?" Derek is studying his cup as though it holds the answers to all life's questions. "It's coffee. It's naturally good, right? For a company with such a good track record for looking after employees, it's weird that they'd fuck up something so basic."

I take another sip and wince. "Do you think they do it on purpose? Like, if they make it bad to drink, we'll spend less time in the break room and more time working?"

He shakes his head. "They subsidize the coffee cart," he reminds me. "And that takes us even further from our desks."

We're both deliberately avoiding the subject of the audit, of course. There's nothing to say, really, and in about five minutes I'm going to have to go and meet with the audit team, so… I take another sip of coffee and wonder if this was the right thing to do, after all.

Yes.

Probably.

Definitely.

Yeah, okay. I just need to get over the nerves. Ultimately, this is going to help. As long as nobody other than Derek ever finds out it was my idea. They'll kill me.

"I came in yesterday and found that my latest assistant tried to approve an emergency concessions order for the park," Derek says abruptly, and I snap to attention.

"Oh." It seems that the hole left by Dimi has given people ideas about expanding operations. Emergency concessions orders are an easy way to skim—or they would be, except any nonstandard order needs to be approved all the way up the chain to the AD's office. I know in some districts, the AD allocates permission to an assistant for that, but Derek never has, not even when his assistant was Dimi. The buck stops at the top. My predecessor allocated permission to an assistant in the past, and now I can't take it back. IT and I have been wrangling over this for nearly a year—they swear they've changed it a million times, but there are three people in my district who have permission, and no matter how many times I ask them *not* to approve anything, to forward it directly to me, somehow that never happens.

"Oh, you were in a meeting and it looked urgent."

"I'm so sorry, I forgot. I'm so used to doing them."

"Whoops! Next time."

The problem, of course, is that since they have permission, it's hard for me to officially sanction them for doing something wrong.

"Yeah, *oh*. She's still on her trial, so I'm going to move her somewhere less dangerous and find another assistant. From outside JU, I think. Maybe bring in some new blood."

I meet his gaze. He's being a little paranoid—I don't think anyone is hovering outside the door, eavesdropping, or that they've planted listening devices, but I don't really have time to get into this conversation now anyway.

"Good plan." I stand. "Let me know if you want another set of eyes on applications. I guess I'd better go meet the audit team."

FOUR

Grant
———

The second-floor conference room is largely unused, with most people preferring to use the bigger boardroom upstairs or the cozier meeting rooms. So it was the obvious place for Ken to put the audit team. It's also relatively private, with the door coming off the corridor not far from the elevator, rather than off the open-plan office space, where people can watch the door from their desks. Sure, there are more people loitering in the corridor than usual this morning, but they can really only hang around with nothing to do for so long before they have to get back to work.

I give everyone assembled a sharp look, especially Toby, the head of events, who knows better. He shrugs and grins unapologetically before wandering off with the rest.

A quick, bracing breath, then I knock on the door. It's actually not closed properly and moves a little.

"Come in!" a woman calls, and I push the door the rest of the way open and step inside to close it behind me. The room is a hive of activity—there's about a dozen people setting up computers, unpacking boxes, and generally just buzzing around.

"Hey," that same female voice says, and I turn my head to see an elegant brunette with a friendly smile. "Are you Grant Davis? If not, you're in the wrong place." She keeps smiling as she says it, but I suddenly have no doubt that if I was just snooping for gossip, she'd throw me out on my ear.

"I'm Grant," I assure her, holding out a hand.

She shakes it. "Diana Wessert. Luke will be back in a second—he just went to check out the closet we'll be using for interviews." She rolls her eyes, and I snort.

"I wish I could say something clever and witty here, but it really is a closet. We were using it as a storeroom."

We're laughing when the door opens behind me. I half turn, glancing over my shoulder at the newcomer, then stop and turn the rest of the way.

This is not good.

At all.

Fuck.

How could I have let this get past me?

Why didn't I check to see who the head of the audit team would be?

Fuck.

His gaze meets mine, then he does a double take. "Grant?"

Luke Durrant.

I force a smile.

"Luke. Hey. Wow, I did not expect to see you here."

"Ditto. I don't know why, but I never thought the Grant Davis I was meeting this morning was you. It's been a long time."

Diana looks between us. "You two know each other?" She sounds delighted by this, and I shoot her a curious look.

"We went to the same college, had some classes together," Luke says, and it's true, but also feels like a knife to the gut.

"So long ago," I manage, then screw up all my courage and add, "I heard you and Matt got married a while back. Congratulations."

His face closes. "We're divorced."

Part of me says, *oh fuck*, because hello, faux pas, but there's another part, the part that was nuts for this guy seventeen years ago, that stands up and cheers.

"Sorry," I mumble. "Well, this is awkward."

Surprisingly, he laughs. "Don't worry about it. Come on, let's get this meeting started, and we can catch up later. Di, I'm going to take Grant back to the small, dark hole that's been allocated as our interview room. You've got things here, right?"

She says something in the affirmative, but I'm not listening. My brain is stuck on the idea that I'm going to be in a *small, dark hole* with Luke Durrant.

It's been a long time since I've had to concentrate on not getting hard in public.

Luke leads the way out of the meeting room, and I deliberately keep my eyes up. It proves a little too difficult, so once I'm clear of the doorway, I pick up my pace to come up alongside him. The storeroom isn't far, and before I know it, we're sitting at a tiny table in a room that can never be mistaken for anything other than what it is. The dark part isn't true, though—the industrial florescent lighting bounces off the walls and is guaranteed to give anyone in here too long a monster headache.

"So," he begins, "have you ever been part of an audit before?"

Okay, strictly business.

"Yes, but only when I was a small cog in a big machine. I've never been audited when I was in charge."

He smiles, but it's a distant, professional smile. "The process is pretty much the same. You might be privy to more information this time around, but we generally don't share much until we have our final findings. We'd also like you to encourage your employees to cooperate as much as possible."

"Absolutely," I say firmly, ignoring the fact that his lips are so amazingly puffy. They were a cause of great distraction to me in college. "They've already been told to be helpful by me and by corporate. If anyone gives you problems, please file an official complaint."

His head comes up, surprise all over his face. "You don't want us to advise you first?"

I shake my head. "No. Everyone's aware that they're required to cooperate. There's no need for warnings." Plus, there are a few people who are likely to be deliberately obstructive, and having me tell them—again—that they need to cooperate will do no good. An official warning from HR, on the other hand, may help. At the very least, it'll be a record of the issue.

He still looks surprised as he makes a note on his tablet. I'd be surprised too, and probably thinking not-too-flattering things about an executive who seemingly hung his people out to dry like that. Hopefully once he starts digging, he'll get an idea of why and stop thinking I'm an asshole.

The meeting goes quickly. Luke outlines the structure the audit will take and what kind of input he'll need from me. I give him all the information he asks for, which he has access to anyway, and answer his questions about who holds what roles within my district. We set up a weekly meeting so he can ask more questions as he and his team find things, and I reiterate several times that the audit team has full access to me anytime they want to know anything. I'm not sure what Malcolm and Seth told him, but by the time he wraps things up, I think he's beginning to suspect I might have had something to do with the audit.

We stand, and I'm just about to say something about catching up over a drink when it hits me: he's the head of the audit team. My job is literally resting on what he discovers. He's *investigating* me. And I'm going to see him probably every day until they're done with my district, and then he'll still be around after that.

Fuck.

Panicking, I thank him for his time and then bolt.

I make it back to my office and slump into my desk chair. Shit. Shitshitshit. Luke Durrant is here. He's single. He's still hot as hell, only now with maturity. He's still just as smart and driven, given that he's risen to a position of such responsibility in a company the size of Joy Inc. And yet, I still can't act on my attraction.

Wait. Maybe he's not single? He said he and Matt were divorced, but that doesn't mean he hasn't met someone else.

Jealousy surges.

I bang my head on the desk. It's been seventeen fucking years, and I'm still tied in knots by this guy. One night. One fucking night was all we ever had, because I was too chickenshit to grab any of the opportunities that came up.

My phone beeps, and I seize on the distraction.

Lunch? I want to hear about your meeting.

Glancing at the time, I text Derek back.

Let me just send an email to Ken.

Talking to Derek is a good idea. I can trust him to keep his mouth shut, and maybe if I tell someone about my unrequited crush, it'll exorcise it.

Sure.

FIVE

Luke
———

That was the weirdest meeting I've had in a long time.

I can't say ever, because... well, I've had some weird meetings. Before I started working at Joy Inc, I was with a small business consultancy, and one of my clients owned a new age shop. He insisted on consulting the cards before making any decisions, including whether or not to offer me coffee before we began our meetings. I don't have anything against people wanting to defer to whatever higher power they believe in, but that was probably taking it too far.

Still, my meeting with Grant ranks right up there.

First... Grant Davis. He's older, a little heavier-set, but in the way that shows he's a man now rather than the "new adult" he was then. The thick black hair and gray eyes are the same, as well as the tall, broad frame. I can't believe he's here—and that it never occurred to me that the Grant Davis who's an assistant director at JU is the same guy who introduced me to Matt seventeen years ago. Sure, it's a pretty common name, but still, you'd think it would have at least crossed my mind to wonder. I guess I've just been too distracted lately.

And then the whole thing about not wanting to be advised if his people are uncooperative. That set off a huge alarm bell. It's pretty obvious, especially when you combine that with the fact that Mal and Seth allocated the order of departments to be audited, that Grant's the AD who expressed concerns to them. That's fine. It's not going to change how I'll do my job. He wanted this audit, so we'll do our best to find whatever it is he thinks is here.

I push open the door to the conference room. I'll tidy my notes from the meeting and discuss them with the team and then think about lunch. These first few days are really going to be about familiarizing ourselves with everything.

The room is already much more organized than it was a few hours ago. Di is fanatical about everything having a place—she's the best person to have as a second-in-charge. I can leave things in her hands for a few hours, a few days, or a few weeks, if necessary, and know they'll be in tip-top shape when I get back.

She looks up from where she's tapping away at her laptop. "There he is. We've all been anxiously waiting for your return," she declares.

Stu snorts. "Speak for yourself."

I head over to the end of the table, which has been allocated as my work area. "Aww, Stewie, you didn't miss me?" I tease. Di and Stu and one of the admins, Natalie, are the only people I brought with me from California. Everyone else is new to working at Joy Incorporated, although I have worked with some of them before in other jobs. I sweated bullets choosing the team for this audit.

As I wake my laptop up and log in, Stu makes a face. "You know you're the center of my universe," he deadpans. "I'm just not as eager as Di to hear all about this guy you apparently went to college with."

"I am," Nick, our lawyer, says. "The look on his face when he saw you says there's a story there, and I am all about the gossip."

I blink.

"What? There's no story, not really. Definitely no gossip. Grant and I were in some of the same classes in college. I was a sophomore; he was a senior. We worked on a group assignment together, went and got food a couple times. One time we ran into some friends of his, and he introduced me to Matt, my ex. I guess we hung out a bit for the rest of the year, once Matt and I started dating, and then Grant and Matt graduated and I haven't seen Grant since." And I had a dizzying crush on him because he was so awesome, and we fucked one night. But they don't need to know that. It's better if I forget *all* about that night if I'm going to be able to work with Grant.

"That's it?" Di sounds disappointed.

"That's it," I confirm. "Sorry, everyone."

"You should be," Nick grumbles. "I expected to hear that you and he had had wild, crazy monkey sex. Or at the very least that you'd *wanted* to."

I say nothing, but the back of my neck gets really, really hot.

"You did!" Stu leaps up from the table, pointing at me in a really obnoxious way. "You had sex with him!"

"Shhh!" I hiss, looking at the door. It's closed, and I really hope nobody was walking past, because Stu is *loud*. The last thing I need is for anyone to think the audit team sits around gossiping about sex instead of working.

I mean, we do sit around and gossip about sex, but it's *while* we're working.

"I… This is a totally inappropriate conversation," I tell the circle of delighted, fascinated faces.

"You *did*," Nick insists. "Right? Please say yes."

Jesus. This is supposed to be my crack team?

"Have you all ever heard of professionalism?"

"Stop trying to distract us." Di props her elbows on the table and leans forward. "Tell us instead all about how you climbed that man like a tree and did dirty, dirty things to him."

I glance quickly at the team members I don't know that well, worried that they'll be distressed by what basically amounts to sexual harassment.

They look just as captivated as the rest.

Heaving a sigh, I give in. "Before he introduced me to Matt, I had a crush on him. We spent a night together. But then I met Matt, and so…"

"You would have been better off holding out for Grant," Di says scathingly, but I shake my head.

"Then I wouldn't have the kids, Di. Things went bad with Matt, but we had a lot of good years." We did. A lot. Fifteen. "And we don't know anything about Grant. He and I may never have clicked like that."

Max, one the admins I don't know well, claps his hands. "It's a second chance! My wife is going to flip when I tell her this."

What.

"What?"

"You and Grant. Meeting all those years ago but not having it work out. Leading separate lives. And now getting another chance to be together. It's like a Hallmark movie."

Is he high? Do I need to enforce the random drug testing policy?

I just stare at him, not knowing what to say.

"It's so romantic," Natalie says. Natalie, who once told

me that romance was for teenagers who didn't have a grip on reality. What the hell is in the water here?

"It's not romantic," I protest. "And there's no second chance at anything. And it's definitely *not* like a Hallmark movie. Grant may be seeing someone—or married. Even if he's not, that doesn't mean he'd be interested in me." As soon as it's out of my mouth, I know I've made a mistake.

"Right, we've got a job to do," Nick says, grabbing a notepad and pen. "We need to find out everything we can about Grant's personal life."

"No! We have a job to do, and it's got to do with Grant's professional life, not his personal one," I insist. "Have you forgotten that we're auditing his department? Even if I wanted to, I can't *date* him."

There are some grumbles and disappointed faces, but thankfully everyone seems to get the point.

"Okay. Now, since I've got your attention, let's talk about work." I begin going through the notes I made in my meeting with Grant. And if part of me is just a teeny, tiny bit disappointed that they let it go so easily, well, I push that part down firmly and sit on it.

Grant

"There's something you're not telling me." Derek's smiling, but his gaze is sharp.

I sigh. I've given him all the business details of the meeting, but have been putting off this part, because I'm not sure after all if it's something I want to share. I should have known Derek would guess.

"It's not work related," I admit.

He shrugs. "If you'd rather not say, that's fine. But

we're friends, yeah? You can tell me stuff that's bothering you. I won't tell anyone."

It *would* be nice to tell someone about this. Especially because the fact that Luke and I knew each other before isn't exactly a secret—Diana knows, for one.

"The head of the audit team—"

"Luke Durrant?"

"Yeah." Sudden dread strikes me. "Do you know him?"

Derek shakes his head. "Not really. He was out here to do a feasibility study the last time we opened a park, but we never did more than say hello in passing." He tips his head to the side, studying me, and then his face lights up in a smile. "*You* know him."

I grimace. "I used to. We were in some classes together in college. I had a huge crush on him. We… we had a one-nighter the night before my grandmother died, then I had to leave town, and I was going to ask him out when I got back."

"So why didn't you?" Derek is avidly fascinated. Seriously, what is it with this place and gossip?

I shrug. "The timing was never right, and then I introduced him to the guy he ended up marrying—and divorcing."

He winces. "Ouch. Not a good association. Was he rude to you?"

"No." I think back over the meeting. "He was mostly just professional."

"And you were hoping for more?" His tone is gentle, and I heave a huge sigh.

"I have no idea. It was just such a shock to see him. I feel really stupid about all of this. I mean, it's not like we ever actually dated. He's… just a guy I hung around with one year. He was dating someone else for most of it."

Derek leans back in his seat, a calculating expression on his face. I know that look.

"You have an evil plan," I try to tease, but it comes out a little flat, and he shoots me a sympathetic glance.

"It's not an evil plan."

"What's not an evil plan?"

We look up as Dimi pulls out one of the other chairs at our table and drops into it. Derek and I decided to just grab sandwiches from the deli in the Village rather than trying to get a table at a restaurant.

"You don't mind if I join you, do you?" Dimi goes on. "This place is packed." He unwraps his sandwich as Derek raises an inquiring brow at me.

"Of course we don't mind," I say. And we don't. I don't. Dimi's good people. And he might have some insight here.

"Good. So, what's the evil plan?"

"I said it's *not* an evil plan," Derek insists, but Dimi just waves dismissively.

"I worked for you for years. All your plans are evil, even if they don't seem that way. There's got to be something unholy about the way they always succeed."

Derek looks like he's going to argue, so I cut in and quickly run down the situation for Dimi. By the time I'm done, he's put down his sandwich and is staring.

"This is not good," he says, and my stomach knots. "I mean for you," he adds. "It's great for us. I get to start the pool this time."

Oh, fuck. I forgot about that.

"No pool," I declare, trying to sound utterly firm. I do *not* want my colleagues betting on my life.

Dimi ignores me. He's pulled out his tablet, and he and Derek are discussing the best way to take bets about my love life—or lack thereof.

"No pool," I say again. "He's the head of the audit team, guys. Plus, he never knew I had a *thing* for him. Don't make this awkward and uncomfortable for me—and him."

They both hesitate, and I know I've won the pool battle. One thing these two *always* are is consummate professionals. I don't relax, though—just because they're not going to start a betting pool doesn't mean I'm getting off scot-free.

"Okay," Derek says, and he sounds disappointed. "No pool. But I do have an idea."

"The evil plan," Dimi and I say together and then laugh.

Derek rolls his eyes. "The evil plan," he concedes. "Obviously it would be unprofessional for you to ask him out while he's auditing you, and it would just make things awkward for everyone. But he's only going to be auditing you for a few months before he moves on to another department, and once his findings on your district are handed in, there's nothing to stop you dating, right?"

I think about it. Officially, he's right. Of course, there's always the chance that Luke is a really bad auditor and won't find anything, which means I'll lose my job.

I decide not to mention that. Besides, what are the odds that he's *that* bad? The Luke I knew in college was meticulous with details and super organized. He can't have changed so much that he'd miss the huge red flags in the recordkeeping for my district.

"Right," I agree.

"So in the meantime, you should rekindle your friendship."

"Did you just say 'rekindle' with a straight face?" Dimi demands. We both ignore him.

"Think about it," Derek continues. "He's here for the duration of the audit, but he probably doesn't know anyone here, right? Invite him out for a drink one night. We can all go. Or Trav and I will have another cookout. Make it casual. Be his friend. Get to know him again."

Fuck me, Derek has good ideas.

"That's brilliant, Derek," Dimi says admiringly. "The best part is, there's absolutely no pressure. If things develop between you, great, but if they don't, he never has to know you were ever interested, and you have another friend. It's almost diabolical."

"It is *not* diabolical," Derek argues. "Where do you get this shit from?"

I tune them out. Dimi's right—it's an incredibly low-risk idea. I enjoyed spending time with Luke in the past, even without the edge of lust, and hanging out with him now is unlikely to be a hardship—like I said, how much can he have changed? So we become friendly again, he finishes auditing my district, I clean house, and then if he's still turning my crank the way he used to, I ask him out.

A small part of me shrieks in protest. That's the part that nearly made an idiot of me this morning and wants me to prostrate myself at Luke's feet and beg him to be mine. It points out that the last time I waited for the timing to be right before I asked Luke out, he ended up with someone else—that I introduced him to.

Note to self—only introduce Luke to guys who are coupled up.

"It's a good idea."

Derek grins. "Great. I'll stop by the conference room later to introduce myself and invite him out for a drink tonight, then."

"Jase and I can't come—we have Monday night dinner," Dimi says. Dimi is a local boy and has dinner with his family every week. I can't imagine what it would have been like growing up in the shadow of this place, in a town built solely to support it, and then moving back as an adult to work here. "It's probably better that we're not all there the first time, anyway," he continues. "It looks more casual, less like we're checking him out."

"Agreed," Derek says, and I get the distinct feeling that control of the situation is slipping out of my hands. "I'll call you later, Grant, and let you know where we're going."

Yep. I've lost control.

As it turns out, Derek doesn't have to go introduce himself later—we literally run into Luke when we get back to the office. He's on his way out the main door as we're about to go in. It's a real meet-cute—or it would be if it was the first time we'd met.

"Hey," he says, looking surprised and a little spaced out. "Sorry. I didn't see you."

"No problem," I assure him. "Have you met Derek?" I need to let my friend work his famous charm.

"Ages ago, but you probably don't remember," Derek says smoothly, flashing his winning smile and offering a hand. "Derek Bryer."

Luke returns his smile and shakes his hand. "I remember. You're one of the ADs here, right?"

"That's right, good memory. How are you settling in?"

Luke huffs and rolls his eyes. Derek's magic mojo has worked, and he's already at ease. I swear, if someone could work out a way to bottle that charm, they'd make a fortune. "If I never have to unpack another box, I'll be a happy man," he jokes, but doesn't mention the audit.

"Sounds like you need a break. Why don't we go get a drink after work? I'll call my boyfriend to meet us. Grant, you're up for that, right?"

"Sure," I say casually, like I haven't been waiting for him to suggest it. This is starting to make me feel a little dirty. Is it wrong to deliberately plan to make friends with someone for the specific purpose of maybe asking them out in the future, and then get your friends involved in the plot?

Luke shakes his head, a cross between regret and disappointment on his face, and my stomach sinks.

"That's really nice of you, but I'll have to take a rain check. It's the kids' first day of school, and I want to head straight home and see how they went."

Every part of me freezes.

What?

He has kids?

"You have kids?" Derek sounds as surprised as I feel. I don't know why we're reacting this way. People have kids, right? And I haven't seen Luke in seventeen years.

"Yeah, I have two." He doesn't add any more, but I'm compelled to ask,

"How old are they?"

He seems a little taken aback, but smiles. "Mila is nearly fifteen and Jordy is eleven." He hesitates, then adds, "They're my niece and nephew, actually."

Oh.

He's parenting his niece and nephew.

He's such a good person. No lie, I fall a little bit more in love with him right now.

"Another night, then," Derek says, picking up the conversational ball. "Or maybe we can have dinner sometime and you can bring them. If you don't think they'd be annoyed to eat with a bunch of boring old men."

Luke shrugs. "They eat with me all the time. Plus, Mila's at that age where everything annoys her, so what's one more thing? That sounds great."

"I'll be in touch, then," Derek promises. "Were you on your way out to lunch? We won't keep you."

There's a flurry of goodbyes, and the next thing I know, Derek and I are in the building and walking toward the stairs. "You have skills," I say finally, and he snorts.

"You don't. What was with asking him the kids' ages?"

I shake my head. "Honestly, I have no idea. I was just shocked to hear he has kids. I wonder how they came to live with him?"

We hit the stairs and take them two at a time. Three flights like that is a bitch, but seriously cuts down the amount of time needed at the gym.

"I'm sure we'll hear the story eventually." Derek shoots me a sidelong glance. "Do the kids change anything for you?"

Should I be insulted by the question? Because I'm not, and I actually take a moment to think about it. Babies freak me out, always have, but I like the idea of having kids. Not that I'd have kids if Luke and I date, but what I mean is, it wouldn't bother me.

I sound like an ass, even in my own head.

"No," I answer Derek, deciding not to share my thought process. Nobody needs to hear that.

"Then the plan is falling into place."

As we hit the second-floor landing and turn for the last flight of stairs, the small part of me that's still crushing madly on Luke sits up and cheers.

SIX

Luke
———

The first day at JU is just as busy and exhausting as I thought it would be, but I still make sure I leave by five. I bring a pile of work home with me to do once the kids are settled after dinner, but I'm determined to eat with them tonight and check in on how they're feeling after their first day at their new schools.

I drag myself in through the door from the garage to the heavenly aroma of a homemade dinner I don't have to cook and the sight of Jordy sitting at the kitchen table eating an apple and some cheese. I should have hired a housekeeper years ago.

"Uncle Luke!" Jordy's face lights up in a grin, and Jus turns from the stove. "Guess what? Three of the boys in my class play baseball, and they said their team needs more players."

"That's great, Jordy. That might be the team I spoke to today." I sandwiched the call in between bites of my lunch. I meant to call last week, but somehow it kept getting away from me.

"You already called?" His delight makes it worth the indigestion.

"You bet. Your first practice is Wednesday. You've missed a few weeks, but they said it's not a problem."

He scrambles up and comes over to throw his arms around my middle and hug tight. "Thanks, Uncle Luke. You're the best!"

I hug him back, my heart warm and the anxiety that's been with me since we first got guardianship of the kids finally easing a little.

"Did you get any homework, pal?"

He nods and steps back. "Yeah, but I already did most of it. Jus helped me. There's just one assignment I need your help with, but it's not due till Friday."

I swear, it's only the first official day and already I can see I'm not paying Jus and Jas enough. "We'll look at it after dinner, even if we don't start it tonight," I promise, and he happily resumes his seat at the table and reaches for another piece of apple.

I look over at Jus, who's smiling. "We're good here if you want to change," he assures me. "Dinner will be ready in about twenty minutes, but it will keep."

That sounds like heaven. "Let me change real quick and then I'll set the table." I want the kids to see that even though we have help, basic chores are still a part of all our lives. "Mila in her room?"

"Doing her homework," he confirms. "She was in a good mood when I picked her up and had a snack down here with Jordy before."

Which means this is not Jordy's first after-school snack of the day. Does the kid have a tapeworm? Is this something I need to worry about? I've tried to remember if I ate that much when I was his age, but if I did, it never registered.

I head upstairs, making a mental note to ask Jus later. It hasn't been as long since he was that age; maybe he'll remember.

Mila's door is open when I approach, which is encouraging. She's sitting on her bed, tapping away at her laptop, and I flash back to my own teen years when my mom would chide me for studying on my bed and warn that it wasn't good for my back. At the time I'd roll my eyes and ignore her, but now as I have the same concern for my niece, I really miss my mom.

Or at least, the mom she was then.

I tap on the doorframe, and Mila looks up and smiles. "Hey, Uncle Luke."

That smile is so beautiful. Every last ounce of tiredness and stress falls away. "Hey. How was school?"

She shrugs, but it's more a teenager thing than anything else. "Okay. It's weird coming in so late in the school year, but I think it will make next year easier. I won't be the new kid anymore."

That's such a mature way of looking at the situation, and it makes me proud, but...

"Was anyone mean to you?" I have to make sure.

She shakes her head. "No, everyone was super nice, but I'm new. They all have their groups and their jokes, you know?"

I nod and enter the room to sit in her desk chair. "Yeah. It's the same at the office." Well, kind of. It's a bit different because I'm in a position of power. "There were these guys today who were really nice, invited us all over for dinner, but I got this feeling there was something going on that I didn't know about."

She frowns. "Do you think they're playing a prank? Do grown-ups still do that stuff?"

Well, that's a can of worms she's not ready for.

"Some do," I admit, "but I don't think these guys are." If it was anyone else, I might think they were cozying up to the lead auditor, but Grant was never like that when I knew him, and Derek's rep at the company is second to none. "I actually know one of them from a long time ago—he went to college with me and Uncle Matt." As always when Matt is mentioned, her expression shuts down, so I hurry on. "It was just that feeling of being an outsider—they know each other really well, and I'm the new guy."

"Sucks," she commiserates.

"Yep. But like you said, it'll get better." I get up. "I'm going to change. Dinner will be ready soon; can you come down and help set the table?"

"Sure." It seems like she wants to say something else, so I wait. "Uncle Luke, would it be okay if I got a job?"

I sit back down. Where did this come from?

"Well," I start, choosing my words carefully, because work ethic isn't something I want to discourage, "I'd prefer you focused on getting settled in at school right now. School and a job wouldn't leave you much time for just… stuff. Being a kid. Maybe this summer you can find something? Is there something in particular you want to save up for?" She gets an allowance, and although it's not extravagant, it's not stingy either. Plus, I pay for all her school stuff and clothes, and she knows that if she needs or wants anything else, she can ask. I rarely say no. They're good kids, and sensible.

She doesn't meet my gaze, which brings all the anxiety rushing back. "No. I just thought it'd be good to earn my own money."

"We'll talk about it again next month," I promise. "I'll ask at work and see if they have anything for the summer that might suit you." JU is huge, and summer is peak season. I don't know all the workings of the company yet, but I know they hire extra staff during their peak times.

"That sounds good. Thanks, Uncle Luke." Her smile is back, although it looks a little forced, and I wish I knew how to fix things for her.

I go change into shorts and a tee, then just sit on the bed for a minute. I've been so worried that this move was a mistake, but it seems like it's going to work out for the best, even though it's early days. That doesn't mean I'm going to stop worrying. Being a parent is *hard*, and I'm so lucky to have great kids, even after all they've been through.

And then there's work. This audit is a huge undertaking that needs all my attention, especially since it's not exactly routine. I haven't told anyone in my team, not even Di, that we're here because Grant has specific concerns. I'm sure they suspect, because we pulled this all together at the last minute and it's never been done on this scale before, but I don't want to bias them by confirming anything. If it's there to find, they'll find it.

Which means I can't afford to be distracted by a sexy, handsome blast from my past.

I haven't been able to stop thinking about Grant all day. Part of that is because I've been working through his files, but mostly I've been traveling down memory lane. Grant when I first met him was funny, flirtatious, and cocky. When we were assigned to work together, I was guilty of judging a book by its cover and assuming I'd carry most of the workload—if not all. He quickly proved me wrong, and honestly, that keen intelligence and his dedicated work ethic were what really attracted me to him. Campus was full of hot, cocky guys, but hot, cocky guys who took studying seriously? Sign me up.

And now he's back in my life. Just as hot, the cockiness mellowed into a mature confidence that I find even sexier, and now with the addition of an air of authority. Talk about a distraction. Memories of that one night rise, and I squeeze my eyes shut to block them out.

It *was* nice of him and Derek to invite me out for a drink. Like I told Mila, I feel like there's something else going on, but that could just be that the invitation wasn't as unplanned as it was supposed to seem, and that doesn't bother me at all.

Sighing, I get up and head downstairs. Whatever happens at work or with Grant, I can worry about it later. Home time is family time.

We don't even make it to the end of the week before my team begins to notice problems.

That's right, only three and a half days. At this stage, we should still be cross-checking what the filing system is and putting together interview schedules. No wonder Grant was willing to put his job on the line—this is a *disaster*.

Stu comes to me first. He was in charge of liaising with the IT department. One of the first things we do with an audit like this is get the accesses, permissions, and backups for all employees. It's a shitload of information, but it can be invaluable—most people don't realize exactly how much of what they do on a work server or device is recorded and tracked. In case you're wondering, it's everything.

"Luke?" Stu's frowning as he takes the seat beside mine. He's just come back from IT—during our morning debrief, he said he had some questions for them.

"What's up? You look like you need coffee."

"I do. With whiskey in it. Luke, I think someone in IT is allocating system access without permission."

"What?" Fuck me. That's *beyond* a disaster.

"Grant Davis has been complaining for the past year that some of his staff have access that he doesn't want them to. It's been fixed a dozen times at least but keeps reverting. IT is officially calling it a system fault, but the department head knows it's hinky. When I spoke to him this morning, he talked in a circle."

I blow out a breath. "What kind of access are we talking, here? And has Grant been filing official complaints, or just whining?" Please let there be a paper trail. Please please please.

Stu laughs. "Oh, it's official. He's logged them all through the system. The first few are marked as resolved, but the other—" He glances at his tablet, presumably at his notes. "—fourteen are still active and have been escalated. They're all for the same thing: three members of his team have retained access to approve purchase orders at the highest level."

"And isn't that a huge, flashing sign," I say dryly. "So Grant complains to IT, IT fixes it, and then someone changes it back."

"Looks like. But they're being sneaky about it. I think we need to bring in an expert if we want to figure out who it is. There's no way I'd be able to work through the code, and since we don't know who in the department we can trust…"

"Yeah." I sigh. "Okay." Seth is not going to be happy about the expense. On the other hand, if people are skimming, putting a stop to it will save a ton of money. So… are people skimming? Or is there something else going on? There's even the possibility that it's all completely innocent—

a genuine system fault. After all, we barely had to scratch the surface to find this. If there were a scam going on, wouldn't they have gone to some trouble to hide their activities?

"Do we have anything else that looks dubious? Who are the people whose access keeps getting bumped up?"

Stu taps his screen a couple times. "Macy Taylor, Hank Jeffries, and Lena Teller."

"Did you say Lena Teller?" Amelia, the consultant who's been going through employee records, looks up from where she's sitting halfway down the table. "Sorry. What are you talking about? Because I was going to talk to you sometime later about Lena Teller."

"What about her?" It can't be this easy. It really can't.

"I've never seen anyone have so many complaints made about them and not have faced any consequences."

The room goes dead quiet. None of us are naïve.

"How many complaints?" I'm almost afraid to hear the answer.

"Thirty-seven in eight years."

"Jesus fucking Christ," Di gasps. "How is she still working here?"

Amelia shakes her head. "Most of them were withdrawn. They remain on record because they were lodged through the system but aren't actually attached to her employee file. It's only because we dump the data and then restructure it that I can see them all. About half a dozen were made inactive because the employees who filed them left the company before they could be investigated. Only four were ever fully actioned. In each of those, Lena was let off with a warning."

"Doesn't JU have a three-strikes policy, same as Joy Inc?" Stu raises an eyebrow at me.

"Yes. She should have been fired when the third

complaint was found to have merit. Were they minor issues?"

Amelia looks back at her laptop. "A lot of them are, but bullying comes up more than a few times. In the early days, she had quite a few warnings for tardiness and one or two for misuse of company time and equipment."

I look at Stu, but he's already tapping away at his tablet, checking Lena's IT logs.

"It looks like not much has changed," he says after a minute. "She spends a lot of time online shopping at work."

Drumming my fingers on the table, I think about it for a minute. This definitely needs to be looked into, but so early in the audit, it would be irresponsible to focus only on one angle.

"Amelia, see if you can find out why all those complaints were withdrawn and why Lena never saw disciplinary action. Do it quietly, though. Stu, track down which orders have been approved by those three and see if any were unnecessary or went missing—you know what to look for. You both have two days to focus on this, and then we'll debrief. Everyone else, if you find anything that might intersect with what Amelia and Stu are working on, make them aware and hand it over. Good?"

"Good," Stu affirms, and Amelia nods.

The knock at the door startles all of us.

"Come in," Nick calls. The door opens and a tall blond man appears.

It's Derek Bryer. I get up and walk around the table.

"Derek, hi. Is there something I can do for you?"

He beams his charismatic smile around the room, and I can practically feel my team falling in love with him. I don't blame them—the other day, I felt pretty much the same way.

"I just came to invite you and your kids to brunch on Saturday."

Oh. That's... weird. Brunch?

My expression must show what I'm thinking, because he laughs. "It was going to be dinner, but Trav, my boyfriend, only gets Monday and Thursday nights off from work, and I figured a non-school night would be easier for you."

"That's really thoughtful of you." It is. A weeknight means making sure the kids do all their homework before I get home from work, then hustling them out the door pretty much right away. Plus, they wouldn't get their wind-down time before bed and would probably end up going to bed late. It's not that big an issue with Mila, but Jordy's really started growing lately and he gets grumpy without the right amount of sleep. A Saturday morning is much easier. "Thank you, we'd love to come." It will do the kids good to see me making friends. Not to mention, it'll do me good to actually make friends. Mine in LA gradually dropped away after Matt left and my life became a frantic mix of work and kids with no time for anything else, and as great as my work friends are, here at JU I don't know anybody who doesn't report to me, and it does impact our relationship.

Derek's smile gets brighter, which I wouldn't have thought possible. "Great! Do you mind if I invite a few others? Dimi and Jason, who work with Trav, and Grant, of course."

Nobody makes a sound, but I can *feel* ears pricking up behind me.

"No problem. Just let me know where and what time. Can we bring anything?"

"Nope." Derek shakes his head. "We've got it covered. I'll text you with the details—you're in the company directory, right?" He barely pauses for me to nod. "Are either of your kids fussy about food? It'll probably just be bacon and eggs and pancakes, stuff like that."

"That's fine, neither of them is very picky." It's only half a lie. Mila will try anything once and eats most foods, but Jordy avoids vegetables like they're poison. It's unlikely we'll be having broccoli for brunch, so he should be safe.

"See you Saturday, then." He aims another grin around the room, and I swear Natalie actually sighs. Then he's gone.

I turn around as the door closes and face my team. There's a mix of knowing grins and expectant smirks, even from the ones who don't know me that well. A word of advice: if you ever have to put together a team to work with, go against all your instincts and pick people you don't feel that comfortable with. When you pick the ones you like and get along with, you end up in situations like this.

"Sooooo…" Surprisingly, it's Nick who starts. I really thought it would be Stu or Di. "You're having brunch with Grant."

"And my kids, and four other people," I say dryly, returning to my seat. "Sorry, but there's nothing salacious about this."

"Oooh, *salacious*." Di puts a hand to her throat. "You're thinking salacious thoughts about Grant."

Okay, there's no point in even trying to defend myself here. It's a no-win situation.

"Don't you all have work to do?"

Yeah, it's the workplace equivalent of telling kids to go to their room, but I've really got no other option.

"Sure, in a minute," Nick says. "I want to know how things went from having to be completely professional because we're auditing his department to you having brunch with him."

Would it look like weakness if I bashed my head against the desk? "You were here," I tell him patiently. "You heard everything Derek said. That's how I'm going to be having brunch with a group of people, some of whom we'll be auditing."

"Some?" Di perks up. "Wait, was that Derek Bryer? The guy whose name was in the news because of the murder at his hotel last year?"

"Yep," Max announces. "He met his boyfriend the same day as the murder."

We all look at him. "How do you know that?" Di asks. Max blushes and shrugs.

"I talk to people. I like knowing things."

A plan unfurls in my mind. "Max, you have a new mission," I announce. "Your job is to collect gossip. Be subtle, but I want to know what the story is with Lena Teller." For her to have had so many complaints made against her, she has to be hated by her colleagues. I suspect the bullying is the reason most of them get withdrawn, but someone will talk to Max. He's got that best-friend vibe.

"Great! My wife will be thrilled. She loves hearing all the gossip." He shoots me a sly look. "She really wants to know anything that happens between you and Grant."

I can't win.

"Okay, look. How's this? While we're auditing Grant's district, things between us remain friendly and professional. I'll see him on Saturday at Derek's, and if he's as nice as I remember, I'll make an effort to reconnect as friends."

There are disappointed frowns around the table, and Stu opens his mouth to argue, but I hold up a hand.

"If it turns out that I still feel attracted to him and his audit doesn't result in him being fired, then when it's done, I'll ask him out like I should have back in college. Okay?" I can't believe I'm negotiating with my team about my dating life.

Not that I really have a dating life.

Maybe I should thank them.

The tiny current of excitement in my stomach at the thought of *reconnecting* with Grant suggests that I should send a thank-you fruit basket.

The frowns have all disappeared, replaced by sunny smiles.

"That's fair enough," Nick says. "Let's get cracking on this audit. The sooner we're done with Grant's district, the sooner Luke can get some!"

On the other hand, this might have been a mistake.

SEVEN

Grant

Saturday morning rolls around fast.

I mean, it's not like I'm nervous about it. Why would I be? It's just brunch with friends. I've done that a million times before. No need for nerves.

Did I fool you? Because I sure as shit didn't fool me.

I need to pull myself together. This is getting ridiculous. I think the problem is that Luke and I never actually dated. If we had, things would be easier now. He'd be my ex, or that guy I dated once or twice and we were better off friends. This unresolved crush and the memories of that one fantastic night are playing havoc with me. Youthful, hormonal thoughts are overtaking my rational mind. It's hard to forget, even all these years later, what being with him was like.

In a word: Hot.

I mean, we were both young and energetic, so that only helped. But my memories of that night center around us not being able to get enough of each other. We went for hours—long, sweaty, writhing hours. At one point we took a break and dozed off, and I woke to Luke's mouth on my cock. I hadn't thought it could get hard again that night, but I'd been wrong. The sex was incredible, and we really only started out expecting it to be a way to blow off steam, but long before we collapsed into sleep near dawn, I was thinking of more. He was just so… perfect for me. Fun. Funny. Smart. Interesting. And we'd just proven our sexual compatibility.

But it never turned into more, and we both moved on, even if I can't get past my crush.

It doesn't help that Luke is still really appealing to me. I've dated widely over the years, but there's still a certain type of guy I'm more attracted to, and Luke's basically it. He's average height, about five nine, and slimly built, which makes me feel all masterful and protective (no snarky comments, please—I already know I'm an ass), with blondish-brown hair that he's always worn short and big brown eyes you could get lost in. Add to that his air of competency and being in charge, and that's it for me.

If I'd met him—or re-met him—under any other circumstances, I'd already have hit on him. But with the audit complicating things, it's best I wait. Derek's plan is good—I should stick with it.

And meet his kids.

I've never really been around kids that much. My brother has two, but he lives in England now and we've never been close anyway. I send gift cards on their birthdays and a big family present at Christmas, but honestly, I'm not entirely sure off the top of my head how old my nieces are. I always have to stop and think about what year they were born.

So… kids are uncharted territory.

Shaking my head, I get out of the car and wander up to Derek and Trav's front door. Trav opens it with a smile.

"Hey, Grant, come in. We're out back."

I follow him through the house and out onto the back deck. Derek turns from his fancy barbecue, which I swear could double as a space shuttle.

"Good morning," he greets, and Dimi and Jason look up from where they're picking at a fruit platter. There are hellos all around, and then I settle into a chair and pour myself a drink from the jug of orange juice.

"There's champagne if you want a mimosa," Trav offers. "We figured with kids coming it was better not to premix."

"Thanks, I'm good," I decline. I need a clear head. Let's face it, my encounters with Luke so far haven't exactly shown me to be intelligent and witty. I'm skating by on the fact that he hopefully remembers what I was like in college—back when I thought I was invincible and the world was my oyster.

Dimi leans forward. "We've told Jason and Trav about the plan."

Jesus. This is going to be a disaster.

"Can you try really hard not to turn this into a humiliating experience for me?"

Jason laughs. I don't know him as well as the others—it's only been a few weeks since we met—but what I know, I like, and he and Dimi seem to complement each other perfectly. Even if I think it's weird to work so closely with your boyfriend. "Sorry, Grant, but they've already made special allowances by not starting a pool. Asking for more is greedy."

Dimi elbows him. "You make us sound awful," he complains, then turns his glare on me. "This is not going to be humiliating. How would that fulfill our goals?"

Goals.

Dread settles in my stomach.

"Please tell me you don't have a list of SMART goals

and a spreadsheet for tracking them," I beg. I know Dimi too well.

He looks away, and I groan.

"Seriously?" Derek sounds slightly incredulous, which is faintly reassuring. "Can I see?"

"I'll send it to you," Dimi promises, then raises an eyebrow at me. "Do you want it too?"

"No," I say firmly. "Yes. Wait." Fuck. The business-minded side of me thinks this is a good idea—a clear outline of targets to work toward. The rest of me thinks it's insane. What the hell did he put for goals, anyway?

I'm just about to ask when I hear the doorbell peal inside the house. All thoughts of goals go out the window, and I turn to stare at the door as Trav walks through it.

"Be cool, Grant," Dimi chides, and he sounds amused. I like Dimi. He's a great guy. But right now, I want to strangle him.

Even if he is right.

I can't keep staring at the door, or I'll freak them out. I make myself turn back to Jason and Dimi and pick up my glass of OJ.

"This is a disaster already," I mutter. Surprisingly, it's Jason who reassures me.

"It's not. You'll relax once they're here. It's always hard with someone you've crushed on for a long time." I want to answer, but the screen door opens right then, and Trav comes out, followed by two kids and then Luke. The kids look a little wary, but Luke is smiling.

"Hi," he says, his gaze skimming over us. Derek comes over from the barbecue to shake his hand.

"Hey, glad you could come." He turns his attention to the kids. "Mila and Jordy, right? I'm Derek."

Jordy sticks out his hand for Derek to shake, and Mila

rolls her eyes. "It's nice to meet you," she says dutifully while Derek and Jordy shake hands, but then she smiles.

"Thanks for inviting us," Jordy announces, sounding very rehearsed, then adds, "Uncle Luke said there would be bacon."

I grin. The kid's got his priorities right.

"There is bacon," Derek assures him. "Let me introduce you to everyone, and then I'll start cooking it." He turns toward the table and points us out one by one. "Dimi Weston, Jason Philips, and of course, Grant Davis, these are Luke, Mila, and Jordy Durrant."

"Marks," Mila corrects, then gives a little wave.

"I beg your pardon, I shouldn't have assumed. Mila and Jordy Marks," Derek amends.

Dimi and Jason get up and move forward to shake hands. I wait my turn, and Jordy looks over at me.

"Why are you 'of course'?"

Huh?

My confusion must show on my face, because he clarifies, "He said you were 'of course' Grant Davis."

Oh. "Your uncle and I have met before," I tell him.

"Actually, Grant and I have known each other for a long time," Luke explains. "We went to college together."

Jordy nods. "It's good that you've got friends here, Uncle Luke." He looks around. "What else are we having other than bacon?"

Trav gestures toward the barbecue. "Eggs, mushroom, sausage, tomato, spinach, pancakes, and toast."

Jordy looks at his uncle, who sighs and says, "No, you don't have to have the mushrooms or spinach." The grin he gets in response stretches from ear to ear.

"Can I help cook?"

From the way Luke's brows rise, he wasn't expecting that, but he shrugs and looks at Derek and Trav.

"Fine by me," Derek declares. "I could use an assistant. My last one dumped me to run a theater company."

Dimi groans. "You were the one who nominated me for the job. And anyway, I've never helped you cook before. Jordy, keep a close eye on the bacon, or he might eat it all before it gets to the table."

Jordy's gaze narrows on Derek, who shakes his head.

"It's all lies. Do you want an apron like mine?"

He studies the apron for a moment, then nods. "Yes, please. Are you sure it's lies? Because I would totally cover for you if you gave me some too."

I swear, I laugh so hard I think I might piss myself.

Luke settles into the chair beside mine. "Was that extortion? Or blackmail? Whatever, I think I might be failing at this parenting thing." He's clearly joking, but my gaze happens to land on Mila's face just as she flinches.

"Nah, that's just ingenuity," I say. "Dimi, you've got a million brothers and sisters—it's normal, right?"

Dimi looks at me a bit strangely, because there was nothing about Luke's tone that indicated he needed reassurance, but he nods. "Sure. We used to trade keeping each other's secrets for all kinds of benefits. Extra bathroom time, each other's desserts, use of the car—or someone to drive us places. Sneaking bacon is for beginners."

Mila laughs, and Luke's face lights up.

"Do you guys want some juice?" I ask, reaching for the jug.

"Yes, please," they say in unison, then both laugh.

"How many brothers and sisters do you have?" Mila asks Dimi while I pour.

"Not a million. Grant has trouble counting sometimes. There are eight of us. I'm number four."

She shakes her head. "I can't imagine having that many siblings. Did you ever just want to strangle them?"

Luke groans. "First Jordy with extortion, now you with homicidal tendencies. Maybe it's genetic. You were both predestined for lives of crime."

This time Mila rolls her eyes. "Stop being dramatic."

"Which school are you at, Mila?" Dimi asks.

"Joyville High. I started on Monday."

"I went there," he tells her, "but it's all changed. They did some huge renovations about five years ago."

Her eyes are wide. "You grew up here? I thought only people whose parents work at JU went to school here."

He nods. "Yeah, that's usually true. My dad worked at JU, but my mom actually grew up here too—both her parents worked at JU. So my family's been here pretty much since the beginning, and we all went to that school."

"That's so cool! What was it like growing up right next door to JU?"

As Dimi fields Mila's questions and draws her out of her shell, Jason asks Luke how he's finding moving to a small town after living in LA. I take advantage of the opportunity to study the kids. They resemble each other but look nothing like Luke. Their hair and eyes are darker, complexions fairer, and the shapes of their faces different. If I had to guess, I'd say they look like the parent not related to Luke.

I think back, but honestly can't remember Luke ever talking about a sibling. He might have mentioned them in passing, but it wasn't important enough for me to take note of and remember for seventeen years—at least, not compared to everything else I know about his home life.

"Don't you think, Grant?"

I zone back in and turn to Dimi. "Sorry, what?"

"Mila was just saying that she wants to get a job, but Luke wants her to wait for summer. I think that's a good idea—don't you?"

Oh, crap. How am I supposed to answer this? I mean, Luke's in charge of her, but I don't want her to hate me right away. That won't help if I start dating her uncle later.

I decide to go with the truth.

"You've just moved here and started at a new school. There's a lot of sh—stuff for you to get used to. It's probably a good idea to wait a few weeks and get settled before adding a job to the mix, and since we're so close to the end of the school year anyway, it makes sense to look for summer jobs."

She doesn't look particularly thrilled, but she nods. "I guess."

"What kind of job are you thinking of?"

Mila shrugs. "I don't know, really. Uncle Luke thinks I might be able to get something at JU."

"Sure," Dimi says. "We hire a lot of people for summer. Most of them are college kids who come to town especially for work, but there's also a lot of local high school kids, and some of those will carry over to part-time work during the next school year."

Her face lights up, which makes me hesitant to burst her bubble, but…

"How old are you again?" I'm pretty sure Luke said she was fourteen.

"I'll be fifteen in June."

"So you're not driving yet."

Dimi winces, and she looks from him to me and back.

"No, not yet. I figured that since Uncle Luke works at JU, I could get a lift with him most of the time, and the rest of the time Jas or Jus could drive me."

"That might work sometimes, but the kind of job you'll have, in one of the parks or resorts, will be shift based. You can't be sure you'll have shift with the same hours your uncle works. You might start at six and finish at two or start at lunchtime and finish at nine. They don't usually give the overnight shifts at the resorts to underage kids, but in an emergency, it's possible you'll be asked to cover from ten to six. I think before you apply, you need to talk to your uncle and... Did you say Jas and Jus?" She nods, and I wonder who the hell they are and how they got stuck with those names. "Uh, talk to them and see if it's feasible." I pull a face. "I'm really sorry to be the one who tells you this."

She's frowning, but she shakes her head at me. "No, it's good that you told me. It's not what I want to hear, but better now than after I've gone through the process of applying and whatever, yeah? I guess Uncle Luke and I need to work it out."

"Work what out?" Luke's conversation with Jason has finished and they've both tuned in to ours. Mila explains, and Luke's expression falls.

"I hadn't thought about that. It could turn out to be a big problem, especially since I haven't worked out yet if your brother is going to have activities. It might be better to try and find something in town. At least that way it's not as far for Jus and Jas to drive you, and you might be able to ride a bike or something." He looks at us. "Does Joyville have a public bus system?"

"Yeah, but it's not great. Where do you live?" Dimi asks. Luke tells him, and I realize with a jolt that he's not far from me—less than five minutes to drive, maybe fifteen to walk.

Of course, almost everywhere in Joyville is like that.

"There's a bus maybe a block away that would take her right down Main Street, so depending where she finds work, that could be useful. It doesn't run that often though, so it's not exactly convenient. A bike would be faster."

"Something to consider," Luke says. "Maybe next week

you could visit some shops and see if anyone is looking for help this summer."

"Or I could talk to my mom," Dimi offers. "She owns a boutique and she's part of the Joyville Small Business Association, plus she knows pretty much everyone and is on every committee that's ever formed. If anyone's looking, she'll know."

Mila gives him big, hopeful eyes. "Could you? That would be so awesome. And then I'll go talk to them myself, but it would be a huge help to know they're already wanting to hire someone."

"No problem." Dimi smiles at her. "My mom raised eight kids, remember? Helping kids get jobs is like her life's work."

"Hey, Mila, come and help us carry!" Jordy calls from the barbecue, and she gets up right away.

"Thank you," Luke says quietly. "I don't know where this whole job thing has come from. She never said anything about it before. I don't want to discourage her, but…"

"But you'd rather she focused on school and being a kid?" Dimi sounds sympathetic. "She might change her mind once she settles in and makes some friends or gets involved in school activities. And if she doesn't, a summer job doesn't necessarily have to lead to work during the school year." He seems to hesitate. "Is she dating?"

Luke goes so white that we all burst out laughing.

"I guess that's a no," Jason says dryly, and Luke chuckles and shakes his head.

"It hasn't come up yet, which both makes me grateful and concerns me."

"What concerns you, Uncle Luke?" Jordy appears at Luke's side bearing a platter piled high with bacon and sausage.

"The fact that Derek gave you such a huge plate to carry," Luke says promptly. "We're lucky our breakfast didn't end up splattered across the deck."

"Hey, I'm not a baby anymore," Jordy protests, but he's grinning as he carefully sets the platter down and scrambles into a chair.

Derek and Mila carry over the rest of the food, Trav comes out with plates and cutlery, and we get stuck into eating.

Conversation lags a little, but I'm okay with that. It gives me time to think. I haven't really spoken to Luke yet, but I haven't made an idiot of myself, either. What I said to Mila probably didn't endear me to her, but she reacted in a mature way that makes me think she won't automatically hate me for being the bearer of bad news.

So far, I'm calling that a win.

EIGHT

Luke
———

This was such a great idea, and I will forever be grateful to Derek for inviting us. The only thing that could make this morning better would be if there were other kids for Mila and Jordy to hang out with. Regardless, they're interacting well with the adults here and it seems like they're having a good time.

Wait… I lied. There's one other thing that could make this morning better, and that would be for Grant to actually talk to me. I don't think he's said more than a couple of sentences to me since I arrived, and I deliberately sat next to him so we could talk. My team is going to bug the hell out of me on Monday, and it'll go better for me if I can tell them we talked.

I'll keep telling myself that, anyway. It's as good an excuse as any. Sitting next to him had nothing to do with the fact that he looks great in casual clothes, much more like the Grant I remember, and up close I can smell his cologne and practically feel the heat from his body.

You believe me, right?

Whatever. It doesn't change the fact that it's going to be hard for me and Grant to renew our friendship if we don't actually engage in conversation. So that means I need to think of something to say to him.

I'm still wracking my brain as we all finish eating. Derek looks longingly at the few lonely pieces of bacon left on the platter.

"I really want those, but I think my stomach may kill me if I try."

"So don't have them," Trav says prosaically, and Derek pouts.

"They're tormenting me. Calling to me."

"I can fix that," Jordy announces, and puts the bacon on his plate.

Derek blinks, and Dimi stifles a laugh.

"Jordy," I begin, because hell, Derek all but said he was going to eat it.

"Thank you," Derek says sincerely. "That saves me from having to make a difficult decision."

"You're welcome," Jordy replies… with his mouth full.

I just shake my head.

"Come on, Jordy," Mila says, getting up and starting to gather plates. "We'll wash up."

Well.

Warmth unfurls in my chest, and a smile stretches across my face.

"You don't need to do that," Trav protests, but Mila waves him off.

"It's fine. You were so kind to invite us." She hands Jordy a stack of plates and grabs another. Jordy's inside and she's just reached the door when she looks over her shoulder and grins cheekily. "Besides, you old guys should rest."

The door bangs behind her to indignant exclamations and laughter.

"They're such good kids," Derek says, leaning back in his seat.

"Thank you. I worry all the time that I'm fucking them up, you know?" That's not something I normally share, but I can't help feeling really comfortable with these guys.

"My brother says the same thing all the time, and he's got good kids too. I think that's something a lot of parents worry about," Dimi assures me.

"Yeah." I search for words. "It's just… they've been through so much shit."

Grant puts his hand on my arm, and the sudden contact sends tingles zooming through my body. *Yep, definitely still attracted.*

"Whatever they've been through, they clearly adore you, so you're doing something right."

"Thank you." My voice is just a little husky, and I clear my throat and try to lighten things up. "Uh, I'm still terrified by the idea of Mila dating, though."

"Is she into boys or girls or both?" Jason asks, and I sit back.

"It's never come up," I admit. Does that make me a bad parent? Shouldn't Mila feel comfortable coming out to me? "She'd know I don't care either way, right? I mean, she knows I'm gay."

"It probably never occurred to her to worry about it," Grant says. "That's a good thing, Luke. You'll find out when she starts dating, anyway."

I smile gratefully at him and pick up my juice.

"And it's not any easier either way," Dimi says gloomily. "I was living at home through four of my sibs dating, and straight or gay, boys or girls, there's always drama. Gay means no pregnancy scares, though."

Somehow, there's juice going up my nose and down my airway. I cough and splutter, hacking away as I desperately try to breathe. Someone thumps my back, and I wave them off. It takes a few minutes, but finally I'm able to slump back in my seat, eyes watering, oxygen rasping in and out of my lungs.

A napkin appears in front of my face, and I take it gratefully and mop myself up. "Sorry about that," I manage.

"No, I'm sorry," Dimi says. "I forgot I was talking about your kid."

"Here." Grant hands me a glass of water, then smirks at Dimi. "Do not speak until he's finished drinking."

I chuckle, then sip cautiously. "I guess she'll eventually start dating." I deliberately avoid any thought of pregnancy scares. "I'm not looking forward to it, but I also worry because she isn't. Don't most kids start nagging their parents about dating by her age?"

Everyone looks at Dimi.

"What? Now I'm the expert?"

"You have the most siblings, and that gives you the widest knowledge," Trav points out.

Dimi rolls his eyes, but when he looks at me, he's smiling. "Don't worry so much. Not all teenagers want to date right away, and even if they do, they don't always find people they like. Mila seems really together for her age, and her classmates might be a bit immature for her taste. You should think about it, though, and be ready for when she asks. Know what you want her curfew to be and what the limits are—do you want to drop her off and pick her up only, or is it okay for her date to drive her? That kind of stuff. The more prepared you are, the less chance that she'll talk you into stuff you don't like."

"Like you did to your parents?" Jason asks dryly, and Dimi snorts.

"Not me. By the time it was my turn to date, Pat, Cait, and Jack had already pulled every sneaky trick in the book, and Mom and Dad were all wised up."

I think it over. He's right, Mila is mature for her age—her therapist used to say it all the time. Horror strikes me. "If her classmates are too immature for her, she's going to be dating older kids, isn't she?"

Silence.

Derek winces. "I mean, it's a possibility."

Ugh. "Great. Something else I have to think about. I am so close to appointing you all as my official support group."

That cracks them up, and by the time the laughter settles, Jordy and Mila have rejoined us.

"What's so funny?" Jordy asks, reaching for a strawberry from the platter still on the table.

"The price of bacon," I tell him. "You're going to have to cut back, pal, or we'll be on the streets."

He sticks his tongue out at me. "You can sell all my stuff, because I'm not giving up bacon."

"Smart-ass."

His cheeky grin is awesome.

"What kind of stuff you got?" Grant asks. "Maybe I can take some off your hands, help the budget." He winks. "Bacon's important."

Jordy wrinkles his nose. "Clothes and shoes and school stuff," he volunteers. "I don't want to sell my PlayStation or baseball gear until things get desperate." He cocks his head and studies Grant. "I was going to offer you some of Uncle Luke's clothes, because he has a loooooooot, but they won't fit you."

"I don't have that many clothes," I mutter, although I kind of do. I don't wear most of them anymore in my new life, but I haven't been able to bring myself to let them go.

Other than to shoot me an amused smile, Grant lets that slide. "You play ball?" he asks Jordy. "I used to play too."

"I'm still learning," my nephew says honestly. "Did you play Little League?"

Grant nods. "Yep. Little League, high school, and college."

What.

That's news to me. Shouldn't I have known that?

"College? Why don't I remember you playing ball in college?" Baseball was a pretty big thing at our school. I've never been hugely into sports, but I went to a few games with friends. Surely I should have noticed one of my classmates on the field?

In fact, I think I even went to one of those games *with* Grant.

"I quit at the end of my sophomore year," he explains. "I was never better than fair, and baseball took up a lot of time that I figured would be better spent on studying. It was fun, though."

"Will you practice with me?" Jordy asks, and my heart leaps into my throat.

"Uh—" I begin, but Grant's already said, "Sure," and I don't know what to do with that.

"I don't think Derek and Trav have any gear," he continues, "but I could come round to your place later, if you want?"

Jordy's beaming face can probably be seen from space, it's so bright and happy, and this is a great way for us to reestablish our friendship, isn't it?

"If you're sure you don't mind," I say, and he shakes

his head.

"Nah, it'll be fun. I'm probably rusty, though, so you'll have to go easy on me."

Jordy rolls his eyes. "That's what Jus said too. Is it like a rule that you have to say you're rusty when you get old?"

I cough to hide my laugh, wondering what Jus would think of being called old.

"Yep," Grant replies cheerfully. "It's in the rule book. Along with 'that music is too loud.'"

Derek throws a blueberry at him. "You forget that I've worked out with you at the gym," he says. "Nobody could play music louder than you."

"That's because I'm old. Hard of hearing, you know." He turns back to Jordy. "Who's Jus? Your coach?"

"Nup." Jordy shakes his head. "He and Jas are our housekeepers. Jus used to play baseball in high school and he's showed me some stuff."

"The Henson twins?" Dimi asks, and Grant turns incredulous eyes on him and huffs.

"Do you know literally *everyone* in Joyville?"

"Yes," Jason answers for him, and Dimi pinches him.

"I swear I don't. Jas and Jus were in the same class as my brother Mike, who also played baseball. I barely know them; I was already living in Atlanta then."

"Does your brother still live here too?" Jordy asks, and I can tell he's imagining his own personal team of baseball coaches at his beck and call.

Dimi shakes his head. "Sorry, no. He lives in Jacksonville now."

Jordy looks at me. "Is that far?"

This kid. I swear.

"Too far for him to come and practice with some kid he doesn't know who already has other people willing to help him," I say pointedly, and to give him credit, he looks a little abashed.

"It would be really cool if you could practice with me," he says to Grant. "Thank you."

Grant grins. "No problem, kid. It'll be fun."

This move is the best thing I've ever done.

NINE

Grant
———

I end up following Luke and the kids home. I don't have any urgent plans for the day—a bit of work, but if I get stuck into that now, I may not surface until it's too late to go over, and I'd rather spend a couple hours playing catch and work later.

Plus, I get to hang out with Luke and his kids, who are pretty cool.

I already knew their house wasn't far from mine, but it's actually closer than I realized. We probably go to the same grocery store.

I park on the street in front and then follow Luke's car into the garage. Jordy scrambles out of the car first and is waiting for me.

"I'll go get my glove and ball," he declares. "There's room in the backyard."

"Maybe we should invite Grant in and offer him a drink," Luke suggests, but the thread of amusement in his voice is strong.

"After," I say, unable to bear the disappointed impatience on Jordy's face. "I'm still full from breakfast, but I bet I'll be thirsty when we're done."

His grin comes back.

Luke unlocks the door into the house and Jordy races past him. Mila and I follow more decorously.

"I'm going to finish my homework," Mila tells Luke.

"No problem. We'll be out back if you need anything. Maybe we can go out for pizza tonight."

Her smile is dazzling. "That sounds good. The kids at school say the place on Harris Street is awesome."

"It is," I agree. "And not just for pizza." Thinking about their cannoli almost makes me hungry again.

"Cool!" She wanders off, leaving me alone with Luke in his kitchen.

He leans against the counter. "Are you sure I can't get you so—"

"Got 'em!" Jordy thunders back in, cutting his uncle off. "Let's go." He grabs my hand and tows me along. Luke mutters something but I don't quite catch it.

Jordy and I play catch for about an hour. He's not bad, especially considering he's just started playing, but it's his focus that impresses me most. The kid's only eleven, but he doesn't throw tantrums when he messes up. A couple times, I can see he's getting frustrated or angry, but he just takes a second, breathes deep, and tries again.

Finally, Luke interrupts. "That's enough for today, Jordy."

Jordy's face sets mutinously, and he opens his mouth to reply, but Luke's not done. "Grant's been really nice to practice with you, but if you overwork him, he won't come back."

The kid seems to consider it, then turns to me and says, "Thanks for hanging out with me."

"Anytime," I assure him, impressed by his maturity. "I

had fun." I really did. I used to get together with friends for the occasional game in the park, but that stopped after I moved to Joyville. I just haven't had time to hunt that kind of thing down. I forgot how much fun just playing catch could be.

"Can I go for a swim?" Jordy asks Luke, and I shiver involuntarily. It's a nice day, but the temp is only in the low eighties—not exactly swimming weather.

"Sure," Luke says. "But not a long one."

"I'll be hungry soon anyway," Jordy informs him, then takes off inside with his glove and ball.

Luke stares after him. "Do you know if it's normal for him to eat like he has a tapeworm? I should have asked Dimi this morning."

I laugh and follow him back to the deck, where he's got a laptop set up beside a jug of iced water and a couple of glasses on the table.

"I remember my mom complaining about how much I ate when I was a kid, so I'm going to say it's normal." I plant myself in one of the chairs. Too bad if he was ready to get rid of me. With Mila studying and Jordy in the pool, I have the perfect opportunity to further the friendship plan.

"That's good enough for me. Do you want some water? Or we have tea and beer."

"Water would be great, but I can pour it." We both reach for the jug and of course our hands collide. Sparks shoot up my arm. Can this moment be any more like a Joy Inc movie? All it needs is music playing in the background.

No sooner do I think it than *music begins to play*. I jerk my hand back and look around. Am I the unwitting victim of some reality show prank?

"Mila's turned on the sound system," Luke says, grabbing the jug and pouring water into two glasses. He seems completely unaffected by *the touch*. "We haven't worked out the zoning yet, so it plays through the whole house and out here. I have to put some time in on that, or it's going to get old really fast."

I force a smile, but I think it looks more like a grimace. "At least she's got good taste in music," I manage, picking up my glass. Maybe the water will settle me. My stomach is seriously churning right now. This friendship thing may be beyond me.

Thankfully, Jordy comes out right then and Luke is distracted reiterating the pool rules. I take advantage of the reprieve to pull myself together.

By the time Luke turns his attention back to me, I've gulped down the water in my glass and refilled it and am feeling a bit more myself.

"Sorry about that," he says with a self-deprecating smile. "I know we're sitting right here, and he's a decent swimmer, but still…"

"Pool safety is important." I nod. Okay. Keep up the conversation. "So… did you have a pool in California?"

"No, not at the house we just moved from. When we bought it, we had to choose between proximity to work and a pool. Since we weren't going to let the kids swim unsupervised anyway, Matt and I figured it would be better for me to be close to work and spend less time in transit."

There's a really awkward pause, then Luke blows out a breath.

"We should probably just get it out on the table, yeah?"

Oh fuck, does he know how bad I crushed on him back in college… that I seem to be still?

"Uh…"

"I mean, it's more weird for us to avoid talking about it. You're the one who introduced us in the first place."

Oh. He's talking about Matt.

"Uh, yeah. I don't know if I'm supposed to be sorry for that or not." I am for my own sake, but Luke presumably loved Matt for a long time—still might, for all I know, even if they are divorced.

He smiles, but it has a sad edge. "No, don't be sorry. Things went bad in the end, but I wouldn't take back any of it—especially since I wouldn't have the kids otherwise."

I blink, and my confusion must show, because he sighs again. "I forget people don't know. Mila and Jordy are Matt's sister's kids. She and her husband left guardianship of them jointly to me and Matt."

He's raising his ex's sister's kids? Is it just me, or is that weird?

"How... uh... Matt didn't..." How do I ask why the kids aren't with Matt now?

Luke runs a hand through his hair and looks over at Jordy in the pool. "Matt never wanted kids. He loved being an uncle, and he loved—loves—the kids, but suddenly being a parent wasn't in his plans. Or mine, really. Our whole lives changed, and he hated that. Then he felt guilty for hating it, because the kids have literally nobody else. It was just this cycle of bad feelings and resentment and guilt. He stuck it out for three years, then he couldn't take any more and left."

I don't know what to say. I know what I want to say, but Luke is seemingly very understanding of Matt's feelings in all this, and I don't think me announcing what a fucking douche he is will sit well.

Also, is it just me, or is Luke superhero material? Seriously, does the guy have any flaws? He can't be human. Maybe that's why I'm so obsessed with him—it's some alien or paranormal charisma. Like in that movie Joy Inc made last year that had all the teenage girls swooning. Only without the werewolves.

I hope.

"Wow," I finally say. "He… just left custody to you?" A horrible thought strikes. "Is it okay that you moved them out of state?"

"Yes," he assures me. "After he left, I realized how precarious my situation was. We were both named guardians in the will, and the courts approved that, but ultimately he's their blood relative, not me, and when Jordy was crying himself to sleep at night because Uncle Matt was gone just like Mommy and Daddy, I couldn't stand the thought of him and Mila having to go through that kind of upheaval again. Matt had cut off contact completely, but I tracked him down through some friends and got him to sign legal papers relinquishing guardianship. Then I adopted the kids. They're legally mine now. He actually surprised me by submitting a character reference in support of the adoption, which I didn't find out about until my attorney told me. He wants what's best for them; he just can't be their parent."

"So he hasn't seen them since he left?" That sticks in my throat. Admittedly, I don't know the kids well, but the few hours I've spent with them has shown them to be pretty amazing. Matt might not want to be a parent, which I totally understand, but to cut the kids out completely? That's not okay. How hard is it to fucking visit a couple times a month or make a weekly phone call?

Luke shakes his head. "I think that's the guilt, you know? He doesn't want to face them after he left them. I'm not in direct contact with him anymore, but we have a couple of mutual friends I stay in touch with just so he'll always have a way to contact me if he wants to see them—and so they can contact him when they get older."

"You're a better person than I am," I say honestly.

"Not really." His expression turns grim. "I was so

angry when he left. He just went to get something from the drugstore and never came home. At least he sent a text, so I didn't have to go through the stress of worrying something had happened. I didn't—don't—understand how he could just walk away from the kids. Even if we hadn't been named guardians in the will, I would have fought for them. I've been in their lives since they were born. Changed diapers, kissed scrapes, sneaked chocolate to them. How could I have let them go into the system, maybe be separated? That happened to Matt and Mandy—his sister—when their mom died, and they hated it. They were lucky to be able to stay in contact until Mandy got her license and could visit Matt." He takes a sip of his water, eyes back on the pool. "I never wanted to be a parent either, not really, but I could never leave Jordy and Mila. I was so pissed off, I donated most of his stuff to charity. The only things I kept were the ones I thought the kids might like someday. First I had to tell them that he wasn't going to be living with us, and then when he made it clear he didn't want any contact, I had to explain that he didn't want to see us either. I tried to make it about me, but they saw through that pretty much right away. Neither of them like to talk about him." He shrugs. "That's what made me get over being so angry. They're kids, yeah? They're allowed to have emotional reactions to things. I need to be stronger than that, the voice of reason. Set an example. So I decided to let the past go."

"That's really mature of you," I tell him. Part of me is wondering if he's really just burying all that anger. He's in a difficult and stressful situation as a single parent to two kids, plus he has a busy full-time career that calls for more than a standard forty-hour week. Taking the time to deal with his emotions after his significant other of fifteen years left him was probably too hard. Much easier to let it go—

on the surface, at least. "It sounds like you've had it rough for the past few years. Have you been working for Joy Inc this whole time?"

"Yeah. I started with them about nine years ago. At the time, I didn't really pay as much attention as I should have to benefits for parents and families. It was a nice surprise when everything went to shit and I found out that our insurance covers therapy for the kids and I could flex my hours and office time to be with them. Matt's company wasn't as good." He shrugs. "Jordy's always loved to boast that I work for Joy Inc, even if it is for the 'boring business part.'"

I smile. "Do you get more cool points now that he's living in Joyville?"

Luke rolls his eyes. "Some, but not as many as if we were actually living at JU. He's also unimpressed that we've been here for nearly two weeks and I haven't taken them there yet."

Pasting on a shocked expression, I tsk. "The horror!"

"I know, I'm a rotten uncle. I usually make him eat his vegetables, too, and I recently limited him to one package of Pop-Tarts per day." He snorts. "That was a total parenting fail on my part—somehow I didn't realize how many of the damn things he was eating."

"Next you'll be telling me that he's only allowed to play video games for a certain amount of time a day," I say, my tongue firmly in my cheek.

"Would you like to learn more than you ever wanted to know about Fortnite?" he asks, and I laugh.

"I can't even remember the last time I played a video game," I admit. "I'm not sure whether to be sad about that or consider it part of growing up."

"Same. We used to play all the time, remember?"

We reminisce for a while about college—video games,

parties, and group study sessions, people we used to know, people we still know. I thought it would be awkward, because it's impossible to talk about that time without Matt coming up, but it's not. I guess Luke telling me what happened cleared the air.

Eventually Luke turns toward the pool and yells for Jordy to get out. He's done that twice already, and both times Jordy managed to bargain for "five more minutes." Next time I need to buy a car, I'm taking that kid with me —he's a champion negotiator.

"He'd stay in all day and turn into a prune if he could," Luke grumbles, but he's smiling. "He's probably only getting out now because he's hungry."

I check the time on my phone, and sure enough, it's edging toward midafternoon.

"I'd better take off." It sounds just as reluctant as I feel. I've been enjoying myself—Luke is just as good company as I remember, and there are worse ways to spend a Saturday than kicked back on the deck, enjoying the sunshine and talking to an interesting man.

Like working. Which is what I need to go do.

"You're welcome to stay. I'm just going to make sandwiches for the kids now, then Jordy and I will probably watch a movie or something else quiet."

Jordy arrives on the deck right then, dripping everywhere. "Can we watch a scary movie?" he asks. "Grant, will you stay?"

"No scary movies," Luke says firmly, passing him a towel. "Last time you didn't sleep for a week. I had my very own personal zombie, but without the fun brain-eating part."

Jordy immediately impersonates a zombie, complete with groans and moans, his towel sliding to the deck. I laugh, and he breaks character to grin at me.

"Will you stay?" he asks again. "There are still good movies that aren't scary."

"I'm sorry," I say, and I really am. "I have some work to do. Can I take a rain check?"

"What's that?" Disappointment shadows his tone, and I feel like a monster. How does Luke ever manage to say no to him?

"A promise to do it another time," Luke tells him. "Maybe we can plan a movie night with Grant." He shoots me an inquiring look, and I swear I see hopefulness in his gaze.

"I'd like that. Next Friday? Since you don't have school the next day, we can watch more movies."

"Yes! Can we order pizza too?" Jordy turns a beseeching gaze on his uncle.

"I thought we'd have pizza tonight," Luke says. "But if you want it again Friday, I guess that's okay. Or we can make tacos."

"Okay, let's rain check," Jordy announces. "Thanks for coming over, Grant." He grabs his towel and darts inside, leaving me and Luke staring after him and wondering how the conversation came to such an abrupt end.

"So…," Luke begins. "Friday night. I'll, uh, touch base during the week to sort out details?"

"Definitely," I confirm, then push my luck just a little bit further. "We should have lunch too. I mean," I backtrack, losing my nerve, "you should have lunch with us. Me and Derek. And probably Trav or someone too. In the Village." Jesus, talk about uncool. Could I have sounded any more like a dork?

Fortunately for me, Luke doesn't seem to notice. "That sounds great. I really liked everyone this morning."

I manage to get through goodbyes and head out to my

car, but it's not until I get home that I finally let myself relax.

"That was good," I say out loud to my empty house that suddenly feels so much emptier. "Derek's plan is good."

I just wish we could move on to the second stage already.

TEN

Luke
———

Monday morning is here before I know it. One thing I never expected about having kids is that the weekend is no longer a time of rest and recreation—or if I do manage recreation, it's not the kind I was used to.

I'm cleaning up the breakfast dishes when I hear a key in the front door, followed a moment later by Jas calling, "Good morning!" It's been less than two weeks that we've had a housekeeper, but already I know that I would cry if they went away. Who knew coming home to a clean house, dinner, and washed and folded laundry could be so good?

"Hi!" I call back, and a moment later she comes into the kitchen. "Did you have a good weekend?" I ask, and she nods as she comes over to help me load the last couple plates in the dishwasher.

"Did you?"

"It was more relaxing than I thought." I close the dishwasher door. "I'm going to change. I'll check if the kids are getting ready on my way."

She's already got her head in the fridge. "No worries.

I'm going to do a grocery run this morning, so let me know if you want anything in particular."

See? Angel.

I take the stairs two at a time. I'm a little later than I wanted to be today, but Jordy was feeling chatty over breakfast and I didn't want to cut him off to finish getting ready. I guess I could have left the dishes for Jas, but I'm still getting used to this whole housekeeper thing.

Tapping on both kids' doors as I walk past, I call out a reminder that they should be getting ready for school. I don't remember getting distracted so easily when I was a kid, but I probably did. I was definitely late for school a lot.

By the time I jog back down the stairs ten minutes later, I'm shaved, neatly dressed, and almost in the right frame of mind for work. In the kitchen, Jordy is packing his schoolbag with the lunch Jas made him.

"Hey, Uncle Luke, I was telling Jas about how Grant came to play catch with me," he says. "And about brunch."

That reminds me— "We met Dimi Weston at brunch," I tell Jas. "He said you and Jus went to school with his brother?"

She smiles. "Mike. Yeah, sure. I've only met Dimi a couple times, but it's impossible not to know the Westons in Joyville. There are so many of them, and Sascha has a finger in every pie. They're good people."

Well, that's good to know, and backs up my impression of Dimi. Not that it really matters, but if I'm going to take parenting advice from the guy, I want to know that he's a reliable source.

I drop a kiss on Jordy's head, hug Mila as she comes through the door, and then I'm off.

I pushed most thoughts of the audit out of my head over the weekend, but as I drive toward JU, they all come flooding back in.

On Friday afternoon, Stu and Amelia both asked me to give them the weekend before they reported. "You're not going to like this," Amelia said, "so I want to connect as many dots as possible before I tell you."

Encouraging, right?

The closer I get to the office, the crazier my brain goes, clicking into high gear. This early in an audit, we really shouldn't have so many red flags. Vague warning signs, maybe, especially since the audit was commissioned because there were suspected problems. But it's only been a week, which tells me that things are bad and nobody's even trying to really hide it.

So we have a status meeting first thing, and then later this morning I'm meeting with Grant to update him on our progress and get his help with any problems we're running into.

My stomach does a weird flip.

Spending time with Grant on Saturday was... really great. I don't want to say amazing, because that makes me sound like a teen with my first crush. I mean, we only talked in my backyard. But it was *really great* to reconnect with Grant and to talk to someone about Matt who wasn't there when it all went down. That's without even considering the fact that I'm still crazy attracted to him... and he was fantastic with Jordy.

But for now, casual friendship is all this can be. Especially since we need to meet about work issues later today. I need to get my head in the game and focus on the audit.

Work first. The rest later.

I stare at Amelia in shock. "You're joking."

She shakes her head. "I wish I was. This is a mess."

"How has nobody noticed this?"

Max pipes up. "They just haven't made a big deal about it. And since there are a lot of different names and they're spread through a lot of districts and departments… it just slipped through the cracks. Like, people know, but they haven't put it together."

I feel a headache coming on. "So." I stop, trying to gather my thoughts. "Lena Teller is Ken Dulles's niece."

Amelia and Max nod.

"And hearsay is that anytime somebody makes a complaint about her, she threatens their job, citing her influence with her uncle."

"Yes," Max says. "But of course it's only hearsay."

"Right." Although it's a lot of hearsay, and we could easily get firsthand accounts. "The part that concerns me most, though, is the number of relatives Lena has working here and the way they seem to get promotions they're not always qualified for. Run me through that again, please."

As Amelia ticks off the data again, a small part of my brain is racing. This is a lot worse than just skimming, although I suspect we'll find that too—Stu looks like he's about to burst.

"So I'm not sure how they're getting these jobs," Amelia concludes, "but given the number of sudden resignations right before these promotions or new hires, I have to assume intimidation is involved."

"Yep." I stare into space for a minute, mentally laying it out. "Can the two of you please draw up a relationship map of all parties of interest? Across personal relationships and company departments, please."

Amelia nods, and Max says, "Of course." He looks so excited that I feel the need to add, "I'm sorry, Max, but your wife has to wait to hear about this. It's confidential for now."

His smile makes me feel like an idiot. "No problem, Luke. She'll enjoy hearing it better when we have the whole story."

Great.

I turn to Stu. "What do you have?"

"Skimming."

"Why am I not surprised? How bad is it?"

"Really bad." He taps his tablet and the screen on the wall comes to life, displaying a spreadsheet of data highlighted in green, red, and yellow. He begins to painstakingly explain what he's done, and my stomach sinks. This isn't just the occasional skim when the opportunity rises—it's systematic and organized. No wonder Grant insisted on an audit.

"And I'm pretty sure there's similar stuff going on in the other districts," Stu concludes. "There are threads that don't quite tie up. But definitely the whole thing loops back to Lena Teller and her circle. A lot of the names on Amelia and Max's list coincide with mine."

"Okay. Okay." I think it over. "Continue to work on this—*quietly*. If you need to take steps that might alert anyone, don't. Let me know and we'll see what other options there are. Is there any indication so far that Ken Dulles actually does know what's going on or is otherwise involved?"

All three of them shake their heads. "None," Stu says. "All signs point to the place being run by the ADs and department heads while he plays golf and has lunch."

I grimace, because although that's better than him being involved in the skimming, it's still not what Malcolm and Seth are going to want to hear.

"Moving on. Di, you're next."

We get through the rest of the briefing, and I'm actually impressed with myself for giving it all my attention. As soon as everyone disperses to continue work, I start a group chat with Malcolm and Seth.

Luke Durrant: Need to talk to you both ASAP.

It's still early on the West Coast and they might both be busy. This isn't urgent enough for me to call and interrupt without warning, but that message will get their attention and hopefully I'll be able to update them sooner rather than later.

Sure enough, it's only been ten minutes when the chat window pops up.

Seth Holder: I don't like the sound of that. Mal's in a meeting until 11:30. We'll call you then.

Luke Durrant: Thanks.

I reschedule my meeting with Grant to later in the afternoon—depending on what Malcolm and Seth say, I may have some very pointed questions for him.

How the fuck has this flown under the radar for so long?

I get a message from Malcolm at eleven thirty-five and take my phone and laptop with me to the interview room-slash-storage closet. They call almost before I have the door closed.

As the video comes up, I sit at the tiny table and split the screen so I can see them and my notes at the same time.

"Good morning," I greet, and Malcolm studies me.

"Is it? You don't look happy, and it's kind of early in the audit process for you to make a report."

"You have no idea. You both need to prepare yourself, because I have very bad news."

Seth groans. "After *one week*?"

I don't bother delaying any more, just plunge right in and lay out what we've found so far. By the time I'm done, Seth's got his head in his hands and Malcolm is sheet white. Maybe I should have eased in after all—they're both in good health, but they are older, and this isn't exactly something to celebrate.

"Are you... I..." Malcolm trails off. "Luke, is the man we put in charge of JU stealing from us?"

"At this stage, we don't believe so. I don't even think he's aware that his niece and her friends are using his name to influence decisions. That said, we're only a week in and our attention so far has been exclusively on Grant's district."

Seth's head jerks up. "You think this is happening across the entire company."

"No." I say it quickly and shake my head. "I met Derek Bryer and his former assistant. There's no way they would miss anything like this, and I don't see them being involved."

"No, Derek wouldn't be," Seth agrees, and they both look a little relieved. "And Grant brought it to our attention... Oh, hell, that's why he wanted an audit. He needed to go over Ken's head."

"There's one thing I wanted to ask," I say, skimming my notes. "The AD before Grant wasn't here that long. Did he mention anything being unusual?"

"No." Malcolm sounds grim. "But he was fired when his incompetence resulted in his park needing to be closed due to permit issues. It's possible he never noticed."

I make a note. "We'll chase it down and see if we can find out." I level my gaze on my bosses. "So... I need some direction from you. We can continue the audit as planned, but I'm fairly certain we're going to start running into roadblocks. The only reason we've gotten this far is that my people are being very quiet and haven't openly investigated anything. As soon as we officially dig into orders and finances, records are going to begin disappearing."

"Continuing as planned seems short-sighted," Malcolm says. "We'll still need the audit, of course, but now mostly to work out the extent of the damage and how to fix it. How many employees would you say were bullied completely out of their jobs?"

I double-check the number, even though it's burned into my brain, and tell him. He looks ill.

"I think we need to reassess," Seth says. "We're no longer operating on 'what will we find.' Luke, is there enough on record to terminate Lena Teller's employment?"

"Yes." No question. She should have been fired long ago.

"What about her cronies? The ones that have the most seniority."

I hesitate. "I'd need another day or so to make sure."

"You have until Wednesday. Mal and I will come out there and fire them ourselves. Ken is going on paid leave for a while, and I want you to figure out a way to ensure all nonstandard orders can be approved only at AD level until you've had a chance to do a full assessment."

"We can probably make it manual." I make a note for Stu to check. "It'll mean a little more work for everyone involved, but they'll survive."

"Do we need to appoint someone to Ken's position in the interim, or are the ADs pretty much running things anyway?" The resignation in Malcolm's voice tugs at my heartstrings. It's easy to forget that for them, this is the family business. It may be a multibillion-dollar global enterprise, but it's also the company their uncle started.

"The ADs are pretty much running things, but I don't think it would be a good idea to remove all oversight. Maybe a weekly teleconference where they can report to you? I know you don't have the time, but it would reinforce for them how serious this is."

They exchange glances. "We'll consider our options. In the meantime, you should start preparing. There's no point in concentrating solely on Grant's district anymore when it's clear there needs to be a company-wide overhaul."

"So… less an audit and more a business assessment and restructure?" That will change the way my team needs to work—and also change the situation with Grant.

"Yes," Malcolm confirms. "But we'll go over that on Wednesday. For now, just make sure we'll have what we need when we arrive."

"No problem. Do you have any objection to me interviewing Grant this afternoon? I won't tell him what the plans are, obviously, but now that we've discovered what he wanted us to know, it might help to find out exactly what information he has."

"Do it," Seth approves. "I think the fact that he brought this directly to us in the first place is fairly indicative that he can be trusted. Find out who else he's talked to about this, though."

"Done. Do you need to be picked up at the airport?" There are regular shuttles to and from JU, of course, and a car service for VIPs, but since this is a surprise visit, I doubt they'll want to use either.

"We'll let you know. Thank you, Luke. This is good work, even if we don't like it."

We end the call, and I sit there for a moment, my mind whirling. This is not what I expected to happen when I came out here for this job.

Finally, I get up and go back to the conference room. My team falls silent and they all watch as I close the door. They know who I was talking to.

"There's been a change of plans."

ELEVEN

Grant
———

Luke Durrant is a fucking beast at his job.
Really.
In one week, he and his team have discovered what took me months to even suspect. Our Monday meeting is supposed to be a list of questions about the functionality of my district and a vague overview of how the audit is going. Instead, he sits me down in that tiny closet, looks me dead in the eye, and asks me who I suspect of skimming, how, and for how long.

I actually sputter, I'm that surprised.

"Come on, Grant. You didn't request this audit because you thought life needed spicing up. You knew we'd find something—you *wanted* us to find it—and we have. Now I need to know everything you do."

He's so fucking sexy when he's all take-charge like this.

I pull myself together. Work now, the rest later.

"I actually don't know much. It's been a year since I got this job, and every time I try to clean things up and improve efficiency, it all goes mysteriously awry—like the damn system allocating approval permissions. I can only get so far with anything before it all takes a huge step back. And whenever I tried looking into issues, files just weren't there. One time I could have sworn they were, but when I went back into the system, things were mixed up and what I needed was gone." I hesitate. "It's definitely skimming? I thought it was, but like I said, I can never pin down what I need. Once someone else approves an order, I have only limited visibility of it."

He frowns and makes a note. "You should be able to track and view every order for your district. It sounds like someone's fucked with your systems access."

What?

What?

"Son of a bitch!" I don't know why this upsets me more than everything else, but it really, really does.

"Calm down," he says. "We'll fix it. But I need you to tell me every tiny detail you have."

I do. And then he asks questions that wring out details I didn't even know I had. People, approximate dates, incidents, bad feelings… he asks about all of it and takes meticulous notes. It's almost shocking to see the contrast between this laser-focused businessman Luke and the slightly insecure parent Luke from Saturday, or the young, let's-hit-the-pub-after-class Luke I remember from college.

"Okay," he says finally, sitting back. "I know I don't need to tell you that everything we've discussed is confidential. We're going to continue for now and you'll be advised if anything changes."

"That's great, thank you." It is. This is better than I hoped, and certainly sooner. And it pretty much means my job is safe, since they found what I wanted them to.

"Just one more thing—who have you discussed this with? In even the vaguest terms."

"Uhhh…" I think about it. "Malcolm and Seth, of

course. And I might have hinted to Derek that something wasn't right, but I didn't give him any details. He did mention that he's had a lot of problems with assistants since Dimi left, and that one of them tried to approve an emergency concessions order. It didn't work, of course, because he's never assigned permissions to anyone." There's a faint hint of bitterness in my voice. I don't mind having to clean up my predecessor's fuckups, but I wish they'd stay clean once I get them that way. Having to redo everything over and over because someone is fucking with me really pisses me off.

"So he's suspicious but has no details?"

I shrug. "That sounds right. I honestly don't think they'll have gotten much foothold in his district. He keeps a really tight grip on things, and Dimi knew every single detail of what was happening, no matter how small. Maybe some small things have snuck through in the last six months, but it won't be much."

Luke nods. "Thanks for the tip."

We part ways, and I head back to my office to get as much work done as possible. It's been a hard slog for the past twelve months, and that won't change anytime soon, but it seems like there's finally a glimmer of light at the end of the tunnel.

Given the bombshell of our Monday meeting, I don't remember until late on Tuesday that I wanted to plan a group lunch for this week. So I start a group chat.

Grant Davis: Hey everyone, how about lunch one day this week?

Simple enough, right? Nice and casual. Replies start popping up within minutes.

Dimi Weston: Sounds great. Thursday works best for Jase and Trav and me.

Trav Jones: Dimi's such a slave driver. Yep, Thursday would be good.

Derek Bryer: Thursday at one? I can't do earlier.

Jason Philips: Works for me. Although Dimi's being a control freak. We could probably manage tomorrow if that's easier for everyone else.

Luke Durrant: Not sure yet what plans are for the rest of the week. Can we hold off setting a time?

I stare at Luke's message for a few long minutes. Tuesday is done. The only reason not to know what plans are for the rest of the week is if something big is about to happen that he can't tell us.

My phone rings in my hand, Derek's name flashing on the screen. I answer.

"Hey."

"Hi. Did you see Luke's message? That's weird, right? Could we have offended him on the weekend or something?" There's a careful blend of concern and suspicion in his voice. He already knows something isn't right. I all but told him the audit was at my request.

"It's weird," I agree carefully. "I don't think we offended him, though. I was at his place for a few hours, and everything was good. Maybe it's something to do with the kids?" As soon as the thought occurs to me, I begin to worry. What if it *is* to do with the kids?

"I hope not," Derek say, echoing my thoughts. "Well, I guess we'll find out eventually. Coffee in the morning?"

"Hell, yes." Knowing that Luke's team has found so much and is actively working on fixing this mess but not being able to actually do anything has my nerves wound super tight. It's only been a day, but already I'm practically fueled by coffee.

We say our goodbyes, and I immediately respond to the group message.

Grant Davis: No problem. Just let us know when things sort themselves out.

Then I send a private text to Luke.

Me: Is this work related or has something happened to the kids?

I just can't shake that niggling worry.

Fortunately, he replies pretty much right away.

Luke: Kids are fine. Thanks for asking. Will see you at work tomorrow.

Oh.

That's pretty telling, because we don't have a meeting scheduled for tomorrow. So... something's in the works.

I don't think I'm going to sleep tonight.

It's a little after one on Wednesday when I hear commotion outside my office. That type of increase in volume usually means there's shocking gossip making the rounds.

I've no sooner thought that than my office door opens and Marly, one of the few people on my team that I trust and actually like, pokes her head in, eyes wide.

"Malcolm Joy and Seth Holder are here."

So that's what Luke couldn't tell us. Wow, they must have left LA before dawn.

"Here in the building, or here waiting to see me?" I ask calmly, and she blinks.

"I-In the building." She looks a little taken aback. "They went in with the audit team."

"Okay. I guess we'll find out what's going on soon enough." I meet her gaze. "I don't think you need to worry, Marly."

Awareness dawns in her eyes, and she comes inside and closes the door. "Are… are you fixing things?"

We've never spoken about this before, and I don't want to say too much now. I trust Marly, but really, how far can that go in this toxic environment?

"An audit usually cleans things up," I say vaguely. She nods.

"So I guess I'd better get on with my work. The last thing I need is to be slacking off while the big bosses are here."

She lets herself out, and I pick up my phone and call Derek.

"You hear?" he answers.

"Yep. All I know is that they're here and in with the audit team."

"Same. Not a good day for Ken to be playing golf."

I frown. "Isn't golf day Thursday?"

There's a sound that I suspect is him putting his feet up on his desk. "Usually, yeah, but word is he decided to play twice this week."

And that's our director. His assistant is probably frantically calling him now, but he never has his phone on while he golfs.

"This is going to be interesting."

An hour later, Derek and I just happen to be drinking coffee in the lobby when Ken rushes in, red-faced, wearing his golfing clothes. The gossip we gleaned at the coffee cart is that his assistant had to call the clubhouse and have them send a caddy out to get him. For some reason, we found that amusing.

Ken hits the call button for the elevator six times in rapid succession, glances toward the stairs, then practically leaps into the elevator when the doors open.

I would not like to be him right now.

"Ready to go up?" Derek asks blandly, and I toss my cup into the trash can.

"Sure." We head for the stairs, keeping our ears peeled for any snippet of information we might hear along the way. I doubt there will be anything truly valuable—Luke's team have kept things locked down tighter than a vault, and the team Mal and Seth brought along went into the conference room with them.

Turns out, I'm wrong about that. We hit the second floor just in time to hear Malcolm say, "We'll call for you when we're ready to see you. I'm sure you have a lot of work to do." The last is accompanied by a derisive head-to-toe look that says very clearly what he thinks of Ken's golfing attire. Then he shuts the door to the conference room in Ken's face.

Derek nudges me, and we move to the next flight of stairs before Ken can recover from his shock and see us standing there. We're halfway up before Derek says, "That was like Christmas."

"And my birthday," I mutter. "Did you see his face?"

"The look of utter stupefaction, you mean? Oh, yeah. I'll be picturing it the next time he pisses me off."

We get to the top and pause.

"There's going to be a shake-up, isn't there?" Derek asks in a low voice.

I shake my head. "I don't know for sure, but I know there's a lot wrong in my district and I think Malcolm and Seth want to be sure it's not everywhere else."

He frowns, and I can practically see him mentally assessing his own district and wondering if he's missed anything important.

"Derek," I say firmly, "if I thought you were having the same problems I am, I would have told you months ago.

There might be something, but it's not going to be debilitating to clean up."

He sighs. "I guess we'll find out soon enough."

Malcolm and Seth call a meeting of all ADs and department heads at four. As we assemble in the boardroom, there's a low-key murmur of concern and dread. It's not a good thing when the big bosses unexpectedly arrive ten days into a company-wide audit, and everyone knows it.

Of course, they also know that my district was the first to be audited, so I'm getting a lot of sidelong glances. I ignore them and settle into a seat beside Derek. Dimi, as manager of the Joy Village Theater Company, is on his other side, and leans across to say, "I'm pretty sure you know more than you told us, and that's fine, but if I'm about to get fired because of a restructure, I'd really like a heads up."

I roll my eyes. "Dimi, you worry too much."

Malcolm and Seth walk in right then, Luke and two members of his team following. One of them is Diana, who I met briefly last week.

The room goes quiet. Diana and the other guy sit in a couple of the empty chairs at the foot of the table, and Luke goes with Malcolm and Seth to the head. Three chairs have been left empty there, in that accidentally-on-purpose way that happens sometimes. One of them was probably intended for Ken, but he's nowhere to be seen, and Luke sits in it like he owns the place.

I stifle a shiver. That austere confidence is very attractive.

"I'm sure you're all wondering what's going on," Malcolm begins, and although nobody dares to breathe an answer, an air of expectation fills the room. "The first thing you need to know is that Ken is on leave for the foreseeable future. Our understanding is that this won't affect you all that much," he adds dryly. "In the event that you do need to escalate anything, Luke Durrant will be acting as our point of contact here. Any instructions he gives are to be treated as though they come from us."

All eyes go to Luke, who lifts his chin in acknowledgment but doesn't smile. I want to grin crazily at him, because what a fantastic indication of their faith in him. I don't, of course.

"At this moment, security is escorting from the building seventeen employees who have been found to be stealing and will ensure they leave JU property. Seth and I have considered this very carefully and have decided at this time not to press criminal charges. Those former employees have been required to sign NDAs, and I know I don't need to remind anyone here about the confidentiality clauses in your employment contracts. A memo will be sent to all employees within the hour with explicit instructions about what to do if approached by the media. We have no illusions that we'll be able to keep this under wraps, but nobody working here will feed the press." He gazes around the table, making eye contact with everyone to underline his point, then focuses on me.

"Grant, we'd like to thank you for everything you've done this past year. A preliminary investigation has made it very clear that any steps you took to improve efficiency and profitability within your district were sabotaged. I can only imagine what a full review will show. We look forward to seeing how things will improve going forward."

"Thank you," I say, because I don't know what else to do.

"As of right now, all nonstandard orders will need to

be approved manually by department heads—that's all of you—and countersigned by a member of the audit team."

That causes a murmur of offended discontent, but Malcolm doesn't pause.

"The audit team will also be reviewing the standard ordering process. In fact, each department will be allocated a liaison from the audit team. You will give them your full cooperation. The focus of the audit has changed, and it will be rolled out across the entire company instead of working one department at a time." He looks at Kiara. "There is going to be a complete overhaul of the hiring and promotions process, and strict attention will be paid to the anti-bullying policy and bullying complaints procedure. All complaints of bullying made over the past five years will be reviewed." Kiara looks shaken and appalled, but she nods.

"Of course."

Elise from marketing half raises a hand. "I'm sorry, Malcolm, I'm just trying to process this… are we absolutely sure all this is necessary? I mean… we have measures in place to prevent theft and bullying."

"We do," Seth says smoothly. "But they're clearly not working."

"Actually," Luke interjects, "if I may…?" Seth nods, and Malcolm makes a be-my-guest gesture. "The measures currently in place do a great job to prevent and manage one-off incidents and petty behavior. What we've discovered is an extensive, well-planned network designed for systematic theft that over the years has added up to an appallingly large amount. From what we've been able to determine, the bullying is almost incidental—a means to protect and further the network. We're still taking things apart and tracing back to the beginning, but once we know how it started and have a complete picture of how it works—"

"So you don't even know exactly what's happened?" Elise interrupts. "Is it possible you've just misinterpreted some incomplete information?"

I glance sideways at Derek and Dimi to see them eyeing me back. Elise has always been kind of a bitch, but this crosses the line into unprofessionalism. Malcolm's face is red and Seth narrows his eyes, but Luke is cool as a cucumber as he says, "I'm sorry, I didn't catch your name?"

"Elise Merrow, head—"

"Of marketing. Well, Elise, the answer to your question is no. We may not have every detail of the operation just yet, but it's pretty difficult to misinterpret the kind of systematic theft we've discovered, and the trail is distinct." He smiles then, but it's cold and frankly a little scary. "Also, this is my job, I've been doing it for a long time, and I'm good at it."

His words hang in the air. By rights, what comes of out Elise's mouth next should be an apology, or at least acceptance of the situation.

"It just seems like a week is an awfully short time to have uncovered a—a *plot*," she rolls her eyes, as though the very concept is too ridiculous for words, "that has been going on for so long without ever being discovered."

"I'll tell you what, Elise," Luke counters, "why don't you come down to the conference room after this meeting, and I'll walk you through every element of *the plot* that we've mapped out. For now, we're sidetracking things, and there's a lot still to go through."

She looks around the table, and seeing no support, subsides. "I'll take you up on that." It sounds almost like a challenge, and I wonder what her problem is.

"Good." Luke looks at Malcolm.

"Uh, before we get back to things," Toby from events says almost cautiously, "may I ask, is the reason Ken's on leave just because he failed to notice what was going on?"

"The reason Ken is on leave," Seth answers, with an edge to his voice as he says Ken's name, "is because a disproportionate number of those involved in this operation are related to him by blood or marriage, and the most common bullying tactic that's been identified in preliminary interviews was to use the threat of him as a hammer. His knowledge or lack thereof of the situation needs to be investigated fully."

I feel as though I've been punched in the stomach, and from his indrawn breath, Derek's reaction is similar. I mean, I always knew Ken was mostly useless as director, but he worked his way up to that job with smarts and a solid reputation. That he's let himself get complacent and left things to the department heads to run is… well, reprehensible and a firing offense, but still, I never would have thought he'd be involved in something like this.

I have to remind myself that he may not be. He's been an absent boss. Why would he have noticed if someone was throwing his name around as a threat? Who would make him aware of that?

"At this stage," Luke says, probably in response to the shocked faces around the table, "there's no reason to believe Ken is involved. Our investigation into the matter is just procedure."

"Thank you," Toby replies, looking about as shaken as I feel. Procedure or not, it's still hard to take. Especially since their investigation is going to shed light on exactly how absent and ineffective a director Ken has been. It's unlikely he'll be coming back from his leave.

Don't get me wrong; that's not a bad thing. A new director, someone hands-on, could push JU to the next level. Sure, it's already the second-largest and most profitable entertainment complex in the world, but there's no reason it can't be *first*. A strong director would have seen the results from Derek's district and pushed the rest of us to match them. Hell, a strong director would never have let me continue like this for a year. There should have been an almost immediate improvement when I took over from the idiot before—

Oh.

I've just remembered something. A bit of gossip I overheard a few weeks after I stepped into the AD job.

I look over at Luke, who's listening to Malcolm explain how the business is going to operate over the next few weeks as they determine what the next steps will be. As though he senses my attention, his gaze flicks to me, and I try to communicate with my expression that I need to talk to him when the meeting is over.

Stupid, huh? If I don't catch him before he disappears back to the conference room, I can just text him. But it feels necessary to communicate with wordless facial expressions.

Luke just looks a little confused.

I guess I'll have to use words after all.

By the time the meeting breaks up, with each department allocated a member of the audit team to liaise with (mine is Stewart, the guy who came in with Luke and Diana) and warnings that we're likely looking at some changes in the future, I'm practically wriggling in my seat. My colleagues seem to be eager to leave, practically climbing over each other in their rush toward the door, but I'm headed in the opposite direction.

Seth is the first one to look up as I approach, and he

nudges Malcolm, who's in conversation with Luke. They all turn to me.

"I'm sorry to interrupt," I begin, and Malcolm manages a tired smile.

"You're always welcome to interrupt us," he says. "Seeing as without you, it could have taken forever to see what was happening."

I wince. "About that."

Luke's gaze searches my face. "Are you about to make this seem worse?"

"No!" I shake my head vehemently. "You might already know this. I overheard it months back, and it never seemed relevant. It's about my predecessor."

"We haven't gotten to him yet. Since he's already left the company, he isn't high on our priority list," Luke informs me.

"Right. Well, when I took over the district, I was… a little surprised that it had gotten into that state in so little time. I mean, Graham Dunne, who was AD before that, was known for running a tight ship. I just figured anyone who could let permits expire and need to close a park probably didn't have the best management style, and…" I shrug. "But then I remembered that he's actually cousin by marriage to Lena Teller, and since she's one of the people I was most concerned about…"

The grim set to their faces says it all.

"We'll look into it," Luke promises. "It might be pure coincidence, or it might be that he was complicit and his underlying idiocy shone through."

"There's no way he would have been allowed to keep his job after his negligence caused a park to be closed, not even if he'd been one of *our* relatives," Seth declares. "So if he was complicit, any plan they had would have been derailed then. Even if Ken is involved, he couldn't have done that without us noticing."

"It's worth noting," Derek says behind me, and I jump and half turn. I had no idea he'd followed me, "that a lot of us thought Grant was the better candidate for the job in the first place. I'm not just saying that because he's my friend. He has a better track record, and that should have trumped longevity at the company. I think you should add that to your list of things to look into when you're reviewing the promotions process."

I blink. Fuck me, I hadn't thought of that. At the time, I'd been so disappointed not to get the job. I'd really thought I had it. Derek's right, my track record is better. People liked me more. When I got passed over, it was like a punch to the gut—and the official reason, that the other guy was just as qualified but had more time at the company, seemed kind of hollow. My results were better, but he got the job because he'd worked here longer? A lot of people told me straight out that it was bullshit. Then a rumor started going around that the real reason was because I'm gay, and two gay ADs might send a weird message. I never believed that, because JU—and Joy Inc.—have always had a highly inclusive diversity policy. Our founder was a gay black man, and while he only came out at the end of his life, his diversity policies were always rock-solid. But a lot of people seemed to buy that, and the indignation on my behalf died down.

Now… thinking back and based on what Luke said earlier about this being a network organized for systemic theft, it makes sense that they manipulated one of their people into an AD role. With Ken being an absent director *and* related to a large number of power brokers in that district—*my* district—they could pretty much do whatever they wanted, not even bothering to really hide. Who was going to look? As long as the invoices match the payments and everything is signed off appropriately, accounting doesn't care. As long as the district isn't operating in the red, Ken doesn't care. The AD is supposed to be the one with their finger on the pulse of the district, and if he was complicit…

And then it all went to shit because he *didn't* have his finger on the pulse, the permits lapsed, and the park had to close for a few days. He got fired immediately, I got promoted, and with all that happening in the space of fifteen hours, nobody had time to cover up what they'd just started bringing out into the open. Once I had full systems oversight, they couldn't simply start moving and deleting files—I might notice. And so began the campaign of sabotage.

It all makes sense.

"Grant, are you still with us?" There's a hint of laughter in Malcolm's tone that's really good to hear.

I shake my head, clearing away my thoughts. "Yes. Sorry. I hadn't thought through some of the implications until Derek mentioned them."

"We're going to map it all out," Luke assures me. "This may actually answer some questions my team has had." He smiles, and this time it's friendly and reassuring and makes me feel warm inside. He has such a beautiful smile, and I return it.

"Is there a pool?" Seth asks, and I blink and switch my attention to him. He's talking to Derek, who shakes his head.

"Grant said not to. His reasons were compelling, what with the audit."

My face goes hot enough to fry an egg on. I can't believe he just said that. I can't believe my boss just asked if there was a pool. Luke is *standing right here*.

I literally don't know what to say.

"I think those reasons have changed now," Seth declares. "I want in on the pool."

"There is no pool," I hiss. "There will be no pool." Luke looks vaguely amused but also a little confused, and I hope that's because he doesn't understand what we're talking about.

"There should be a pool," Malcolm argues. "Grant, you can't expect special treatment like this."

The look I give him could incinerate steel, and he laughs.

"What kind of pool are you talking about?" a voice asks, and we turn to see Diana and Stewart.

I close my eyes. This is it. It's all over.

"Uh…" To give him credit, Derek sounds a little uncomfortable, but that doesn't stop him. "When we found out that Grant and Luke used to know each other—"

"Wait. They knew each other?" Seth sounds delighted. "When? How?"

"We went to college together," Luke explains. The way he avoids my eyes and the slight flush on his cheeks indicate that the penny has dropped and he finally gets it.

Talk about mortifying.

"I introduced him to his ex-husband," I add in a desperate attempt to make the situation so uncomfortable that the subject gets dropped.

No such luck.

"If they knew each other, that changes everything." Malcolm rubs his hands together, positively gleeful. "We definitely need a pool."

"Oh!" Diana's eyes light up. "A pool on when they'll hook up? Yes! We'll be in on that."

"Di!" Luke's indignant exclamation has no effect.

Diana is already tapping on her tablet, muttering about odds. "This is ridiculous," he insists, looking right at me.

My stomach sinks.

Sure, this situation is right up there with that nightmare about going to work naked, and having your colleagues and your bosses set up a betting pool about your potential love life right in front of you and the guy who didn't know you had a thing for him is dire, but I'd still had a vague kind of hope that in a few weeks, maybe a month, I could ask Luke out and he might say yes.

That hope is pretty much shattered now. Ridiculous is not an encouraging word.

In the next second, Luke steps up to me, slides a warm hand around my nape, and pulls my face down to his. My stomach explodes in a tornado of butterflies as our lips meet.

I can't believe this is happening.

I can't believe how good it feels.

My heart beats so fast, I think it might actually burst out of my chest. Luke is a *damn* good kisser, and when he pulls away, I have to force myself not to yank him back for more.

After all, we have an audience.

An audience that has gone completely silent.

I want to see what they're doing, but I can't take my eyes off Luke. I don't want to take my eyes off Luke.

"Dinner?" he murmurs. "I'll be here late tonight, but tomorrow?"

Dinner with Luke?

"Yes."

Our audience erupts into cheers.

Jesus fucking Christ.

Luke turns on them. "You all need to get a hobby."

"We have one," Stewart says cheerfully. "Running a

pool on the development of your love life." He looks thoughtful. "Maybe we should set up a weekly status meeting."

Fuck my life.

But… Luke kissed me. And we're going out. My work issues are getting solved. So maybe my life is pretty damn good after all.

TWELVE

Luke

I kissed Grant in the boardroom, after a very important meeting, while my bosses watched.

What the fuck is wrong with me?

Not the kissing Grant part. That was great, and I'm glad I did it. I'd planned to do it eventually anyway—the timeline just got sped up when I saw how embarrassed he was by the betting pool. But doing it at work in front of our colleagues and bosses… that was an impulse I just don't understand. I managed to avoid an inquisition from my team right after, but you can bet your ass it's coming.

Sighing, I get out of my car and go into the house. It's a little after nine, and I could actually still be at work, but I couldn't ask Jus to stay later than this with so little warning. Especially since I'm going to need either him or Jas to stay tomorrow night so I can go on my date with Grant. Which technically I don't have time for this week, but some things you just *make* time for.

I find Jus in the living room, watching TV.

"Hey," he says, turning it off. "Long day?"

"Never-ending." I drop my laptop bag on an armchair

and sink down to sit on the arm. "How was everything here? How was Jordy's practice?"

He shrugs. "Jordy's great. He had a fantastic time and has decided he's going to be a professional baseball player. He's actually pretty good, especially given he's never really played before, and he gets along well with the others. One of the kids invited him to a birthday party this Saturday—I put the details on the noticeboard—and there was talk of summer baseball camp."

A sense of calm settles over me. I would work a thousand exhausting days like this to know that Jordy's happy.

"And Mila?"

Jus hesitates, and that calm evaporates.

"She was a little moody," he admits. "I mean, I know that's normal for a teenager"—I bite back a smile at hearing this from someone who's really not that far beyond his teens—"but she seemed a little moodier than usual."

"Okay. I'll go let her know I'm home, see if she wants to talk about it. Thanks, Jus."

He gets up and looks at me appraisingly. "Have you eaten? There's leftover pot roast in the fridge. I could warm it up."

"You made pot roast?" Hell, I really lucked out in the housekeeper category.

He shakes his head. "Jas made it. Mine always comes out dry, no matter what I do."

"So does mine. Thanks, but I've eaten—we ordered in at around seven."

"I'll head out, then, unless there's something you need."

"No, we're all good. Thanks, Jus." I need to tell him about tomorrow night, but that would make it *real*.

More real than having the CEO and CFO of Joy Incorporated know?

"Actually, could either you or Jas stay late tomorrow night?" I blurt.

"Sure. Work's out of control, huh? They didn't give you much time to settle in." He makes a sympathetic face.

I don't know why, but my face and neck get insanely hot, and I know I've gone bright red.

Jus looks startled, then grins knowingly. "Ohhhhhhh. Not work, then."

If possible, I blush harder. Jesus, what's wrong with me? I'm thirty-six years old, not sixteen.

"Don't worry, I can stay late. I can even stay overnight if you want. The couch is pretty comfortable."

I shake my head firmly. "No, thanks." Although I can't say I'm not tempted. "I was reminded recently that Mila is going to be dating soon, and I don't want her thinking casual sleepovers are okay." Yet. Not until she's older. Maybe ninety.

Jus's eyes widen. "Fuck, I didn't even think…. She's just a kid!"

As glad as I am to know he thinks of her that way—not that I really thought he didn't, but apparently being a parent makes a tiny part of you paranoid—I chuckle as I remind him, "She'll be fifteen soon."

His face sets. "I'll talk to Jas. If she starts showing an interest in any boy, we'll ask around and make sure he's okay."

I'm touched—and a little amused—by his protectiveness. "Or girl. I want to be prepared if she hooks up with a bitchy girl."

"Boy, girl, or whoever, we'll make sure Mila's okay."

He says goodnight and heads out, muttering to himself about kids growing up so fast. I don't quite know what to make of it—after all, he's barely more than a kid himself, and he's known Mila and Jordy for about two weeks.

On the other hand, I knew them for five seconds before I fell head over heels.

I make my way upstairs and along the hallway. Jordy's door is halfway open, the way he likes it, and through it I can see that he's out like a light in his standard starfish sprawl. Further down the hall, light streams from Mila's open door. She normally has it closed, and I've learned that an open door is an indication that she wants to talk.

I lean against the doorframe and knock. She looks up from her Kindle. Music plays softly, one of the indie bands she likes that I've now heard a million times. I'm thankful for her taste in music—it's not quite like mine, but it could be worse.

"You're home," she says. "Was today as tough as you thought?" I told the kids when I got home on Monday night that this week would be a long, rough one, so they wouldn't be surprised if I was late home. I feel like telling them stuff like that sets an example for them to tell me stuff. So far, it seems to be working.

"Yes, but there was also a surprising turn of events." Should I tell her about my date with Grant? She seemed to like him on Saturday, and she was okay with it the two times I've dated (that's two dates, by the way, each with a different guy, neither worth a second evening away from the kids) since Matt left. On the other hand, Grant and I might be better off as friends, and it might be a good idea to wait before introducing the kids to the idea of him as more.

I ignore the fluttering sensation that tells me Grant and I will *not* be better off as friends.

"I'm waiting to see what happens with that," I settle on. "Hopefully it'll turn out the way I want."

She nods and her gaze slides away.

Fuck.

"Everything good with you?" I ask lightly, and her attention comes back to me.

"Yeah. Just… there's… uh." She shakes her head and starts again. "I've been invited to this party Friday night."

Uh-oh. While I'm glad she's making friends and people are inviting her places, she's never before been reticent about asking me if she could go somewhere, so this is probably not a good sign.

"Okay…," I prompt.

"The thing is, the girl whose house it's at is… not that nice. She's been kind of a bitch to me, actually. Not in a bullying way," she rushes to add when I straighten. "She's just not a nice person."

"All right." I'm a little confused. "So why did she invite you?" And does Mila want to go to this party or not? What's going on here?

My niece turns a bright shade of pink—probably the same color I was when I told Jus about my date—and the penny drops.

"She didn't invite you." I walk into the room and sink down onto her desk chair. I think I need to be sitting for this.

"There's this guy…"

Yep. It's begun, and I am not prepared.

"…he's been really sweet, introducing me to people and stuff. He asked me to go with him, but I don't think Bria—that's the girl—would be really happy if I turned up, and it would be soooo embarrassing if she said something mean in front of Jamie. But I don't want to say no to Jamie in case he thinks I don't like him. What should I do, Uncle Luke?"

Wait, this is about her asking me for advice? Not permission to go to the party? Oh, hell. It just got *worse*.

I take a deep breath. "First, and you are not allowed to

roll your eyes when I say this, if you don't want to go, then you shouldn't let your fear of what Jamie thinks change that." I hold up a hand when she opens her mouth. "Let me finish. I know you're an intelligent young woman, but it concerns me that you don't want to say no in case it influences his feelings. If you genuinely don't want to go to this party, there are other ways—verbal ways," I add hastily, "to let Jamie know that you... like him." I try not to choke on the last two words. I need to get used to the idea of her dating.

There's an expression of teenage condescension on her face, but she nods. "I get it, Uncle Luke. I'm not going to let anyone pressure me into doing something I don't want to just so they'll like me." The "duh" is clear in her tone. I ignore it.

"Good. So... restate the problem?"

This time she does roll her eyes. "You're *such* a business consultant," she sighs. "The problem is, I kind of do want to go to the party. I like Jamie"—the blush returns—"and most of the other kids going are really cool too. They've all been friendly and I'd like to hang out with them."

"But you're worried that if you go, this Brianna girl—"

"Bria," she corrects.

"Sorry. This Bria girl will say something catty to you and potentially embarrass you in front of Jamie and the other kids."

"Nobody says 'catty' anymore, Uncle Luke."

"Are you seriously picking on my vocabulary while I'm trying to help you?" I pick up her stress ball from the desk and lob it gently at her. "Show some gratitude."

She tosses the ball back. "Don't mess up my stuff, please. Fine. Yes, I'm worried Bria will embarrass me in front of everyone."

"Hmmm." I lean back in the chair, trying to focus on

her problem—the party—and not mine—her date. "Wouldn't it be more embarrassing for *her* if she says something mean in front of everyone? You said they're all nice kids."

"Yeah, but I can't take that risk. It's not like I know what she'll say."

Patience. I try to remind myself what it was like to be a teenager. "Let's change tack," I suggest. "This might all be a completely moot point."

She eyes me warily. "Why?"

"I haven't said you can go to the party yet. And I'm not going to until I have more information about Bria, her parents, the party, and Jamie."

She rolls her eyes, just like I was expecting her to. "Uncle Luuuuke." It's an exasperated sigh, but I actually like hearing it. There was a time, right after Matt left, when she never argued with me or expressed any kind of displeasure or exasperation… presumably for fear that I'd leave too. I love knowing she feels confident enough to whine at me like a normal teenager.

"Tell me about the party first," I suggest. "Will it be supervised?"

She shrugs and looks away. "I don't know."

"You don't know, or no, it won't?" She's still only fourteen. I'm not letting her go to a party that could end up being a kegger. There are some things I *do* remember about being a teenager.

"I really don't know," she admits. "Jamie asked me today if I'd go with him. Before that, I didn't really pay attention when people were talking about it because I knew Bria would never invite me."

I don't bother to suggest she could have asked Jamie for details. I'm not that clueless.

"Is there anyone…," I begin, but don't bother finishing

when a look of horror crosses her face. Right. She's still the new girl, and she doesn't want to be uncool and ask if there will be parents at a party. "That doesn't leave us with a lot of options. I guess I could drop you off instead of Jamie's parents, and if I don't like the look of things or if Bria's parents aren't there, you—" I stop short. There's something about her expression.... "Is there something you haven't mentioned?"

She looks at her lap and mumbles something.

"Mila?"

Sighing, she lifts her head and says, "Jamie was going to drive us."

Jamie was?

So Jamie is sixteen.

I hope.

"What grade is Jamie in?" Please don't let him be about to graduate.

"He's a junior," Mila rushes to assure me, and while that's better than what I was thinking, it's not really. He's still driving. He still wants to date my kid. And take her places. In a *car*. Where they'll have a certain amount of privacy.

Oh, hell no.

My face must show what I'm thinking, because Mila says, "You can't say no just because he's older than me. That's not fair. Uncle Matt is older than you."

That throws me off, because Mila doesn't talk about Matt. Ever. She's really pulling out the big guns.

"Actually," I choose my words carefully, "as your uncle and your parent, I can say no for whatever reason I want." Her mouth sets mutinously. "However, I understand your position on this and I want you to understand mine so we can come to a mutually agreeable outcome." And if we can't, she'll just have to abide by my wishes.

She still looks pissed but nods grudgingly. "Go on."

"I don't know Jamie, and I'm reluctant for you to get in a car with anyone I don't know, but especially someone with limited driving experience, and even more so with that someone being a teenager. Teenagers are proven to be occasionally volatile and driven by hormonal surges, which can manifest in reckless driving." I try to sound as factual as possible. "That leads to my second concern. The age gap between you isn't big, and if you were a freshman and he a junior in *college*, I wouldn't be worried. But while you're both at…" I grope for the right term. "…hormonally unstable stages of development, he's a little further along, and—"

"Oh my God, are you talking about *sex*?" Mila's eyes go wide. "Uncle Luke!"

"Believe me, I don't want to have this conversation any more than you do. To put it bluntly, I'm worried that Jamie might be sexually active and could potentially pressure you into having sex before you're ready." Or at all. Because she's my baby niece and she shouldn't be ready until she's a legal adult at the very least.

"He wouldn't do that," she declares. "And even if he tried to, I'm not an idiot! I just said before that I wouldn't let people pressure me into doing things I didn't want to."

"You did," I agree. "But Mila, I'm also worried that you might want to. I'm not saying you should never date or have a boyfriend," I continue as she opens her mouth indignantly, "but these things sometimes happen faster when you're with someone who has more experience." I really hope she doesn't ask me how I know that. Because I was not that much older than her when I "dated" a college guy.

"I think it's really unfair of you to judge Jamie when you don't know him." She folds her arms the way she always does when she's being stubborn. I'm going to have to change my approach if I want to avoid a fight.

"You're right," I agree, and there's a certain amount of satisfaction in seeing her jaw drop. "I should meet Jamie before I make a decision about this."

"No! Oh my God, Uncle Luke, are you trying to make me a laughingstock? He asked me to go to a party, that's all! I can't tell him he has to meet my uncle before I even know if I can go."

"What did you tell him?" I ask.

"That I had to check with you first," she mutters. "And that was embarrassing enough."

"Why? Did he make you feel bad about it?" If he did, she's never going on a date with him, no matter what I have to do to stop it.

Reluctantly, she shakes her head. "He just smiled and said 'no problem,'" she admits. "But *I* was embarrassed, having to say I needed permission like a little kid."

It's my turn to want to roll my eyes. "You're fourteen," I remind her gently. "I'll bet most of the kids in your class need permission to do stuff. But we're getting off topic."

"If the topic is you having to meet Jamie before I can go to the party with him, then it's dead and we're never resurrecting it," she declares with suitable drama.

"That's fine. I'm still not inclined to let you go to the party at all, since we don't know if it's supervised."

"Uncle Luuuuuke." She pouts.

"You weren't even sure if you wanted to go," I remind her, and she heaves a sigh.

"Life is hard."

I bite my lip to keep myself from laughing. "I know, honey," I say solemnly. "I can't decide for you if you want to go, but I can give you your options, okay?"

Taking a deep breath, she nods. "Hit me with them."

"You can choose not to go to the party. Tell Jamie it's my fault, if you like. I don't mind being the bad guy. If he likes you, he'll ask you out again."

She looks a little dubious, so I keep talking.

"You can choose to go to the party, but I will drive you and pick you up, and if I don't like the look of things, you're not getting out of the car."

Her eyes go wide. "Unc—"

I hold up my hand. "Let me finish. Your third option is that you can choose to go to the party with Jamie driving you, but first you need to find out that it will be supervised, I need to talk to the adults supervising it and be happy with what they say, and I need to meet Jamie and like him. If any one of those things doesn't happen, you're not going."

"Those last two options *suck*." Mila crosses her arms again.

I shrug. "You can always choose option one."

She glares. "This brings me right back to the original problem. You haven't helped at all, Uncle Luke, you've just given me more things to decide!"

I lean back in the chair and study her. "Okay. Do you want my honest opinion on what you should do?"

"Am I going to like it?"

I laugh—I can't help it. "I don't know."

She waves a hand, giving me permission to continue. Smart-ass.

"Take option one. You don't like this girl, you're worried she's going to be a bitch, and you don't like the options that will allow you to go to the party. Tell Jamie your uncle's a dick and won't let you go, and then ask him and a couple of other kids if they want to come here for a swim on Saturday afternoon." That will give me a chance to meet Jamie and see how he acts around my niece without Mila being "humiliated."

I know I've made the right call when her face lights up. "Really? You'd be okay with that?"

Do I want to spend my Saturday afternoon after a really long week overrun with teenagers? No. But I smile and say, "Sure. Not more than a dozen kids, though, all right?"

Her brows come together, and I know she's mentally counting. "That's fine. That's perfect. Thanks, Uncle Luke!"

I wish her goodnight and leave her in a much happier state than when I arrived. I'm halfway down the hall when something occurs to me, and I turn around and retrace my steps.

"Mila," I say, sticking my head back around her door. "What's Jamie's last name?"

She blinks. "Boyd. Why?"

"No reason. Good night."

I close the door and pull my phone out of my pocket to send Jus a quick text.

It was boy trouble. Do you and Jas know anything about a high school junior called Jamie Boyd?

He texts me back in less than a minute.

Nope, but we'll ask around.

I can't ask for more than that.

THIRTEEN

Grant

To say Thursday is a weird day would be understating it. For one thing, my whole district is in upheaval. Seventeen of my staff were escorted from the premises yesterday, our director "went on leave," and a company-wide memo went out reminding all employees that they're not to gossip to the press. Luke and his team have basically been put in charge of operations, which makes a lot of people nervous, and I spend a big part of the morning visiting my park and resorts, reassuring my people that their jobs aren't on the line.

That's not even mentioning The Date. Which I'm trying not to think about, because it's so distracting that I won't get any work done.

I stop in the Village on my way back to the office. It's lunchtime, I'm hungry, and Dimi's been blowing up my phone all morning. If I get the inquisition over with, he might leave me alone.

Maybe.

To say that he's pissed he left the boardroom before Luke kissed me is like saying a hurricane is just a little storm. I get the feeling that his frustration is compounded by the fact that everyone who was in the boardroom at the time agreed not to gossip about it, and that Derek swore him to secrecy.

I find him with Jason and Trav in the Joy Village Theater Company office, which is basically a tiny suite of rooms attached to the theater. The three of them are in earnest conversation when I open the door and step in.

Unfortunately, the conversation is about me.

"The man of the hour!" Trav grins. "Boy, do we have questions for you. Got time for lunch?"

"I'm starving," I admit.

"Sit," Dimi orders, pointing through a door. "Derek's on his way and he's picking up food."

I raise an eyebrow as I follow him into the conference room. "Should I be offended that you didn't invite me?"

"No." Jason sits across from me. "Dimi was planning a council of war. You would have been better off not showing up." He winks to show he's joking… I hope.

The outer door slams and I hear Derek's voice, then he and Trav come into the room, laden down with takeout bags from the taco place here in the village.

Derek stops short. "Grant. Uhhh."

"Don't worry." I wave tiredly. "Jason already told me about the council of war."

"Yeah, no. That's not it. I didn't know you'd be here, and when I ran into Luke on my way out of the building, I dragged him along. He's just on a call."

I swear, Dimi's face lights up. "Excellent."

I roll my eyes. "Why is that a problem?" Aside from the fact that I haven't spoken to Luke yet since The Kiss. And The Date is tonight.

Derek eyes me, then smiles. "Great, then." He sets the food on the conference table and starts opening bags.

The outer door opens and closes. "Hello?" a voice calls, and I force myself not to shiver. I think I fail, because Jason smirks across the table at me.

"In here," Dimi says, going to the open door, and a moment later, he steps back to let Luke pass him.

"Hi," he says, his gaze sweeping over us all. I'm sure I'm not imagining that it stutters a little on me. "Uh, I don't want to be a dick, but I don't have a lot of time. I really shouldn't have come, but Derek kind of insisted."

"I really did," Derek agrees, handing me a wrapped taco. "Come and sit. I've got to be back for a meeting, so we won't hang around long."

Luke takes the seat beside me, and my entire right side tingles. I shoot him a sideways glance, only to find him doing the same. Our gazes meet… and we break out in laughter.

It's ridiculous. We're both grown men, and we're acting like teenagers.

I lean over and kiss him on the cheek, and he grins. "Thank you. Pass me a taco?" I do, and while he's unwrapping it, I glance up and see four dumbstruck faces.

"That's a good look on you," I tell Dimi, and he shakes himself out of it and flips me the bird.

"I have questions," he declares. "Derek tells me the pool is on hold until we work out what's going on with you."

"I'd prefer you just forget the pool entirely," Luke says, and takes a bite.

Jason snorts. "Good luck with that." He gets an elbow to the ribs from his boyfriend.

We get through lunch with Dimi and Trav asking nosy questions that Luke and I mostly deflect. Occasionally, Dimi tries to throw us off by slipping in a question about work—he knows I was involved somehow in the audit hoopla, and he wants details. In the end, Luke says, "Stop asking him about that, Dimi. He's not allowed to talk about it just yet." Which basically confirms everything Dimi's been wondering about without me having to say a word.

Finally, Dimi sits back, fiddling with the wrapper from his taco. "You guys have really cheated me. No pool, no company gossip... come on, you've gotta give me something."

"This is a side of you I do not like," I tell him. "Fine. You can tell people that Luke and I are going on a date."

He brightens. "Thank you. Oh, Luke, before I forget, I'm going to email you a list from my mom of businesses in town that are looking for summer help. But Mom also said the summer day camp program is looking for high schoolers to be junior counselors, and Mila might be interested in that too."

"That sounds great, thank you. Please tell your mom I'm grateful." He seems a little distracted, though.

Derek gets up. "Welp, watching Dimi go all master inquisitor has been fun, but I have to get going. Grant, you'll give Luke a ride back to the office, yeah?" He bends to kiss Trav and doesn't notice me flip him off. Not that I mind driving Luke, but Derek's heavy-handed matchmaker antics are not appreciated.

In the next minute, he's out the door, and Luke and I help clean up before we leave. It's not until we're in my car and pulling out of the lot that I ask, "Is everything okay?"

He smiles over at me. "Yeah. I just... Mila had this whole drama over a party, and I somehow agreed to let her have friends over on Saturday." He gives me a quick rundown of the situation.

"You're a better person than me," I admit as we turn into the parking lot for the administration building. "I can't see myself volunteering to host a pool party for a bunch of teenagers."

Laughing, he teases, "So you don't want to come over on Saturday, then?"

I do. The thought strikes hard. We're going out tonight, and I promised Jordy I'd be there for movies tomorrow night, and yet I also want to spend Saturday with one eye on a group of teens, as long as Luke is there.

Fuck, I've got it bad.

Trying not to let it show too much, I grin. "We'll see. I guess you'll need reinforcements, and I've always been willing to take one for the team." It's only after the words are out that I realize how suggestive they are, and the back of my neck gets hot as I park the car.

Luke leans over, intent unmistakable on his face, and butterflies ramp up in my stomach. I'm smiling by the time our lips meet, and so is he, and it's the weirdest, happiest kiss I've ever had.

"I'm so glad we're doing this," he murmurs against my mouth, draws back a little, and then drops a gentle kiss at the corner of my lips.

"Me too. So, tonight? I'm guessing you want to go home and check on the kids first?" I've never been a parent, but Luke seems like a dedicated one.

"Do you mind? I wasn't home until late last night, and I left early this morning and yesterday, so I haven't spoken to Jordy since Tuesday night." He's wearing a faintly guilty expression, and I realize that his date invite, impulsive as it was, didn't take into account what a busy week this would be for him.

"We can skip tonight," I offer, trying not to sound reluctant, even though a little voice is screaming that I'm an idiot for even suggesting it. The thing is, if I'm going to date Luke—and more—I have to be prepared to factor in his kids, right?

He shakes his head. "No, I don't want to do that. I—I feel like this has been a long time coming. Just let me go home first and see the kids real quick, and then we can have dinner."

I try to think outside the box. "What if you have dinner with the kids and then we have drinks later? We can plan an actual dinner date for another time."

He surprises me by kissing me again, this time hard and fast. "You're such a great guy. Have dinner with us, and we'll go out after."

A family dinner? "Are you sure?"

"Yes," he declares. "Can you be finished with work by five thirty? The kids usually eat a little after six. And I'll make plans for after." The way he looks at me promises that whatever those plans are, they'll include some adult time.

"I'll look forward to it."

I wish I could tell you I spent the rest of the afternoon daydreaming about what Luke and I would be doing on our date, but the truth is, my afternoon is just as chaotic as the morning was, and I barely have time to sneak off to the bathroom. Stu, my liaison from the audit team, told me that we'd take a coffee break at some stage to talk about my relationship with Luke and then dug right in to work. He promised to interfere as little as possible with day-to-day routine, but since my district is a mess and I now have the opportunity to rebuild things the way I want them, there is no day-to-day routine right now. I've told my people that their priority is the guest experience—even at the expense (no pun intended) of profitability. I can work on getting that sorted out later; the most important thing now is making sure there *is* a later, and that means happy guests.

By the time Luke knocks on my office door at five thirty, I'm beginning to think I might have a handle on things. At the very least, I have a to-do list as long as my arm, and only a few people I trust that I can delegate things to. But it's a start, and at least now I know my plans won't be sabotaged.

"Ready to go?" Luke asks, and I grin at him.

"Yep." I grab my laptop and phone and follow him out, wishing we didn't both have cars here. It would've been nice to ride with him.

A surprising number of people say goodnight to me as we walk through the building to the front entrance, and I know it's because Luke's with me and they're hoping to meet the head of the audit team and maybe get some inside news on what's happening.

Or at least, that's what I thought before Toby from events hails us in the lobby.

"Off for your big date? Have a great time!"

Fuck me.

Luke and I exchange glances but say nothing. I smile and wave at Toby as though he didn't just share my business with half the building at top volume. Dimi must be better at manipulating the gossip mill than I thought. With him being at the Village and having a full schedule this afternoon, I was sure news would take a little longer to reach the admin building. That'll teach me to doubt the efficiency of the JU gossip mill.

Luke waits until we're outside before he says dryly, "I hope the kids haven't heard already. I really wanted to tell them myself."

"Good luck with that. I'm just hoping the news hasn't made it to my parents in Wisconsin yet."

He snorts, and we part ways to go to our own cars.

When I pull up out the front of his house, Luke's just getting out of his car in the garage. He's left the door open for me and waits for me to walk up the driveway and join him.

"Uh, before we go in," I begin, suddenly a little nervous, "it's okay if you don't want to tell the kids we're going out. I mean… if you want me to just be here as a friend tonight. I don't mind."

"I mind," he says firmly, and kisses me. I swear, I will never get used to this feeling. It's like freefalling. His lips taste better than anything else, ever. My vision is a little hazy when he pulls back. "You and I are dating, and I'm happy for everyone to know it."

Is it wrong that those words make me half hard?

I'm frantically thinking about brussels sprouts and slimy drain mold as I follow Luke into the house. Fortunately, that does the trick.

There are two strangers in the kitchen, one checking a pot on the stove, the other sitting at the table, folding napkins. They look alike enough to be siblings, and it doesn't take a lot of intelligence to guess that they're Jus and Jas. I thought they traded off shifts, though?

"Fancy seeing you both here." There's a sarcastic edge to Luke's voice, and the twins grin.

"Sorry," Jas says. "When Jus called and said you were bringing home a date for dinner, I got nosy. But I have important information to make up for it." She gets up and offers me a hand. "I'm Jasmine, but you can call me Jas."

"Grant." I take her hand. "Nice to meet you."

Jus comes over from the stove and I shake hands with

him too. "We're not usually this invasive," he assures me. "Or we are, but you'll stop noticing."

I snort. "I work at JU. Invasive is my way of life. Is there something I can do to help?"

Jus waves a hand dismissively and turns back to the stove. "Nah, I've got it. Sit down and hear Jas's update on the boy Mila likes."

What? I look sharply at Luke. "Mila likes a boy? What do we know about him?" I feel a weird surge of protectiveness. I don't know Mila well—hardly at all, really—but she's Luke's, and she seems like a good kid, and apparently that means I give a shit about her life.

Luke raises an eyebrow. "Right now, I know that his name's Jamie Boyd and he's a junior. Jas and Jus were going to ask around for me."

A junior? But Mila's not even fifteen yet.

I frown.

"Sit," Jas says, and there's a kind of long-suffering indulgence in her voice that makes me feel like an idiot. "The kids could come in anytime."

Luke and I meekly join her at the table.

"Okay, so my friend has a sister, Lisa, who's a sophomore at Joyville High, and she asked some questions for me. I was getting text updates until about five minu—" The phone on the table chimes, and she glances at the screen. "I'm still getting text updates," she amends, picking up her cell and tapping the screen. A grin spreads across her face, and she says to Luke, "According to the high school rumor mill, Mila's uncle is incredibly overprotective of her because she's an orphan, and she's not going to the party tomorrow night because she doesn't like to make him worry for things that aren't really important."

A laugh escapes me. Luke buries his face in his hands.

"She's good," Jus says admiringly from the stove, and

Luke groans.

"I feel like there's something about that statement that should get her grounded, but I don't know what." His words are muffled by his hands. I reach out and tug them away.

"She doesn't need to be grounded," I tell him. I mean... maybe the dig about the party being unimportant was a little unkind to whoever's hosting it, but not beyond acceptable.

He sighs and looks at Jas. "Tell us about Jamie."

She smiles. "Jamie's excellent boyfriend material. He gets good grades, plays baseball, which will thrill Jordy, and is very popular at school. He had a girlfriend for most of last year, and they've stayed friends since they broke up in November. She's dating a friend of his now. He's been dating on and off this year, but it hasn't gone beyond casual with anyone." She leans back and spreads her hands. "I don't know the kid personally, but my friend's sister is pretty grounded, and if she says he's a good guy, I'm inclined to believe it."

Silence.

"Does it make me a douche if I say he sounds too good to be true?" Jus turns off the stove and moves the pot to the draining board.

Luke huffs a laugh. "I guess we'll have to meet him and form our own judgments. It's good to know he's not a delinquent or anything, though. Thanks, Jas."

"Have you thought about dating rules yet?" I ask, remembering what Dimi said last weekend, and Luke shrugs.

"Not until last night. I've got a few things in mind now." He half turns in his seat to take in both Jas and Jus. "The most important one is, if Mila has a boy here, they stay downstairs. No boys in her bedroom, ever."

"No problem," Jas agrees.

"Doors will stay open, too," Jus adds.

The sound of footsteps thundering down the stairs brings the conversation to an abrupt halt, and a second later, Jordy comes in.

"Grant! Jus said you were coming." He looks me over doubtfully. "Did you bring a change of clothes?"

This kid….

"Sorry, no. I came straight from work."

"You and Grant can play catch another time," Luke says, then turns to me. "Are you still coming for movie night tomorrow?"

Feeling warm from the inside out, I nod. "If I'm still welcome."

"Of course." His gaze says something more, and the warm feeling switches to burning hot. He returns his attention to Jordy. "Maybe tomorrow night."

Jordy grins from ear to ear. "Cool! Are we eating soon, 'cause I'm starving." He rolls his eyes at me. "Uncle Luke won't let me have Pop-Tarts after school anymore."

Jas nudges him. "You mean he won't let you have *six* Pop-Tarts after school."

"Thank you, Jas. You make me sound like a tyrant," Luke scolds Jordy playfully. "I'm sure you had two Pop-Tarts and something else as well."

"An apple, cheese and crackers, and a ham sandwich," Jus recites. "Jordy, will you help Jas set the table, please?"

As if on cue, my stomach growls. "Sorry." How embarrassing. "It smells amazing in here." It's not even like I usually eat at this time. Most nights, I'm still at work. "Uh, I'll just go wash up, and then I'll help set the table."

Jordy gazes at me with something akin to worship, and I gotta say, it doesn't suck. If offering to spend a couple minutes putting out silverware will make him like the idea of me with Luke, I'll take on that chore for every meal I eat here.

"I'll show you the downstairs bath," Luke offers. I follow him out of the kitchen, and only a few feet down the hall, he pulls me into a powder room, shuts the door, and pushes me up against it.

I don't have time to be surprised before I have an armful of him, his mouth seeking mine needily.

"You're amazing," he mutters between kisses. "Thank you for trying to impress my nephew."

For a long minute, I forget that I'm supposed to reply. Words? Huh? His tongue is so much more interesting, not to mention his body in that suit. My hands stray away from the safe zone.

It's the sound of a door slamming somewhere that drags us back to reality. I lean my forehead against his, both of us panting.

"Dinner," I manage. "Kids."

"Yeah." Luke sucks in a deep breath and pulls away. "I'm going to change clothes. Can't wait for our date later."

Yes! Our date. Where we can be alone. In private.

"I've got a really nice bottle of champagne at my place. We could have drinks there." It was a Christmas gift from a friend I never see who's always trying to impress me with the amount of money his wife's family has. I have no problem accepting his gifts and sending appropriately gushy thank-yous if it makes him happy.

To my regret, Luke shakes his head. "No, I have something in mind. We might be really late home, though. Is that okay with you?"

Stay out late with him? "Sure."

He flashes a smile that promises all kinds of delicious things. "I'll see you in a few minutes." He slips out, leaving me to lean against the door and count to a hundred in an attempt to get my erection to go down.

When I'm finally in a fit state to be around other people, I wash up and head back to the kitchen. The table is set, and Mila has joined Jordy and the twins.

"Hi, Mila," I say casually. "How's school?"

She shrugs. "It's been good, thanks. I'm making friends. Did Uncle Luke tell you about Saturday?"

Saturday? Does she mean her friends coming over? "Ah, he mentioned you're having friends over."

Disappointment crosses her face. "Oh. So he didn't invite you to hang out with him and Jordy?"

"Jordy is going to invite two of his friends," Luke says as he enters. "And Grant is more than welcome to join us if he wants, but I don't know how enjoyable he'll find supervising a teenager's pool party."

He's not wrong, but I'm happy to do anything if it means time with him. Plus, think of the points I'll earn—and how nicely he might be inclined to thank me for keeping him company.

As Jordy exclaims over how awesome it will be and decides who he's going to invite, I smile over at Luke and tell Mila, "I'm happy to come and keep your uncle company."

"Oh, yay!" Mila cheers, and as if we'd rehearsed it, Luke and I both turn skeptical looks on her.

"If you think Grant's company is going distract me from keeping an eye on you, you're sorely mistaken," Luke says dryly.

Her face only falls a little. "We're only going to be swimming and sunbathing." She sounds exasperated in a way only teenagers can. "Just don't be uncool, yeah?"

I bite my lip to keep from laughing at the look on Luke's face.

"Dinner!" Jus interrupts, and the edge of laughter in his voice is pretty indicative that he timed the interruption deliberately.

Dinner is a revelation. I've said before that I never really thought about having kids, that if anyone had ever suggested it, I'd be supremely uninterested… and a little put off. I still feel that way when I think about having a baby in my care, or a little kid. But older kids like Jordy and Mila… I think I could be okay with that. And I don't just mean because they're Luke's and I'm already thinking about Luke and me in terms of forever, even though we only met again less than two weeks ago.

We're halfway through the meal and have just heard about Jordy's day in great detail and Mila's in a few sentences when Luke clears his throat and glances at me.

"Uh, so Jus is going to stay here with you tonight while I go out with Grant."

"Okay." Jordy shoves another forkful of food into his mouth, but Mila's attention is piqued.

"Are you going out, or, like, *out* out?" She looks between me and her uncle, and I'm suddenly nervous. What if she doesn't like the idea of me dating Luke? She seems okay with me, but there's a difference between someone being a casual acquaintance and dating your uncle.

I feel like there's a joke in there somewhere, but I'm not quite sure what it is.

Luke meets her gaze steadily. "*Out* out. On a date."

Jordy's fork meets his plate with a clatter. "You're going on a date with Grant?"

Shit. I thought for sure Jordy would be okay with it.

"Yes," Luke says.

A wide smile splits Jordy's face. "Cool." He goes back to his meal, but I don't let the relief take over. There's still Mila's reaction to worry about.

She's studying me like I'm… I don't know. Some kind of thing she'd study with a blank look on her face. I try not to let my fear show. Maybe I can't deal with kids after all. Are they like animals, sensing fear and knowing when to attack?

Yes, maybe I'm being just a little hysterical. I paste a friendly-yet-casual smile on my face and reach for my water glass.

"Okay," she says finally. "Will you be gone overnight?"

"No," Luke and I say in unison. Not that I wouldn't be thrilled to have a sleepover with Luke, but I know he wouldn't leave the kids overnight at the last second like this.

"Why not?"

Jesus. Did I say I could be okay with older kids? Clearly, I was wrong.

"Because it's our first date and we both have work tomorrow." Luke's answer is perfectly composed. He may worry about this parenting thing, but it looks to me like he has it under control. "Before we go, I'll give you the list of places Dimi sent me that are looking for summer help."

Mila shoots her uncle a look that says she knows she's being purposely distracted but goes along with it. "Thank you. Have you looked at it? Did there look like there was anywhere interesting?"

"It's a summer job, not a lifelong career," Luke says dryly. "I doubt any of them will be thrilling. Oh, except maybe the camp counselor job. That could be fun, I guess."

"Jus and I used to do that," Jas pipes in. "It *is* fun." She turns to Mila. "You didn't say you wanted a summer job."

Mila shrugs. "Uncle Luke wasn't really keen, and then his friend's mom was going to ask around for me, so… I was waiting to see what they said."

"I don't know what else is on the list, but working for the summer camp program is awesome. We did it all four summers through high school and then two more when we were home from college."

"Is it a sleepaway camp?" I ask, intrigued. I had no idea there was a summer camp in Joyville. Of course, I don't have kids, so it's not something I would ever have looked into.

Jus shakes his head. "No, a day program. Sports, crafts, stuff like that. There are different streams you can enroll in to suit your interests, or you can do a general program and get a bit of everything. The baseball camp Jordy's teammates are doing is part of the program."

"Can I go, Uncle Luke?" Jordy asks, pushing away his empty plate.

"Sounds good to me." Luke glances at Jas. "Who do I need to call for more information?"

"I'll get the details for you." She raises a brow at Mila. "Do you want me to get a junior counselor application form for you?"

Mila appears to consider it. "I think so. It's helping to organize and supervise the kids?"

"Pretty much," Jus affirms. "Some grunt work too—setting up and cleaning up. But mostly you get to help with the activities. There will probably be a bunch of kids from your school doing it."

Those are the magic words. "I'll look at the list of other places, but I guess it can't hurt to apply. If nothing else, it will be convenient for you guys, since Jordy will be there anyway."

"How very considerate of you." Luke's face is completely straight, and I bite my lip. Who knew trying not to laugh was such a big part of parenting?

FOURTEEN

Luke

I'm really nervous about this date, not least because it's been a long time since I organized a date. Like… seventeen years. The few dates I've been on since Matt left, the other guy planned. This is the first date I've asked a guy on and planned as a non-student adult. So… yeah, this is a big thing.

Lucky for me, Grant is… I don't even have words. He was so great with the kids at dinner, even if he seemed a bit uncomfortable once or twice… but who wouldn't be uncomfortable with Mila asking pointed questions? So even if my plans turn out to be a dud, I know it's not going to ruin things. Kissing him yesterday—and every time since—was one of the best things I've ever done.

We say goodnight to the kids and Grant suggests that we take his car and he'll drop me home after.

"Where are we headed?" he asks once we're belted in and he's started the engine.

"Back to JU. The Chateau resort." A thought strikes me as he drives down the street and turns onto the main road. "That's not one of yours, is it?" A first date at a place where he's the boss would not be conducive to my plans.

He shakes his head. "No, that one's Derek's."

"Phew. I guess I should make an effort to learn who looks after what."

Checking his side mirror, he changes lanes. "You've been here two weeks and there are more than twenty resorts. Cut yourself some slack." He clears his throat. "Uh, so dinner went… well."

Aw. Is he feeling insecure? "Dinner went great. The kids love you." I sneak a glance at him and see his cheeks pinken.

"Jordy does," he agrees, "and the feeling's likewise. Mila seems like a tougher nut to crack."

I shrug. "She's a teenage girl. I mean, she's awesome and a lot more mature than some other girls her age, but she's still a teenager. Believe me, if she didn't like you, I would have heard about it."

"Okay. That's good." He laughs. "Man, this conversation is weird. Like, this is our first date, and already we're talking about your kids liking me. And I've been thinking abo—"

The abrupt way he cuts himself off and the flare of color on his skin tells me more clearly than words could have what he's thinking.

I reach over and take his hand. "Me too. I…" Fuck, do I want to put myself out there like this? Maybe he cut himself off because he's not willing to commit to his feelings just yet, even if he does *feel* them.

Be brave, Luke.

"I know it's kind of fast to start thinking about how we all fit together as a family, and I know you probably never planned to join a readymade family, but my mind keeps going in that direction too. I guess… maybe it's because we knew each other before? We're just... counting the time between then and now as a time-out. So we're not two weeks in, we're, what... eight, nine months in?" Fuck, does that mean I need to talk about *that night*? I should. We can't keep ignoring it.

I take a deep breath.

"Was it bad?" Grant blurts. "I mean, fuck, I mean... Forget I said anything." I'm pretty sure he whispers "Fuck" again.

Yeah, we need to talk about that night.

"Do you..." I pause and clear my throat. "Do you mean, was that night in college when we hooked up bad?" I keep my gaze fixed through the windscreen. A big part of me wishes I wasn't holding his hand right now. I feel so exposed, but it would send the worst message if I let go now.

"Yeah." The word is a croak.

"Why would you think that? Oh my God, was it bad for you?" I was so sure he'd had a great time. I did.

"What? No!"

Against my will, I begin to laugh. Grant lets go of my hand, and I whip my head around to apologize—fuck's sake, I'm *laughing* while we talk about us having sex—but he's wiping tears of laughter from his eyes. Relief floods through me.

"Does this feel like a comedy of errors to you?"

"Yes," he manages to gasp. "Wait." Changing lanes, he pulls over and puts the car in Park. "Maybe we should just talk this out."

"Okay." I pull myself together and prepare to put my cards on the table. "All those years ago, I had a thing for you. That night was awesome, and I was planning on more. Then you were gone for a week, and the next time I saw you was when you introduced me to Matt, and you seemed... I don't know. I just assumed you wanted it to be a one-night thing, and I was grateful we could still be friends." I stop kind of awkwardly, because he's looking at me like I've said the sky is green.

"Man, we were dumb shits," he declares, and I laugh again. "All those years ago, I had a thing for you." Fuck me. He did? "That night was... amazing. Then my mom called the next morning to tell me my grandmother had died, and I went home for the funeral and to help out. And when I got back, I... just didn't know what to say. You didn't say anything either, and it seemed like maybe you just wanted a one-night stand between friends... and then you met Matt."

I let my head drop back against the headrest. "This is unbelievable. Things could have been so different if we'd just used words instead of assuming." How different could my life be? If I'd been "with" Grant when I met Matt, I wouldn't have been open to his flirtation. I never would have gone out with him. Maybe Grant and I would have fizzled out and Matt and I would still have hooked up later, but... maybe not.

He snorts. "Like I said, we were dumb shits." He pauses. "Don't take this the wrong way, but I'm kind of glad it worked out like this. You probably wouldn't have the kids if we'd been smarter back then, and, well... I don't think I was really ready for something long-term and adult. I probably would have been a dick at some point and it would have ended badly. I'm a better person now."

I can't speak for a moment. Is he real? Like... really real? Can I actually have this guy in my life?

"I'm glad we met again," I manage. I wouldn't give up the kids for anything, but it fulfills something deep inside me to have him back in my life—something I didn't even know I needed.

He smiles at me, then puts the car back in gear and pulls onto the road.

It takes me a minute to pull myself back together, but then I ask, "So how did you end up here at JU?" and the rest of the drive passes in idle chatter.

Once we reach the Chateau, we leave the car with the valet and enter the five-star, French-inspired hotel.

"Where to?" Grant asks, glancing around the opulent lobby. "I always forget how nice this place is."

"It really is. Uh, the terrace bar."

The corner of his mouth tips up slowly. "Good choice. Very romantic."

My dick twitches.

We take the elevator up, and yes, the terrace bar is indeed very romantic. It's an entirely outdoor space, overlooking the manmade river that flows through JU, which is currently lit by pink and blue floodlights. There is a plethora of potted trees with twinkle lights in them separating tables into intimate little cocoons, giving the illusion of privacy. It's exactly what I hoped it would be when I checked it out on the website.

The host greets us pleasantly, his welcoming expression turning slightly puzzled as he takes us in, as though he thinks he should recognize us but doesn't. Or Grant, at least.

"We have a reservation," I tell him. "Durrant."

Awareness dawns, and his gaze flicks to Grant again, his smile broadening. "Of course! Welcome. We have your table ready."

Um… is that weird? Not that they have the table ready, but that he's acting like we're celebrities? It's weird, right?

I'm supremely conscious of the eyes on us as we walk across the terrace. Not the guests—they couldn't care less.

But the bar staff are watching us and murmuring to each other and grinning. What the hell?

Grant leans over and mutters, "Dimi's been busy."

Oh, fuck me. My team is going to *kill* me if they realize they're the last to know the details of this date.

We finally, *finally* make it to our table—and wow. I asked for a special table, and boy, have they delivered. We've got the best table in the place—the view is amazing and we're shielded from prying eyes (mostly).

"Thank you," I tell the host, whose name badge I can't read in the dim light. I'll have to find out his name later, because if the service continues like this, I'm definitely leaving a five-star rating.

"The menu is on the table," he advises, "and your server will be with you shortly. Is there anything you need in the meantime?"

"No, everything is great," Grant says. "Thanks."

The guy leaves as we settle into our seats, and with the sigh of the water below and the muted hush provided by the foliage around us, it feels as though we're in our own magical world.

Just us.

Our waiter bustles in, shattering the moment, but that's okay. I'm going to have a lot of these moments with Grant.

We order drinks, and then when they run out, order more. Our conversation doesn't falter, and it ranges over a wide range of topics. We don't agree on everything and spend a good twenty minutes debating the merits or lack thereof of a certain popular TV series, but even when we're bickering, it's… nice. Comfortable.

As the evening progresses, I become more and more aware of how small these bar tables are. How close we're sitting. How often our knees or ankles brush under the table. How Grant uses his hands when he talks, and how I want to reach out and take one, hold it. How his lips curve when he smiles, and the way his eyes crinkle when he laughs.

The way he looks at me.

The way he reaches out and pushes my hair back when the breeze ruffles it.

His touch on my face.

I can't breathe.

"Sorry to interrupt," our server, Leanne, says, and she really does sound sorry. "We're closing in fifteen minutes. Can I get you anything else?"

Grant and I look at each other. "No, we're good, thanks," I say, and then when she's gone, I ask, "Do you need to get home, or…?"

"I have time."

I take a deep breath. "I heard that some of the suites here have great views."

"I heard that, too. Do we… want to see if it's true? Maybe have another drink? You still haven't told me what you thought of the latest *Star Wars* instalments."

We settle the bill with only a minor disagreement that seems to thrill the staff. I end up winning, due mostly to the fact that I lean in and whisper, "Do you really want everyone talking about this tomorrow?"

Down at the check-in desk, we're greeted by name with a beaming smile. Word gets around fast. Getting a suite may not be a great idea—everyone will know about it before we even make it to the elevator.

Grant bites his lip, then leans over the counter and lowers his voice. "Hey, Shana, could you do us a huge favor? The terrace bar is closing and we just want to have another drink before we head home. If we check in to one of the entertainer suites for an hour or so, can you keep it secret until lunchtime tomorrow?"

She gives him a look that clearly wants to know how big an idiot we think she is. I wonder why lunchtime tomorrow is his cutoff. What's so special about then?

Grant sighs.

"Okay," I try. "The thing is, Shana, this is our first date. If you tell people we checked in, they're going to think we're both easy." I flash my winningest smile. "I've got two kids at home, and I don't want them to think I'm easy."

"You've got kids?" Her jaw drops.

Oh. I guess that hadn't gotten around.

"You can tell everyone you know that I have two kids and they get along really well with Grant if you keep the suite a secret until lunchtime," I bargain.

An agonized expression crosses her face as she considers it, and then finally—*finally*—she nods.

Grant wastes no time in getting us checked in, and a few minutes later, we're back at the elevator, Shana picking up the phone. I watch her as the elevator doors close.

"Is she already telling people about my kids?"

Grant nods. "It'll be all over the hotel before we even check out. By the time the parks open, everyone will know."

Holy fuck.

"I thought gossip was bad at head office in LA. This is next level."

"Yep. Impossible to keep a secret around here."

A thought occurs to me. "Is that why you asked her to only keep us being here secret until lunchtime tomorrow instead of just keeping it secret?"

"Pretty much." The elevator doors open, and I follow Grant out into the hallway. There are only a dozen doors on this floor. "There's no way she would have agreed to keep it secret indefinitely. At least this way she'll see us check out as well, and when she tells the story tomorrow, she'll be able to say we were only here for a little while." He bites his lip. "We probably could have saved ourselves all this trouble and just gone back to my place." Hesitating in front of a door, he looks over at me. "We still could, if you want."

"No." I shake my head firmly. "It's bad enough that negotiating privacy threw off our momentum. I'm not delaying this time with you any further."

His smile is so beautiful. He scans the key card and the lock disengages.

The suite is gorgeous, complete with balcony and view. I go to raid the minibar. "Soda okay, or do you want something else?" I don't want either of our brains foggy for what comes next. I'm nervous, but in a good way. My memory of that first time with him is totally hot, and things can only be better now that we're older, right? I mean, maybe not as energetic….

"Soda's good." He opens the french doors onto the balcony, and the hushed whispers of the night flood into the room. I pour our drinks and follow him out.

He's rearranged the chairs at the tiny café table so we can sit beside each other, looking out over the river. His presence and warmth beside me, so close that our shoulders are touching, is… wonderful. All the stresses of the last few weeks—months—*years* just melt away in this quiet moment with him.

I sigh.

"Okay?" he asks softly, and I turn my head to see him looking at me. The dim light and shadows play over his face, and lust surges through me—along with something else, something harder to define... Affection?

"Yeah. Just… glad to be here with you."

My words hang in the air, and that smile I love so much spreads slowly across his face. I don't know who moves first; maybe it's completely mutual, but when our lips meet, it doesn't matter anyway.

It starts slowly, sweetly; the touch of mouths, the hesitant sweep of tongues. There are two chair arms between us, keeping us from doing more, but there's something about this almost innocent kiss that turns me on more than a more explicitly sexual one would have.

I want more. Want to be closer. Want to touch his skin and feel him pressed up against me.

I pull away. "Inside?"

He smiles.

In the suite, we don't bother with lights, veering straight into the bedroom, letting the outside glow illuminate the way.

There's a lot of potential for this moment to be awkward—the "we're still fully dressed and we came in here to have sex" moment. But I won't let it be. I want this too much.

I grab Grant's hand and pull him to a halt a few feet from the bed, then attack his shirt buttons. He makes a startled, laughing sound and takes over, leaving me free to strip off my own clothes—although I'm slowed down by the fact that I keep pausing to watch as his delicious body is exposed. For a nearly forty-year-old man with a desk job, he's in great shape—not six-pack gym junkie shape, but fit and toned all over. Not gonna lie, I love that he's bigger than me. It's always been a kink of mine.

"Hurry up," he says when he's naked but I'm still wearing pants, then turns and strolls over to the bed, giving me a fantastic view of his ass.

I get naked real quick and chase after him, getting my hands on all that skin.

"Mmm," he moans appreciatively, bending to kiss me,

and we topple sideways onto the bed, limbs tangling, hands touching, mouths attached.

When I was younger, sex was all about the race to penetration, but now that my days of out-of-control hormones are behind me, I've developed a real appreciation for frottage. Especially when it involves whole bodies. Skin-on-skin friction, muscles coming into play, full-body worship.

And Grant's so good at it. We're both gasping, hard as posts, our dicks weeping copiously by the time I break free of our kiss and ask, "Wanna fuck? Or like this?"

He hesitates, thinking about it as he undulates against me, making my eyes roll back for one blissful moment.

"Yeah, fuck," he gasps. "Okay?"

"Oh yeah." I draw back a little, then swoop in for another kiss, just because I can't resist, then pull away. Before we left the house, I took a trip to the bathroom and grabbed some condoms and packets of lube, and now I scrabble through the pile of clothes to snag them from my pants pocket. When I turn back to the bed, he's lying on his back, watching me, jacking himself slowly, a smile on his face that makes me feel all melty inside.

My cock, however, stays rock-hard.

I toss the condoms at him as I rejoin him on the bed and tear open a packet of lube, but he stops me.

"Let me?"

I nod, even though it's been a long time since someone else prepped me—Matt never liked to do it—and he races to get the condom on and then pushes me back onto the mattress.

I go willingly, pulling my legs up to give him better access, and he lightly traces his fingers across my stomach, making the muscles contract, then down the crease of my thigh, *just* avoiding my dick, which pulses with need.

The lube is cool, his fingers hot, and he gently opens me up, taking care to do a good job without making it feel like a prostate exam.

"You're so hot," he whispers. "I always thought I was exaggerating the memory, but…"

I gasp as he twists his fingers in a way that feels particularly good, and he smiles.

"Ready?"

"Fuck you, get in me," I pant, and his laugh is a bit unsteady.

He withdraws his fingers, and then his cock is there, pressing in, and I relax, push out, eager for him to fill me, to finally have that feeling again, to have it with *Grant* again.

I groan as he works his way in, and his breath bursts from him in a small explosion.

"Fuck, Jesus, Luke."

"Do it. Go. Please." Neither of us can manage whole sentences.

He begins to move, looking into my eyes, and even in the dimness of the room, the connection of our gazes is… electrifying. Almost as much as the connection between our bodies. I shift the angle of my hips, and suddenly he's hitting just the right spot, and my moan this time makes him grin wildly between pants.

Propping himself on one arm, he reaches between us and grabs my dick, stroking me in time with his thrusts, and the dual stimulation is too much, too amazing.

"Let go, babe," he grunts. "Come with me."

So I do.

FIFTEEN

Grant

Have you ever had everything in your life suddenly start going right? As I walk over to Luke's place midmorning on Saturday, the sun is shining, the birds are singing, and everything in my life is perfect.

Well, maybe not perfect. But headed in that direction.

Work? Problems identified, troublemakers removed, recovery in progress.

Love life? *Amazing*.

Luke and I reluctantly dragged ourselves home at nearly one in the morning after our first date, partly to confound the gossips, but mostly because Jus was waiting for him.

Yesterday, we managed to sneak away from our respective offices to grab lunch together—mostly privately, although we got a lot of sideways glances from the employees at the café we chose. I'm not totally sure why people are so interested in us. Sure, I expected some gossip, but the level of fascination seems a bit extreme.

I make a mental note to ask someone.

Last night was movie night, and that was a lot of fun.

Jordy kept up a running commentary through both movies, despite Luke's exasperated pleas for him to stop, and Mila joined us too, although she was glued to her phone with a slightly fatuous expression, and then disappeared ten minutes into the second movie when her phone rang. Luke told me later that this is not usual behavior for her.

By mutual agreement, I didn't stay last night, even though the plan is for me to be there today. The kids seem to be okay with me dating Luke, but we're going to give them some more time to get used to the idea. Just in case.

I get to Luke's front door and find it open, Jordy standing just inside, ball and glove on the table beside him. "Finally!" he declares, pulling me through and closing it. "I've been waiting *forever*."

Awww. Who wouldn't be happy with a welcome like that?

"Can we play catch?" he asks, looking up at me earnestly.

"That's why I'm here early," I assure him. "Let me just say hello to your uncle."

"I'm here." Luke comes into the entryway. "Jordy, let Grant get into the house at least." He leans up and kisses me, his lips soft and warm and delicious, and something in me settles. It's been less than ten hours since I saw him last, but I missed him.

Jordy sighs, the weight of the world on his preteen shoulders, and I grin against Luke's mouth before pulling back. "Hold my place," I whisper, then turn to Jordy. "Come on, then."

He cheers, grabs his glove and ball, and gallops off through the house, clearly expecting me to follow.

"I'll see you later," I tell Luke. "What time are Mila's friends coming?"

Luke rolls his eyes. "It was supposed to be this afternoon, but about an hour ago, she told me that she was thinking we should have a cookout for lunch… since it would be the easiest way to feed everyone."

My lips twitch. "It's good that she's testing boundaries," I remind him. One of the things we talked about the other night was how worried he's been about the kids, that he feels Mila has grown up too fast. "Do you need me to run out to the grocery store?"

He shakes his head. "I'll go now, while you're playing with Jordy. Mila's cleaning her room. I'm not sure why, since I've told her several times that nobody is allowed upstairs today."

"She's probably trying to distract herself," I suggest, although I really have no idea.

"Gra-ant!"

Luke laughs. "You'd better go. I'll be back soon. Call me if there's any—"

"I will. Relax. Just make sure Mila knows I'm here and you're going." I kiss him again, just because I can, and then head through the house toward the back yard where Jordy is waiting impatiently.

An hour and a half later, Jordy's friends have arrived, and the three of them are cannonballing into the pool while Luke and I watch from the deck.

"I feel as though this might be a catastrophe waiting to happen," I say idly as the boys begin a game where they leap into the water seconds apart, almost on top of each other.

Luke snorts. "When I called their parents to ask if the boys could come early, Micah's dad said, 'God, please, yes,' and Carter's mom asked if she could bring me anything."

"Like what?" I'm fascinated by this glimpse into parenthood.

"I don't know." He shrugs. "From her tone of voice, I'm guessing anything up to and including a kidney was on offer."

"Have you ever felt that way about the kids?" I guess I can see why a couple hours off on a Saturday would be appealing.

Silence.

I glance over to see a conflicted expression on his face.

"Hey—"

"No, it's fine. The therapist said it's a normal part of parenting, but I still sometimes feel guilty about it. I mean… they have nobody else. I'm literally it. And Mandy trusted me with her babies. How can I want a break from them?"

I turn that over. "Your therapist has probably said everything that needs to be said on this," I finally concede. "You're a great parent to them, Luke. It's fine to want a Saturday morning to yourself occasionally." I hesitate. "There's really nobody else? Grandparents, aunts, cousins?"

He shakes his head. "Matt and Mandy went into the system when they were teenagers and their mom overdosed. Their dad went to prison for aggravated assault before Matt was even born and never bothered to come back when he was let out. Bill was a surprise baby to older parents who'd never planned to have kids. They both died before Jordy was born. There's a great-aunt of Matt's in a nursing home in San Francisco and a couple of second or third cousins on Bill's side, but nobody the kids have actually met and nobody who even came to the funeral. They sent flowers. I kept the cards in case the kids want them one day."

He looks so sad. I don't ask about his family, because I already know. He was pretty open about it back in college, that his parents kicked him out when he came out at sixteen. He spent the next few months sneaking from friend's house to friend's house to sleep and shower. It's actually a testament to his friends that he stayed fed and with a roof over his head for so long before their collective parents and the school realized something was going on. At that point, he was incredibly lucky—he lived in a small town, one of his teachers was a registered foster parent, and since he'd been making such an effort to continue attending school and keep his grades up regardless of his circumstances, the authorities decided the best solution all around would be to keep him in a familiar environment. He's an only child, and although he spoke fondly of his hometown and the people who supported him, and emailed and called them regularly, when I met him, he hadn't been back in over a year.

"The kids have you," I tell him firmly. "And based on the way they reacted Thursday night, they're secure in that knowledge."

He brightens a bit. "That's true. They were fine with Jus—both sound asleep when I got back."

"Because they know you're always coming back." I want to kick myself the second the words are out. It's not like the kids' parents planned not to come back. And did I have to remind him of the fact that Matt *didn't* come back?

He just smiles and takes my hand, so I guess he took the words in the spirit they were intended.

"Thank you. I like to think I'm a reasonable man, but my insecurities get away from me sometimes. It's nice to hear these things from someone else."

We hear the doorbell peal before I can reply, and then the distant sound of Mila's feet thundering down the stairs.

I've heard Jordy do that several times, but never Mila—she's always much calmer.

Luke smirks, as though he can read my mind. "She used to do that all the time. It's only the last few years she's been more restrained." A shadow crosses his face, then clears. "It's nice that she's excited."

A couple minutes later, the screen door opens and teenagers stream out. Inside the house, the doorbell peals again.

"I'll get it," Mila says, her face alight with a happy smile. "Everyone, this is my uncle Luke and his boyfriend, Grant."

The screen slams behind her as she goes back inside, and the teenagers chorus hellos, but I'm frozen.

Boyfriend?

Are we…?

We've only had one date. I've been very carefully avoiding applying any kind of label to describe us, but if someone had forced me to, it wouldn't have been boyfriends. It's too soon, right? I mean… it's kind of adolescent to call Luke my boyfriend after one official date and a couple of hours in a luxury hotel room, right?

It is.

That doesn't change the fact that the word feels so incredibly right. It just clicks into place inside me. And… that's where we were headed, right? Luke was never going to be just a hookup to me, and I doubt he'd have encouraged me to spend so much time with his kids if he intended me to be just a hookup.

So… boyfriends.

I sneak a look at Luke, but he doesn't seem to have even noticed Mila's descriptor. He's smiling at the assorted teens, accepting their thanks for the invitation, generally being the awesome person he is.

More kids come outside to join the first lot, and hell, it seems like there's a lot of them. I do a quick head count, and including Mila, there's eleven. I guess it's some kind of amplification effect? Teenagers in a group have an overwhelming presence? How the hell should I know—this is my first real opportunity to spend time with non-adult people since I was one myself.

"Why don't you all get in a swim before we start on lunch?" Luke suggests, looking at Mila. "Play nice with Jordy and his friends."

"Don't worry, Uncle Luke," one of the girls says earnestly, "we'll be nice to them."

I blink. Because… what?

"Did you just call him Uncle Luke?" one of her friends asks, sounding as bemused as I feel.

The girl shrugs. "I don't know if his last name is the same as Mila's,"

she defends herself.

Luke and I exchange glances.

"You can all call me Luke," he says, and with a round of acknowledgments and smiles, the kids troop off the deck toward the pool. Mila runs back inside, and the next thing I know, music is blasting through the outside speakers. One of the boys lets out a whoop.

I sink back into my chair. "You know, Mila will probably kill us if we stay out here," I mutter.

Luke drops down beside me. "Yeah, I know. I figure we can get away with being here for now since we were already out here when they all arrived. And then there's lunch—since we're cooking out, we have to be out here, right? And cleanup. But after that…"

"Jordy and his friends might have gotten bored of the pool by then, too." Which is a shame, because the older kids might feel more constrained to behave with Mila's little brother hanging around. Or not. I try to think back to myself at sixteen.

"We'll deal with it when the time comes," Luke decides. "Now... which one do you think is Jamie?"

I shoot him a glance to see him watching the group with narrowed eyes, and bite back a smile. "I don't—"

"Hey, Jamie, catch!"

"Well, that was fortuitous timing," I say dryly as Luke and I both zoom our attention in on the tall, dark-haired boy in board shorts and a T-shirt who reaches up to catch the inflatable ball another boy just threw to him. I try to see him the way a fifteen-year-old would, and I guess he has appeal, although it's hard for me to see anything but a teenager. He's got the kind of looks that mean he'll be an attractive man... when he grows up. Hair a little messy, a quick grin, dimples.

"I hope he really is a good kid," Luke says with an air of impending doom.

"We need to stop staring at them." I make myself turn away, shifting the chair a little so it isn't so easy for my gaze to drift back that way.

"I have to keep an eye on Jordy and his friends," Luke insists, and I laugh.

"Come on, Uncle Luke. Look at me, or I'll start to feel ignored and neglected."

Sighing, Luke drags his gaze away from the pool and focuses on me. "Fine. Let's talk about how you got all weird when Mila called you my boyfriend."

Fuck.

"Could we not and just pretend we did?" Talk about an awkward conversation. Plus, is this really the best time to have it? With a dozen kids only twenty or so feet away?

He shrugs. "We can if you want." There's an edge to

his voice, and it suddenly strikes me how this might look to him.

"No! I mean… I just thought this isn't really the time or place to talk about it. But we can. I want to. I—It's still early days for us, and I was… surprised when Mila called me your boyfriend." I'm sweating bullets now, and not because of the warm spring sunshine. I keep my gaze steadily on Luke, trying to guess what he's thinking. "But I liked it. Like it. It feels… right." I need to stop talking.

He swallows hard. "Yeah. It does." He clears his throat. "And yeah, this probably isn't the right setting. Just… know that I like it too. I know it's been a bit intense lately, and I come with a lot of baggage, but we can go as slow as you like."

"The way we've been going is just fine," I tell him firmly. "And if the baggage you're referring to is the kids, I happen to think it's pretty awesome. They are, I mean. If they're okay with how things have been these last couple days, I'm good with it."

He smiles, and it seems almost shy. "Good."

SIXTEEN

Luke
———

Have you ever lamented how slowly time goes, then realized weeks have passed seemingly in the blink of an eye? That's how I feel at the beginning of June.

Yes. June.

April and May seemed to stretch out in a series of meetings and the millions of tiny decisions that need to be made when you're sifting through a company's policies and procedures, but at the end of each week, I wondered how it could possibly be over already. There never seemed to be enough time for everything—probably made worse by the fact that I was trying to cram a sixty-hour workweek, two kids, and a new relationship into a very limited number of hours.

You know what, though? I wouldn't change any of it.

The kids are done with school. The summer camp program starts next week, thank all that's holy, because it didn't take long for them to get bored. Mila, after finding out that several of her new friends—including Jamie—would be working there, applied and has been hired as a junior counselor. Jordy considered his options carefully and elected to enroll in the baseball program but made me ask the camp organizers if he could switch to the general program later if he wanted to. Honestly, I don't think he'll want to—his baseball obsession is still going strong, fed by the time Jus, Grant, and Jamie spend playing with him.

Yes, I said Jamie. My fifteen-year-old niece has a boyfriend, and he's proven willing to hang out with her little brother. Am I thrilled about the situation? Well… it's hard to complain. He's been polite, respectful of the rules (of which I set many), will play ball with Jordy, makes Mila smile… what kind of person would I be if I complained about that? On the other hand, he's a seventeen-year-old boy dating my niece. So I'm conflicted.

Grant tells me I'm being ridiculous, but last time Jamie was over and we caught him watching a little too closely as Mila left the room, it wasn't me who cleared my throat and gave him a death glare. That kid went *white*. I've never seen a look like that on Grant's face before, not even when he found out the extent of what had happened in his district.

Which brings me to how things are going with Grant. If this was a movie, there would be cartoon hearts floating above my head while romantic music played. With things as busy as they are at work and me having the kids at home, the whole concept of finding time to date kind of fell by the wayside. We still occasionally sneak an evening out, just us, but mostly our time together is by the coffee cart at the office, at a JU eatery for lunch, or at my place—Grant comes over most nights to have dinner with me and the kids, and then we settle into my home office to get in a few more hours of work while the kids finish their homework and watch TV before bed. It may not be quality time, but it's still time we spend together.

We initially talked a lot about him staying over, but when it finally happened, around mid-May, it was because of a tree branch. It had started storming not long after dinner one night. Grant hung around a little later than usual, waiting for conditions to improve—his place isn't far from mine, but I still didn't want him on the road in that. He'd pretty much just decided to risk it when a massive branch from the old live oak in the front yard came down right across the end of the driveway. Neither of us particularly wanted to go out and try to clear it in the wind and rain, so the decision was made. We had this half-baked idea about him sleeping on the couch, but Mila called us both idiots, and Jordy asked why he would do that when we were boyfriends and I had a king-size bed. Since then, Grant stays over probably three or four nights a week. He's very careful to give the kids some time alone with me, although I honestly think it's getting to a point that they don't care. They've begun automatically including Grant in nearly everything now—Jordy was devastated when he realized Grant hadn't already planned to attend his elementary school graduation ceremony, and it was only quick reassurances that *of course* Grant wanted to come that saved the day.

Grant's been factoring the kids more and more into his life, too. Aside from his sudden protectiveness of Mila, it was his idea to celebrate Jordy's graduation by taking him and his two best buddies to JU for the day and giving them a behind-the-scenes VIP experience. He spends countless hours playing catch and video games with Jordy, and he's helped Mila with her math homework more times than I want to count. He's also stepped into the role of occasional taxi driver when she meets up with her friends after dark, since one of my firm rules is that Jamie is *not* allowed to drive her anywhere until I say otherwise. That's a very unpopular rule, by the way, but since the result is that she and Jamie mostly hang out at home where Jas, Jus, and I can keep an eye on them, I'm okay with her holding a grudge about it. I'll revisit it when—if—she and Jamie have been together a while longer.

So… yeah, the past two months have dragged out, filled with so many things I couldn't begin to recount them all, but yet have flown by in the blink of an eye. My life is good, though.

Today is an important day, because Malcolm Joy and Seth Holder have flown out for a series of meetings to assess where things are. My team has worked super hard and made great progress, but unfortunately, that progress just shows us how much work there is left. It's kind of good, I guess, in that it means I'll be officially assigned to JU for at least as long as I'd originally thought. With the kids so happy and settled here and Grant and me hooking up, it would be a real pain in the ass to have to move back to LA anytime soon. And it's not like there are a lot of other options—I'm a business consultant, and Joyville is a town built solely to house the employees of JU. It's not like there are a bunch of other big businesses and industries headquartered here. If there's no job for me at JU, there's no job for me in Joyville.

So… yeah. Eventually, probably sometime next year, there's going to be a tough decision to make. But not yet, and who knows what the future holds?

I check the schedule for the day as I wait for my team to settle in. We're kicking off with a quick meeting, then Malcolm and Seth will join us for a full briefing on everything that's been found and done so far and our recommendations for the next steps. After, there's a meeting of the management team for me, Malcolm, and Seth, where we'll basically go over all those points and invite input. *That's* going to be loads of fun—there are a few people who really resent my presence here and the interim authority I've been given. They've been throwing attitude and roadblocks my way for the past two months, and I can guarantee they'll stir things up in the meeting.

Bring it on.

Later this afternoon, Malcolm and Seth will be meeting individually with each of the ADs and department heads, which theoretically should give me time to actually do some work, but realistically, it's likely I'll be asked to sit in on at least a few of those sessions. Today and tomorrow are going to be long days and will result in a long to-do list that needs to be handled over the next couple of weeks.

"Okay, let's get started." The only way to tackle a full day is to actually get on with it—procrastinating gets nothing done.

We quickly review where things are. Nothing has really changed since our full team meeting on Monday—a couple of places where we have more detail, but nothing significant—which is good, because it means we're ready when Seth and Malcolm join us. I give a brief overview and then let my team run down the full briefing. Gotta admit—I feel a real sense of pride as they do so. Man, they're good. I don't pretend that I can claim any credit for their intelligence, diligence, and attention to detail, but I *can* claim credit for recognizing how awesome each of them is and recruiting them for this project. They have the answers to nearly every question, and for the few they don't, it's because we haven't gotten to that area or issue yet. By the time it's my turn again, I'm confident that Seth and Malcolm will agree with our recommendations.

Malcolm leans back in his chair. "So we're completely sure that Ken had nothing to do with this fiasco?"

"Absolutely," I assure him. "He's negligent, but he wasn't knowingly involved in any of the skimming, not even indirectly."

"That's a relief," Seth admits. "Well, we'll officially terminate his employment with the payout his contract calls for. Are you okay to continue as you are while we initiate a search for a new director?"

"Yes." I actually have thoughts about the search, but that's a conversation for another time. "I also think we should hold off on any official restructuring until the new director comes aboard. We can draw up our ideas and plans, but since they're the one who'll have to execute them, it makes sense to get their input from the get-go."

Malcolm nods. "Agreed. In the meantime, the audit can continue as it has been." He looks around the table. "I guess we're done here."

As the meeting begins to break up, Seth says, "Stu, this is yours," and takes a white envelope from his laptop bag. It's suspiciously thick.

Uh-oh.

I look at Stu, and sure enough, he's flushed and is avoiding my gaze.

"What's this?" I ask lightly, even though *I know*. "A payoff?"

"Don't get huffy, Luke," Malcolm says gleefully. "We all respected your and Grant's wishes and didn't start a pool here at JU."

"Starting one in LA isn't exactly better," I point out, but sigh. It's done now. "What was the bet, anyway?"

Stu takes the envelope and shrugs. "Nothing exotic. That you'd make it more than a month."

I eye the thickness of the envelope again. "Really? You made that much off something that simple? What were the odds? My colleagues in LA must not think much of my relationship staying power."

"It's not that," Seth assures me while everyone else snickers. "They just know how hard you work and that you prefer to spend your free time with the kids. They haven't seen you and Grant together, so they based their bets on PG Luke."

What?

"PG Luke?" Am I being classified like a movie? Because some of the stuff Grant and I do is definitely not fit for a PG audience.

"Pre-Grant," Di explains. "The guy who had minimal social life. He was decent enough to work with, but he never snuck off for coffee breaks with his guy or got caught doing nasty things in the utility closet."

Heat floods up from my collar. "I don't know what you're talking about," I manage. "I've *never* done anything nasty in a utility closet." That she can prove, anyway. And it was only once. Okay, maybe twice—it depends on how you define "nasty."

She shoots me a superior, knowing glance, and the avid gazes from the rest of my team—and my bosses—are a pretty clear indication that I need to derail this conversation, fast. How did she find out about the utility closet, anyway? I would have sworn nobody saw us. Either time.

"Anyway," I rush on, "it's time for a coffee break, and I think it should be Stu's treat, since he's suddenly flush with cash."

Stu rolls his eyes but he's smiling. "Fine. If it makes you feel better, I'll pay for coffee. What does everyone want?"

WE'RE WELL into the management meeting when my phone vibrates in my pocket. My coffee is long gone, lunch has been provided and consumed, and I'm craving more coffee—or something stronger. Everyone here at JU knows I'm in this meeting—it's not like a visit from corporate head office can go unnoticed—which means it's either an emergency or to do with the kids. They never call me at work unless it's important, so either way, I need to take this call.

Fuck.

Seth's speaking, so I catch Malcolm's eye and lift my hand to the side of my head, thumb and little finger extended to imitate a phone handset. He nods, and I slip out of the boardroom as unobtrusively as possible.

In the hallway, I pull out my phone with the intention of calling whoever it is back, but it's not a number I know. In fact, the area code is California. I frown. Could it be someone from head office? Maybe trying to reach Malcolm and Seth? At least it's not the kids—a knot in my stomach unravels. The last time I got a call about the kids at work, Jordy had broken his leg.

I'm just debating whether this actually needs a callback or not when the screen lights up and the phone begins vibrating again, the same number flashing on the display.

"Luke Durrant," I answer, hoping it's not something stupid.

"Hey… it's me."

My gut turns to ice. It feels as though my heart has stopped beating, my chest suddenly too small for my lungs to expand and give me air.

Matt.

My ex-husband.

I can't find words, and he must take that as a bad sign, because he says quickly, "Don't hang up. I'm sorry to call when you must be at work, but I thought it would be best to have this conversation away from the kids."

Red-hot rage fills me, melting away the ice and destroying the iron bands around my chest. I breathe deeply. *He* thought he had the right to make *any* sort of decision about my kids, even one as inconsequential as this?

The petty, stupid thought kills my anger. I should be grateful that he was that considerate. Mila may have mentioned him a time or two, but she still doesn't like to talk about him. Who knows how she would have reacted if he'd called me while I was with her?

"I appreciate your consideration," I manage, "but this really isn't the best time. I was in a meeting."

"I'm sorry," he replies instantly. "This can wait. When can I call you back?"

Is he serious? The first in-person contact we've had since he left and he thinks I can just wait to hear what he wants?

"I have a few minutes right now, if it won't take long."

He hesitates. "There's a lot I need to say," he says slowly. "Apologies and… stuff. But what it comes down to is that I'd like to visit."

The iron band around my chest is back, tighter than ever, even as part of me, deep down, sits up and cheers. Matt's seen the light—he wants to visit.

"We're in Georgia." It's all I can think to say.

"I know." Of course he knows—that's why I've always made sure certain mutual friends know how to contact me. So Matt could always find us, if he wanted to.

Apparently, he wants to.

"Uh…" I force myself to focus. Right, the meeting. "Now's really not a good time to talk about this. Can you call back in"—I look at my watch, mentally calculate how much longer the meeting will go for—"an hour?"

"Sure, of course. I'll talk to you then."

"Wait!" Fuck, I don't want to lose contact again. He sounds like he'll call back, but who knows what will happen when I hang up? He might change his mind. "Uh, where are you calling from? Can I reach you on this number if something comes up and I miss your call?"

"Yes," he promises. "But if you miss my call, I'll text so we can set up another time."

"Okay. Okay. Thanks. I'll, uh, talk to you later." I need to get a grip, but the world seems to be spinning.

"Talk later."

The call ends, and I look around. There are a few people coming down the hallway, and one looks at me a bit oddly. I can't bring myself to force a smile or a nod. Instead, I turn away and reenter the boardroom, trying to be quiet and nondisruptive.

As I sink into my chair, Malcolm catches my eye. He's frowning. "Okay?" he mouths, and I make myself nod, realizing I must look as unsettled as I feel.

That won't do.

Straightening in my chair, I make an effort to tune back in to what Seth's saying.

"…any current member of staff with the required qualifications and experience is of course welcome to apply, but we will be beginning an executive search concurrent with the internal application period."

Oh—he's talking about replacing Ken. He and Malcolm mentioned to me earlier that they'd prefer to hire someone outside the organization, who can come into the situation completely bias-free of all the drama that's been happening. Their other thought was to offer the job to Derek, but ultimately, they'd prefer to transfer Derek to head office when he's ready for a change. I have to agree with them there, and honestly, I don't think Derek would accept the role. He's really invested in his district right now, and I'm pretty sure his and Trav's long-term plans have them leaving Joyville, either for New York or the West Coast.

I glance around the table, checking to see if anyone looks particularly interested, since Seth and Malcolm have already asked me to be on the hiring panel. When I get to Grant, I see he's looking steadily back at me, concern evident in his expression. I'm obviously not doing a great job of hiding how off-balance I feel.

I throw him a reassuring smile, although my gut clutches as I realize I need to discuss this with him. How do you tell your boyfriend that your ex-husband is coming to visit?

I make it through the rest of the meeting, but I totally let myself down in terms of keeping it together. I can barely concentrate and have to force myself not to check the time every thirty seconds. I don't want to miss Matt's call in case he does have some kind of freak-out and decides not to try again later... but part of me does. The kids deserve to have him in their lives—he's their only remaining blood relative and a tie to their mother—but things are going so well now. Everything is smooth and calm at home. Ginger has been talking about reducing the kids' session frequency because they're doing so well. I don't want anything to upset that.

Besides, what can possibly come of this? Best-case scenario: Matt comes to visit, the kids are pleased to see him, they stay in touch via phone while we're living here and then occasionally see him when—if—we move back to LA. Worst case: The kids refuse to see him. Or Matt just never calls back and I never hear from him again. Either way, I need to step up and deal with it.

Malcolm closes the meeting, and in the rush of everyone getting their things together and leaving, he and Seth turn to me.

"Is everything alright?" he asks.

Considering how much of my personal life has been

dragged through the company in the last few years, the *last* thing I'm going to do is whine to my bosses. "It's fine," I assure him. "A personal thing. I need to make a call—do you need me for now?"

He doesn't seem convinced, but Seth says, "We can survive without you. Let us know if there's anything we can do."

I hesitate, touched. That's a really nice offer, especially considering he doesn't know what the problem is.

Before I can answer, a hand lands on my shoulder, and a second later, Grant is standing beside me.

Malcolm and Seth both smile. "We'll leave you to it," Malcolm says, obviously of the opinion that whatever the problem is, I'll turn to my boyfriend for help.

I manage a smile and a "Thank you," and then they're gone and I turn to Grant.

"What happened?" he asks, his gaze searching my face. "Are the kids—"

"They're fine," I assure him, my heart melting a little at his clear concern. I sink down into the nearest chair, and Grant sits beside me. "Matt called."

He blinks. "What? Wow. Uh… wow."

I huff a laugh. "Yeah, that about sums it up."

Grant blows out a breath. "I was *not* expecting you to say that." He shakes his head, then seemingly pulls himself together. "What did he want?"

I shrug. "I told him I couldn't talk and that he should call back"—I glance at the wall clock—"in about ten minutes, but he said he wants to see the kids." Something niggles at the back of my mind—something about that statement that's not right—but I can't pinpoint it and it doesn't seem that important anyway, so I let it go.

Grant nods slowly. "Okay. Uh, okay. Do you… want

me to…?" He seems uncomfortable, and it hits me in a rush that he's asking if I want him to sit in on the call.

I smile genuinely, then lean over and kiss him right there in the boardroom with the door open.

"Thank you, but I'll be fine. It's just a phone call. I'll come past your office later and tell you what he says." I'm not willing to discuss this with him at the house, where the kids might overhear.

He nods. "Okay. You know where I am if you need anything." He looks around. "Come on, you don't want to be here for the call—anyone can just walk in. Do you want to use my office instead of your storage closet?"

I shake my head as I get up and follow him to the door. "No, it's fine. Thanks, though."

We part ways in the hallway, and I have to admit to feeling a tiny bit of trepidation as we walk away from each other. It would be awfully nice to have Grant holding my hand during all this, but he's got work to do and this is something I should handle myself—initially, at least.

I stick my head into the conference room to let the team know I have to take a call, then close myself into my office-slash-interview room-slash-storage closet, put my phone on the tiny table, and sit down to watch it.

Thankfully, it doesn't take long before the damn thing rings, that same California number on the display. I snatch it up, then hesitate for a long moment before answering it.

"Luke Durrant." I cringe. Seriously? I know it's him, so why didn't I just say "Hi, Matt"? Or even just "hello"?

"Hey, Luke. Is this a better time?"

When he called before, I was so shocked to hear from him that I didn't really process much else, but now, the sound of his voice sends shockwaves through me. It's the voice that promised to love me always. The voice that soothed me when I was sick, laughed when I was being funny, and whispered sweet nothings when we were alone together. Hearing it again, knowing all that is gone... feels weird.

"Luke?"

"Ah... yeah. Sorry, I got distracted. Yes, this is a good time." I need to concentrate. This is important, and I have to give it my full attention.

"Good. So... I guess I want to start with an apology. Walking out the way I did was... I can't even think of a word for what a douche move that was. I honestly don't expect that you can ever forgive me, but I really am sorry and I hope we can move forward."

I struggle to find the words I want. "I appreciate that," I say finally. "You're right, I'm not sure I can forgive you, but I do understand why you did what you did. And I'm very grateful that you supported the adoption. Your letter made a difference to the judge."

"Well, there's nobody better to raise the kids," he says. "I had no doubt that they would be safe and loved with you—I couldn't have left otherwise."

That's like a slap in the face. So if I'd been a less competent and loving parent, he would have stayed?

"How are they... Mila and Jordy?" He sounds a little tentative now.

"They're good. Great, actually. They were a bit unsettled for a while, after... well, after, but this move has been just what they needed. Jordy's relaxed, no more nightmares, and he's taken up baseball and harangues everybody into playing with him. Mila's got a pretty good group of friends now and she seems very comfortable with them. They've even started a slumber party circuit—one house every Friday night. And she's got a boyfriend."

"A boyfriend!" The shock in Matt's voice makes me feel a lot better. "But she's only..."

I let him trail off as realization sets in. "Yeah, she's fifteen now."

"Wow." He sounds hoarse and clears his throat. "Uh... wow. I guess I knew that, but I just didn't want to... acknowledge it."

A laugh escapes me. "I know that feeling."

"Do you... do you think they'd want to see me?"

And there it is, the crux of the matter.

"I don't know," I tell him honestly. "Until recently, Mila wouldn't even say your name. Jordy was kind of wrecked right after you left. Like I said, they're both doing a lot better now, but I really don't know how they'll react."

He sighs. "I guess I deserve that. Could you talk to them about it? See what they think?"

I don't want to.

Shaking off the instinctive reaction, I make myself say, "I'll talk to them. I can't promise it will be tonight—I want them both to be in a good place, and I want to ask their therapist if she has any thoughts on the best way to approach the topic. But I will talk to them."

"That would be great. I, uh, I'll wait to hear from you, but can I text you in the meantime? There's so much..."

I want to say no, but I also want to say yes. I'm beginning to think I should have visited the therapist myself to talk about my feelings after Matt left—because I clearly haven't processed them well.

"Of course. Uh, I don't want to rush you off the phone, but I'm still at work and..."

"Say no more. Thanks for talking to me, Luke. Talk again soon."

I sit and stare at the phone for longer than I want to admit to. I'm not sure what I expect it to do, but it's brought me all sorts of chaos this afternoon.

Finally, I pick it up and call Ginger's office. She's with a client, but I leave a message with her receptionist for her to call me when she can. Then I leave the closet and go to check in with my team.

"You okay, Luke?" Di asks, concern all over her face. "You're so pale."

"Is everything alright with the kids?" Stu demands, and I force a smile.

"Everything's fine. Just something I wasn't expecting. We all good here?"

Both their gazes examine me searchingly, but finally Di says, "Yes. Malcolm and Seth would like you to join them if you're able, but they specifically said it was fine if you couldn't."

I nod. "I need to go check in with Grant, and I'm expecting a call at some stage, but other than that, I'll be in with Malcolm and Seth if you need anything." I'm out the door before either of them can say anything further.

Taking the stairs up to the executive floor helps to settle the nervous energy coursing through me, and by the time I knock on Grant's open door, I feel almost totally in control.

He gets up and comes around the desk to meet me. "Hey. How'd it go?" He closes the door behind me and turns to lean against it.

I shrug. "It was both better and worse than I expected." I slump down in the visitor chair. "He apologized for leaving, which came out of left field but was nice to hear. Asked about the kids. Asked me to talk to them about him visiting."

Grant comes over and perches against the desk in front of me. "Did you agree?"

I sigh. "Yes and no. I think it would be good for the kids to have contact with him, but I don't want to force it on them. I said I wanted to talk to Ginger first, and that any conversation would have to wait until I thought the kids would be receptive. He was okay with that, which I guess is a good sign."

"Yeah, sounds like it. You called Ginger yet?"

"Left a message." I nod.

"So that's all the technical stuff... now tell me how you feel about it."

My sigh this time is broken by a chuckle. "I don't know," I admit. "I thought I'd let go of all my anger about this, but today proves that I haven't. I want to smash his fucking face in for abandoning me and the kids. I want to ask him *why*, and really understand what it was. I want to tell him to stay away from us, but I also want to see him again... because it took me so long to get used to him not being around. I'm... angry and confused, and this whole thing just makes me feel so tired."

He leans down and kisses my forehead. "I know, babe, and I'm so sorry. I wish you didn't have to deal with this mess of emotions. I'm here, yeah? Anything you need."

I reach out and snag one of his hands. The warmth and strength of it feels so good. I knew he'd come through for me. That's the kind of person Grant is.

"Thank you. It helps, having you here to support me. And see through my bullshit."

He grins. "Also, just saying, if you decide you *do* want to take a couple swings at him, I'm also willing to offer an airtight alibi."

My laugh is cut off abruptly when my phone rings. I'm almost afraid to check the screen.

"It's Ginger. Hold on." I answer. "Hi, Ginger. Can you give me just one second? Thanks." Putting my hand over the microphone, I look back at Grant. "I'll probably have to talk to the kids tonight. Can I call you later?" It's the cowardly way of asking him not to come over tonight, even though I really, really want him there, both to hold my hand while I talk to the kids and then after to fuck me until I can't remember my name, let alone anything else.

His smile is warm and understanding. "Of course. I'm only a few minutes away if you need anything."

I smile back, helpless to resist, then take my hand off the microphone and wander out of Grant's office as I begin my explanation to Ginger.

I WAIT until dinner is done and has been cleared, Jas long gone, before I clear my throat and ask the kids to come into the living room.

Ginger's suggestion was to be completely straight with them and encourage them to do the same. She said they were both doing amazingly well, and if they hadn't had anything shitty happen today, then there was no point in holding off. Since conversation over dinner was happy and enthusiastic, I really have no excuse to delay.

Except my fear that this will kill that happiness.

"Is everything okay?" Mila asks, sounding worried as she follows me in. Jordy, bouncing ahead, has already claimed an armchair. I settle into the other one, and Mila curls up on the couch.

"Yes." I say it firmly, wanting to be clear that this is a goddamn safe environment for them, that it always will be, and that I'll never let anything happen to them. "Everything's fine. I got a call at work today that I need to talk to you about."

Jordy's eyes widen. "I'm not moving again!" he bursts out. "I like it here. I'm not going back to California!"

I blink. Wow. That went bad fast.

"Uncle Luke," Mila begins, and she's pale, her fingers

worrying nervously at a throw pillow. I hold up a hand to stop her.

"We're not moving," I declare. "Not now, anyway. I can't guarantee we'll be able to stay here forever, but it's going to be at least Christmas before we need to think about it, okay?"

Mila nods, and I turn my focus on my nephew. "Okay, Jordy?"

He nods, scowling a little, and I know he's not happy that I didn't make a forever promise. I sigh. This is already not great, and I haven't even told them yet.

"So I got a call today," I try again. "It was from Uncle Matt."

The pillow drops from Mila's hands. If I thought she was pale before, it's nothing compared to the ashen color she turns now.

"What did he want?" she demands.

"To apologize." Ginger suggested that starting with that might make the kids more accepting of everything else. "He knows it wasn't right for him to just leave like that, and he wanted me to know how sorry he is."

Mila looks unconvinced, but Jordy heaves a sigh. "It's good that he's acknowledging his mistakes," he says, and it sounds so much like something he would have learned at school that I have to bite back a hysterical laugh.

"He also wanted to know how we were, especially you guys. He already knew we were living here, so I guess he's been talking to some of our old friends."

"What did you tell him?" Mila's voice is strained, barely above a whisper. I don't like that, and I hesitate before answering.

"That we're doing really great. That we like Georgia and that Jordy plays baseball now and you're giving me gray hair by dating." She doesn't crack a smile. "It was a real shock for me to hear from him," I say honestly. "At first, I wasn't sure how I felt. I guess I'm a little bit angry still that he left. That's okay. I'm allowed to be angry. But really, after so long, there are other things I'd rather focus my energy on than being angry."

Jordy gets up and comes over to squish into the chair with me. I get the feeling he'd like to sit on my lap, but he's really too big for that now, so squeezing us into the armchair like sardines is the next best thing.

"Let's sit on the couch," I suggest. Partly because we'll be more comfortable, but also because I don't want Mila on her own like that. We move and settle quickly, and Jordy snuggles up to my side and holds a hand out to his sister. The move is almost unconscious, an instinctive need for comfort. Mila takes it and holds on.

"I don't want to be angry," Jordy announces. "Mostly it still makes me sad when I think about Uncle Matt. And… sometimes I'm scared."

Jesus, I'm not prepared for this.

"Scared?" I ask carefully, and Jordy shrugs, studying the wall across the room as though it holds the answers to the secrets of the universe.

"Mom and Dad are gone. Then Uncle Matt was gone. If I think about it too much, I worry that maybe you'll be gone, too."

I'm pretty sure he's talked to Ginger about this, that it's part of the fear of abandonment she discussed with me. "I can't promise that nothing will ever happen to me," I say reluctantly, wishing I could. "What happened to your parents was a horrible tragedy, and sometimes stuff like that happens, no matter what we do to prevent it. But I can promise that I will never, *ever* leave you by choice. Not ever, no matter what. You're going to be begging to move out and go to college, and I'll call you every week and you'll roll your eyes and ignore the call and then tell me later that you were busy studying. Okay? You two are stuck with me forever, and when I'm an old man, one of you is going to have to look after me."

Jordy giggles, and the sound is like music. "Okay," he says, his voice full of smug satisfaction, and a little bit of my tension eases. "I won't be studying at college, though. I'll be playing ball."

I muss his hair. "College athletes need to keep their grades up, wise guy, so you *will* be studying. But there's time before you need to worry about that."

He snorts, but subsides against me, seemingly reassured. I look over at Mila. She's still holding Jordy's hand, still pale, her expression slightly pinched.

"What else did he want?" she asks, and I'm a little taken aback.

"Uh… well, he said he'd like to see you guys. That's completely up to you," I hasten to assure them when Jordy stiffens again. "Maybe you could start with a phone call."

"You seem very eager for us to be in contact with him," Mila accuses. I blink.

"I—I think eager is the wrong word. He's your mom's brother, and I think it would be… nice to be in touch with him. But the decision is yours." I'm making a mess of this somehow, and I don't know how. Mila looks decidedly unhappy.

"I'll think about it," she says finally, and I nod.

"Of course. Take as long as you like. You two should talk about this, and maybe you could talk to Ginger about it, too. You're in charge of what happens next."

"I don't mind talking to Uncle Matt on the phone," Jordy volunteers. "But I want you to be there."

"Yes. Of course. If that's what you want, no problem."

"May I be excused?" Mila asks, still looking unhappy. I meet her gaze.

"Yes. Mila, if you don't want to talk to Uncle Matt, you don't have to."

"Okay. Thanks. I'm going to read." She unfurls herself from the couch and walks sedately from the room, but a second later, I hear the thunder of footsteps racing up the stairs, and sigh.

I guess it could have gone worse.

Jordy looks up at me. "Mila's mad."

"Maybe," I concede. "I think she might also be a bit unsure of what she wants to do. Being confused can make you feel mad."

He considers that. "Like when I can't work out how to target a new launcher in Fortnite and it makes me want to throw the controller at the TV."

"Something like that," I say dryly. "Please don't throw anything at the TV."

"I'll try." He gets up and heads toward the door, then turns and looks back. "You're not going anywhere tonight, are you?"

My heart breaks. Just shatters into a million pieces.

"No. I'll be right here."

"Good."

A moment later, I'm alone in the living room, my head pounding with a tension headache, mentally consigning Matt to hell for putting me through this and wishing Grant was here.

As though thinking of him conjures him, my phone beeps in my pocket, and sure enough, it's a text from Grant.

Hope everything is going well. I'm here if you need to talk.

A surge of longing takes me over, and without thinking about it, I tap to call him. He answers on the first ring.

"Hey. You okay?"

For a moment, I'm speechless. His voice goes right through me, easing my headache, loosening all my knotted muscles. He's a miracle drug.

"Luke?"

"Yeah. Uh, yeah, I'm okay. Just… wishing I'd had to do anything else tonight. Seriously, cleaning the gutters in a blizzard holds more appeal."

He huffs. "That bad, huh?"

"Not really." I sigh. "There was no yelling. No tears. Jordy's feeling a bit insecure, but he seems open to at least talking to Matt. Mila said she'd think about it, but I wouldn't want to stake my life on her answer. I'll try to talk to her later, make sure she knows it's okay."

He hesitates.

"What?" I ask.

"Nothing. I swear. Just… it doesn't surprise me that Mila's a bit wary."

"Me either, I guess." I wriggle around and swing my legs up so I'm stretched out on the couch, one arm behind my head. "There was no way her feelings about Matt were going to change just because he called. If she agrees to talk to him, he's going to have to work really hard to get back on her good side."

"I think it's more than that," Grant says slowly. "In some ways, I think she's even more insecure about losing you than Jordy is. It might be an idea to remind her—both of them—that you adopted them and they're legally your kids."

My jaw goes slack. "Wait. You think she's worried that Matt will want to take them?"

"I don't know." I can almost hear his shrug. "But it can't hurt to reassure her that it's not going to happen."

Fuck. Fuck fuck fuck. I never even thought of that, not even when Jordy said he was scared I'd be gone.

"Good point. Thanks." My voice is suddenly tight, and of course he hears it.

"I've upset you. I'm sorry, that's the last thing I intended."

"No, I needed to hear it. I think you're probably right—it's just something I didn't really want to think about." I sigh again. "I could really do with a hug right now." That slips out—I didn't mean to say it aloud.

"All right, that's it. I'm coming over." Determination makes his voice forceful, and I can't deny that a part of me goes weak with relief.

But…

"No. I need to talk to Mila again. And there's a chance Jordy will have a nightmare tonight."

Grant hesitates. "Okay, how about this: I'll come over after the kids have gone to sleep, and if Jordy has a nightmare, he and I can swap beds."

Longing rises strongly in me. "Okay."

"Okay." His voice softens. "Go talk to Mila, then make yourself a cup of that tea you say you hate but always drink when you're stressed. I'll be there in a few hours."

A laugh bursts from me, because I really had thought that I'd managed to keep that secret from everyone. It's not even like I've drunk it many times since I met Grant.

"I'll see you later."

We end the call, and I lie there staring at the ceiling for a long moment, then sit up and swing my legs off the couch. Time to be a grown-up.

Mila's door is closed, and I hesitate before knocking. I can hear a low murmur, which means she's probably on the phone, but this is a conversation we really need to have, so I tap lightly and wait for her response.

I count off four seconds before she says, "Come in."

Inside, she's curled up in bed, still fully dressed, holding her phone in front of her the way she does when she's FaceTiming someone.

"Hey. Can we talk for a minute?"

She bites her lip, avoiding my gaze. "I'm talking to Jamie."

"I don't think he'll mind if you call him back." I put a little bit of steel in my voice.

"It's cool, babe," Jamie's voice says from the phone. I try not to wince. I'm still getting used to hearing my baby niece get called "babe" by her boyfriend. "I'll talk to you later."

Mila looks distinctly unimpressed, but says goodbye and ends the call, dropping the phone to her lap. I walk into the room and sit in the desk chair.

"I just wanted to remind you that no matter what you decide, whether you choose to talk to Uncle Matt or not, you're legally mine and nobody can take you away without proving I'm an unfit parent. And they'd be pretty hard-pressed to do that."

She looks startled, then her face flushes and her eyes fill with tears.

"Oh, hey now." I get up and go sit next to her on the bed, taking her in my arms. She curls up against me, buries her face in my shoulder, and cries.

I just hold her, completely at a loss. The last time I felt this utterly useless was after Mandy and Bill died, when I held nine-year-old Mila and five-year-old Jordy while they cried and had no idea how I could possibly make things better for them. Surely I should have known she was feeling this way? What kind of parent am I that I didn't realize my kid was so worried about something?

Eventually her sobs taper off to hiccups, then to

unsteady breaths. I hold on, letting her decide when she wants to pull back, and when she looks up at me with wet, puffy eyes, my heart breaks all over again.

"I'm so sorry," I say hoarsely. "I'm sorry."

She sniffles. "Why are you sorry?" It comes out rough, and she clears her throat.

"Because I should have seen you were worried about this and made sure you knew that it was okay."

A damp laugh bursts from her. "You're so ridiculous sometimes, Uncle Luke. How were you supposed to know if I didn't tell you?" She looks away. "I didn't want you to know. I… I just figured that it would be okay. I mean, if Jordy and I did well at school and didn't get in trouble, as long as nothing happened to you, there would be no reason for them to put us in foster care."

"Foster care?" There's a slight tremble in the words, and I'm so proud of myself for not shouting them in horror.

She shrugs. "That's what happens, right? When there are no parents or other family. That's what happened to Mom and Uncle Matt. They got separated. I didn't think anything like that could happen to us, because we had you and Uncle Matt, but…"

But Matt left.

Her uncle.

Her blood kin, who she should have been able to rely on to keep her and Jordy out of the system.

"Mila—"

She holds up a hand and lifts her still teary eyes to mine. "I know you didn't need to keep us. When Uncle Matt left, nobody would have blamed you if you'd called Child Services or whoever. We're not any relation to you. If Mom and Dad hadn't died and you and Uncle Matt had divorced, you wouldn't have kept contact with us. And I know how hard it's been for you, raising us on your own. You've given up your life. I know you would never just leave the way Uncle Matt did, because you're not that kind of person. But I didn't want you to regret deciding to keep us… and I remember the lady from Child Services who talked to us after Mom and Dad died, and then again after Uncle Matt left. She kept asking us if we wanted to go live with a family and have a mom and dad instead of you… and I wanted to be ready for anything, just in case."

Pain tightens my chest.

"Is that why you wanted to get a job so badly? So you could have some money put away?" Oh my God, my kid thought she needed to stash money in case… what? The government took her and her brother away from me? In case she had to look after herself and her brother on her own? I feel sick.

She nods.

I make myself take a breath and think carefully about what to say next.

"I'm glad you know that I would never leave. And nobody can take you from me. Legally, I'm your dad. They would need to prove that I've neglected you, that you've been mistreated or that being in my care endangers you. Ginger, your friends, your teachers… they're all people who can testify that you're safe and happy with me. So the chances of you ever going into foster care and being separated from Jordy are so slim that you don't need to worry about them." I take another deep breath.

"Mila, you said that nobody would have blamed me if I'd called Child Services when Uncle Matt left. That's not true. I would have blamed me. I never could have lived with myself, and I would have spent the rest of my life hating myself and missing you. I was the fifth person ever to hold you when you were born. I have loved you since you were a baby—same for your brother. I loved your parents. Your mom was a sister to me, even if there was no blood between us. If your parents had lived and Matt and I had divorced, yeah, I wouldn't have seen you as often—but I still would have seen you. Your mom and I used to joke about it, remember—she'd tell me if I ever got sick of her brother, I had to promise that I'd still have lunch with her once a week. Your parents left guardianship of you and Jordy to both of us, not just Uncle Matt. Yes, it's been difficult sometimes, especially after Uncle Matt left, but I *did* need to keep you. There was no other option for me. I could never have lived with any other option. I don't have any family except for you, and I could never let you go. I don't feel like I've given up anything, not a single thing. Understood?"

There's a tremulous smile on her lips and she opens her mouth to speak, but it's my turn to stop her.

"One more thing. In the event that something happens to me, my will specifies that guardianship goes to Uncle Matt. If he's unwilling or unable to take you, it goes to Janie and Lana. I've talked to them a lot about it, and they promised to love you and take care of you." Janie and Lana used to live next door to Mandy and Bill. They refused to lose touch with the kids after they came to live with me and Matt, and even after Matt left, they doggedly maintained contact with birthday and Christmas gifts and the occasional visit. It's not like they're super close to the kids, but they're not strangers, either—and they're a connection to the past that might bring the kids comfort if their lives are turned upside down again.

Mila nods. "I'd rather have you."

"Oh, baby, I'd rather be here for you. Believe me, the only way you're going to anyone else is if I'm not alive to stop it happening. And I wish you didn't ever have to think about this, that we didn't have to talk about it, but unfortunately, you know that bad stuff can happen. I just want you to know that no matter what happens, you and Jordy are not getting separated."

She nods again, taking a shuddery breath.

"What… what happens if… I mean, you've never really dated anyone before now. Grant is great—Jordy and I really like him—but… Would… Does…" She trails off in a frustrated jumble of words.

My heart sinks.

"I don't exactly understand," I admit. "I thought we agreed that I would never leave you."

"We did. I know that. But what if… Well, Grant never signed on to be a parent to half-grown kids."

"That's true. But he knew when we started seeing each other that I was a parent. That doesn't change just because we're in a relationship." I hesitate. "Has Grant given you the impression that he doesn't want—"

"No! God, no. Grant's great. He… he's been great. But… I guess I worry that he'll get sick of us. I don't want you to be alone, but I don't want him to hate us because he's stuck with an instant family."

Jesus fucking Christ, how much has Mila been holding in? I really wish Ginger was here to moderate this conversation.

"I can't speak for Grant," I say honestly. "But he's an adult, and he's entered into this relationship with his eyes wide open and completely aware of our situation. He really likes you guys, and he likes spending time with you. He cares about you. It was actually him that thought you might be worried about being taken away from me."

Her eyes fill again, and she dashes the tears away impatiently. "I'm getting sick of crying."

I chuckle and lean over to kiss her cheek. "I want you

to be happy, Mila. I want you to feel safe and secure. If—if you're really worried that Grant—"

"Uncle Luke, if you're about to offer to break up with Grant because I'm feeling insecure, you're the dumbest man alive."

This time I laugh outright, relief settling over me like a heavy blanket. "Okay, good. But promise that you'll talk to me if you have concerns. Or at least talk to Ginger."

"I will," she assures me. "I'm going to call Ginger tomorrow, I think. I'm still not sure if I want to talk to Uncle Matt again, though."

I stand. "Take your time to think about it. The decision is yours and it doesn't need to be made in a hurry." I head toward the door. "I guess you want to call Jamie back."

"Yeah." She tilts her head. "Do you like Jamie, Uncle Luke?"

Fuck me, what a question. "Well… he's a good kid. I don't dislike him. But I'm still getting used to the idea of you having a boyfriend. Why?"

She shrugs. "No reason. Just curious. I like him."

I snort. "I should hope so. I love you, baby girl."

Her smile is radiant, one I haven't seen from her in years, since before Matt left. "Love you too, Uncle Luke."

I'm sacked out on the couch with my eyes closed when I hear a key in the front door. I don't move. It's Grant, of course—I gave him the key a couple weeks back.

The door closes quietly, and then soft footfalls approach. They pause—I'm guessing in the living room doorway—and then continue. A moment later, the couch depresses as he sits beside my hip.

"'M awake," I mumble, but can't quite drag my eyes

open.

"I know." He leans down and kisses me gently. "Come on, let's get you to bed."

I make a sound of protest. "Don't wanna move."

He laughs. "Just keep your eyes closed, then."

The next thing I know, I'm being hauled up off the couch, his arm around my waist as I'm planted on my feet. I grumble and sway, my head dropping to his shoulder to nestle into the curve of his neck. He smells so good.

"All you have to do is shuffle along," he says, dropping a kiss on my head. "I'll steer you."

Of course, by the time we get to the top of the stairs, I'm mostly awake. I pull away from Grant and sigh. "Waking up is hard."

"Life sucks," he agrees, and leads the way to my bedroom. I manage to kick off my shoes and strip down to my boxers, then collapse into bed.

I hear Grant moving around, picking up my discarded clothes and putting them away, and I should protest, tell him he doesn't need to do that... but it feels nice to be looked after.

I drift off, and the next thing I'm aware of is Grant sliding into bed with me. I can no longer see any light from behind my closed eyelids, and I roll over and snuggle into him. His arm comes around me, and his breathing slows and steadies.

"You were right," I mumble sleepily. "Mila was afraid of being taken from me. The social worker suggested she might like a family with two parents, and she's been worried about it ever since."

Grant's arm tightens and an explosive breath escapes him. "Wow. I know they're only doing their jobs, but shit like that makes me mad. Poor Mila."

"Yeah. That's why she wanted a job so bad."

"Is she okay now?"

I shrug in the dark. "I think she will be. I made it pretty clear what would need to happen for them to be taken from me and how unlikely it is, and also what provisions are in my will. She'll talk to Ginger, too—I already texted her and warned her what to expect. I still don't know what she'll decide about Matt, but she seemed happier when we were done talking."

"Good."

The silence stretches in the darkness, comfortable and warm, safe. I stir myself once more.

"She's afraid that you'll get sick of having an instant family."

Grant sits up and turns on the bedside lamp. "What?"

I squint up at him. "She likes you and she's happy that we're together, but she's worried that—"

"Yeah, okay. Did you tell her that's bullshit?" His frown is fierce.

"I told her you cared about both of them and that you were an adult who knew what he was getting into."

"Good. Do you think I should talk to her?"

I close my eyes. "If the moment presents itself. I don't think you should force an awkward conversation."

A moment later, the light goes out and I feel him settle beside me again. "I don't like that I'm the cause of her feeling bad."

"You're not," I assure him. "It seemed like a general kind of worry, since she's already so insecure about this. And she told me I'd be dumb if I broke up with you."

He chuckles. "She's so awesome."

Sleep has almost overtaken me when he speaks again.

"I did know what I was getting into. And I'm glad I'm in."

"I'm glad too." I smile into the dark.

It's nice to be looked after.

But… it's also nice to look after others.

I roll over and snuggle up to Grant's side. I'm sleepy, sure, but this shouldn't take too long.

I start by lightly stroking his chest, then let my fingers wander downward. He shifts, catching my hand. "You're tired, babe. You should sleep."

"I will. In a minute. Wanna do this." I pull free of his hold and close my hand around his cock. It's already half hard in anticipation. I give him a light squeeze, then roll back over and fumble in the nightstand for the lube. When I close my hand around him again, he groans.

I was right—it doesn't take long to get him off, especially once I start whispering to him with every stroke.

"You're so fucking hot."

His mouth opens on a gasp.

"Love your big, hard dick."

"Baby," he moans, thrusting into my grip.

"Can't wait to have it in me again."

"Anything… anytime…"

"Nobody's ever fucked me like you do."

His head thrashes on the pillow as I tighten my fingers.

"I want you to fill me up with your come."

I know he's close. Shifting, I bring my other hand into play and tickle lightly over his sac and back toward his taint.

"I want you to fuck me until I can't remember what it felt like without you."

He comes so hard, his back arches and he slaps a hand over his mouth to hold in a shout. After, as he lies there panting, I clean us both up and kiss him, and he pulls me to him and holds me close.

Yeah. This whole looking after each other thing is amazing.

SEVENTEEN

Grant
———

It's nearly the end of June before Mila agrees to talk to Matt. He called or texted Luke every day for a week after that first call, not in a harassing way, just touching base and reiterating that he wanted contact with the kids. Mila and Jordy both had phone sessions with Ginger within the first few days, and Jordy decided he wanted to talk to his uncle but he didn't want to upset his sister. Mila, unsurprisingly, encouraged him, saying she wouldn't be upset at all.

It still took a few days for Jordy to make up his mind for sure, and when he finally agreed, it was with the stipulation that Luke had to be part of the call too.

Since then, he's talked to Matt three more times, the last two times on his own, and he's occasionally mentioned him in general conversation. He seems comfortable with the idea of Matt being a peripheral part of his life.

Mila, on the other hand, struggled hard. Even after her talk with Luke and several phone sessions with Ginger, she was torn about letting go of her anger and resentment. I can't say I blame her—being abandoned by your only blood relative has to hurt.

I struggled too—with whether or not I should talk to Mila about my relationship with Luke. In the end, I asked Luke for Ginger's number and set up a phone appointment with her. She's the professional, right? And she knows the kids probably at least as well as Luke by this stage, although in a different way. She couldn't tell me anything Mila had said, of course, but after I laid out the situation in a brutally honest way that made me feel completely vulnerable, she was able to give me some tips for dealing with the situation. I haven't said anything to Mila, but if it comes up, I'm confident I can handle things.

Well, somewhat confident.

Luke had to tell Jus and Jas, and as great as they are, I know it really wasn't fun for him to have to explain that his ex-husband who abandoned him with two children now wanted to be a part of the kids' lives again. The twins have totally come through, though, keeping an eye on the kids' moods and making sure things are as normal as possible. I'm pretty sure Mila has taken Jas into her confidence, which is great, although Jas is keeping mum on the subject.

Tonight over dinner, Jordy asked Mila if she'd talk to Matt with him. She hesitated, then shocked us all when she agreed. So now I'm nervously pacing the kitchen while Luke hovers in the doorway. He wants to listen and make sure everything is going okay, but he also doesn't want to make the kids feel self-conscious. I know exactly how he feels. We're both supposed to be reviewing information about possible candidates for JU's new director. The official hiring committee was appointed two weeks ago—Luke, as the interim director, me and Derek, as ADs, and the heads of HR and events, representing the functional departments. Kiara, the head of HR, has been managing the actual executive search process and ensuring interested parties do actually meet our requirements, but that still leaves a lot of information for the rest of us to go through prior to interviews, which begin next week. It's been narrowed down to six people at this stage. Malcolm and Seth have requested that we recommend at least two for them to choose from. If we can't do that from the current six, the search will continue.

So… it was supposed to be a busy evening anyway, but now neither of us can focus.

"Uncle Luke!" Jordy shouts, and Luke is racing down the hall so fast, he loses his balance and nearly slams into the wall. I abandon the groove I'm wearing into the kitchen floor and follow more sedately down the hall, stopping short of the living room door, just out of sight.

"…come for the Fourth of July?"

My stomach clenches. It's so weird, I haven't heard Matt's voice in seventeen years, but I recognize it instantly. We were friends, yet I can't help the instant antagonism that rises in me. I'm surprised by it—I knew I was angry over the way he left Luke and the kids, but the intensity of what I'm feeling now is deeper than that.

Shoving it down, I concentrate on what's being said.

"Uh… sure. We're having a party on the Fourth, but otherwise don't have plans for the weekend. There's a small motel and a couple of B-and-B's in town, if you don't want to stay at JU."

A small part of me stands up and cheers. Good for Luke, setting boundaries.

"Oh. Uh, I guess that would be more convenient. JU's not right near the town, is it?" I'm kind of pleased to note that neither of the kids offers Matt the couch.

"It's about a half-hour, maybe forty-minute drive, depending on where exactly in JU you start from. You'll need to hire a car anyway, because public transport around here isn't great."

"Okay. Let me sort out the details, and I'll let you know what my plans are. It'll be good to see you all."

I back away and turn to go back to the kitchen. Okay, so Matt is coming for the Fourth. The kids asked Luke and me a week ago if we could have a party for the Fourth—and yes, it made me feel like the king of the world to be included in the request and the planning. We decided on a cookout and pool party, Jordy and Mila inviting about half a dozen friends each—and their parents, if they wished to come. Luke's very conscious that with the number of hours he works, he hasn't really had a chance to do more than say hello to Jordy's friends' parents, and he hasn't even met some of Mila's. He figured this would be a good way to get to know them better. We also asked Derek and Trav and Dimi and Jason, of course, plus Luke's audit team. It adds up to quite a lot of people, but they'll likely be coming and going over the course of the day; plus, it'll be good for us to be social.

Mila comes into the kitchen as I'm filling a glass with water. There's a tense look to her that concerns me.

"Hey. All good?"

She shrugs. "Yeah, I guess. Can you drive me to Jamie's?"

"Are his parents home?"

She snort-laughs. "Yes, Mr. Overprotective, his parents are home. You can even come to the door and check."

I love that she's comfortable teasing me like this, and I don't want to wipe the smile from her face, but…

"Is everything okay, Mila?"

She looks out the window "Yeah. I just… want to think for a bit."

Well, I can't blame her for wanting the comfort of her

boyfriend's presence. Fuck knows, any time I'm stressed lately, I home in on Luke like a heat-seeking missile.

"Okay, let's go."

We go out the front door, since my car's in the driveway, waving to Luke and Jordy as we pass. They're deep in conversation, but Luke mouths "Thank you" to me.

Jamie lives just a little too far for walking to be convenient, which is an annoyance for Mila and a relief for my control freak, overprotective boyfriend. I leave Mila alone with her thoughts on the drive. Considering tonight was the first time she even agreed to speak to Matt, she probably feels a bit overwhelmed by the idea of him visiting in less than two weeks.

I pull up out the front of Jamie's house, and she turns to me. "You want to come to the door, don't you?"

My sheepish grin says it all, and she laughs. "Come on. Between you and Uncle Luke, I sometimes feel like I'm only five years old."

"If you were only five years old, we probably wouldn't worry so much about your 'playdates' with Jamie," I tell her, getting out of the car. Her indignant squeal is music to my ears.

The front door opens before we reach it, a sign that Jamie's been waiting. There's an anxious expression on his face that relaxes when he sees Mila smiling. She flounces up to him, lifts her face for a kiss, then announces, "Grant wants to make sure your parents are home."

Jamie grins at her, and in that moment he looks so besotted that my heart clutches a little. Aren't they too young to be feeling so strongly? It's just going to make them hurt so much more if—when—things don't work out.

"Sure," he says. "Come in, Grant. Mom and Dad are having coffee."

I end up staying for coffee with Jamie's parents, a nice

couple who assure me they're planning to come to our cookout on the Fourth. I'm glad—they seem like people Luke and I could be friendly with, or maybe even friends. Jamie's mom assures me they can make sure Mila gets home later, but I decline, citing Luke's overprotectiveness. "He'll be fine once he meets you," I promise, and she chuckles understandingly.

By the time I get back to Luke's, Jordy has gone up to his room and Luke is trying to make headway through the paperwork we left on the kitchen table. He looks up when I come in.

"She okay?"

I nod. "Processing, I think. She was glad to see Jamie."

"Thanks for taking her. Jordy wanted to talk."

"He okay?"

Luke snorts, probably at the similarity of our questions. "Yeah. It kind of sank in hard that he's going to see Matt again and it threw him off-balance."

I slide into the chair opposite him. "How are you feeling about it?"

He sighs, then laughs a little. "I honestly don't know. I... I guess I'm still angrier than I thought." He scrunches up his face. "A month ago, I thought I was all mature and shit, letting go of my anger toward Matt. I felt so superior—and actually, I'm still so insanely angry with him. I'm angry that he acted like he had to carry this huge burden. I'm angry that he left. I'm angry that he's been supposedly living a happy life since then. And I'm really, *really fucking angry* that he's calling now and thinks an apology will make any difference. That he thinks he can just drop in for a visit and it will all be okay." He sucks in a deep breath. "That he had the nerve to seem surprised and hurt when I didn't invite him to stay with us. I mean... *come on!*" He stops abruptly, looks over at me, and smiles sheepishly. "Sorry. I didn't mean to just…"

I reach across the table and grab his hand. "Hey, I asked. And I did want to know. You've been so concerned about the kids that I feel like you've forgotten that you get to have feelings too. And I know you want the kids to make their own decisions on this, but that doesn't mean you can't vent to me."

Luke pulls his hand free, gets up, comes around the table, and plants himself in my lap. I barely have a chance to get my arms around him before his face is buried in my neck.

"I love you," he mutters. "I love you I love you I love you."

Every muscle in my body locks up tight. I know he feels it, because he lifts his head and leans back a little to look me in the eye.

"I love you. You're… everything I ever wanted and never deserved. I never want to be without you again."

I'm moving before I know it, my mouth on Luke's, up from the chair, pushing him back on the kitchen table, heedless of the paperwork, our laptops, intent only on kissing him, touching him, him him him—

Except he's not just him.

A thud from upstairs shatters the moment.

"I'm okay!" Jordy yells cheerfully. "Just dropped something."

I pull back, breathing hard, and meet Luke's gaze. In the next second, we're both laughing.

"Sorry," I say, straightening and helping him off the table. "I got carried away."

"Feel free to do that anytime you like… when the kids are sleeping over with their friends." His face turns solemn.

"I… uh, I know we've talked about this already, but this is what it's—"

I put my palm over his mouth. "Stop. I know. And I'm good with that. The way you are as a dad is a huge part of why I love you."

The words feel incredibly right, and the way his expression softens behind my hand and his eyes warm makes everything inside me settle.

Jordy comes thundering down the stairs in his usual manner, and I drop my hand and take a step back. Luke turns to sort out the mess on the kitchen table, rescuing my laptop from where it's balanced precariously close to the edge, and Jordy comes in.

"Do you know an easy way to open a piggy bank?" he asks.

"Smash it," I tell him. "But why do you need to open it?"

He rolls his eyes in a way that reminds me of Mila. "It won't smash; I tried that."

So that's what the crash was.

"Why do you need to open it?" Luke repeats my question, and Jordy sighs as though he's the most put-upon child on the planet.

"I need money, Uncle Luke."

"For…?" Luke seats himself calmly, his attention still on Jordy, who squirms a little.

"Stuff."

I clear my throat to hide a chuckle and go to the sink to get some water. "Stuff like…?" I have a funny feeling this could go on for a while.

"It's a secret."

Uh-oh.

I turn and look at Luke. He looks at me. We both turn to look at Jordy.

"It's my money," he says defensively. "I saved it myself."

Luke nods slowly. "That's true. You've been saving it for a long time, and to be honest, I'd like for you to keep saving it. Is this secret something that I can buy for you?"

Jordy immediately shakes his head. He looks uncertain. "I need to talk to Grant," he says abruptly. "In private."

There's a flash of hurt in Luke's expression, but it's gone in an instant. He stands. "I'll go change into my pj's," he offers, stopping to drop a kiss on Jordy's head on his way out. "Love you, pal."

"I love you too, Uncle Luke." Jordy waits until he's gone, then sits at the table and looks at me expectantly.

So I join him.

"What's up?" I really hope this isn't going to tax my kid management abilities.

"I want to buy a present for Uncle Luke, but I can't unless I can get my money. He can't pay for his own present!"

Ohhhhhhh.

What a relief.

How sweet is this kid?

Fuck me, have I forgotten Luke's birthday?

No. It's in October. I'm positive of that.

"Okay, this is a problem we can solve," I assure him. "Uh, I just have to say, I'm pretty sure Uncle Luke would rather you save your money than spend it on a present for him."

Jordy shakes his head stubbornly. "He works really hard and he's been taking care of us by himself. My friend Jack said that his mom won't even talk to his dad anymore and when it's his dad's weekend his grandma has to be inter… intem… I can't remember the word."

"Intermediary?" I suggest, suddenly getting an idea of what brought this on.

"Yeah, that's it. Uncle Matt was Uncle Luke's husband and he left, and Uncle Luke is being really nice to him. Jack says that's gotta be hard for him, so I thought it might be nice…" He trails off and stares fixedly at a point on the table.

I swallow hard. "I get it. Does… uh, does it have to be a gift you buy? Because I think your uncle would appreciate it just as much if you made him breakfast one weekend. Or cleaned your room without being asked."

Jordy looks doubtful, and I bite my lip to hide a smile.

"Well, what kind of gift did you have in mind?"

He screws up his face in exactly the same way Luke does, and my heart skips a beat. It's a learned mannerism, of course, since there's no genetic tie between them, but it says more clearly than anything else could that they're family.

"I don't know," he admits. "I thought I'd see how much money I had first and then decide."

There's an easy solution here, of course. I can offer to pay for whatever Jordy decides to get Luke, Jordy's savings will stay safe, and knowing Luke, I'll find some "extra" cash in my wallet after he realizes what the money was for. But this is something Jordy seems to feel strongly about, and if he really wants to spend his savings on a gift of appreciation for his beloved uncle…

I stand. "Let's have a look at this piggy bank."

Jordy's face lights up, and he leaps up to lead the way. We pass Luke at the bottom of the stairs.

"What…?"

"We're going to see what it'll take to break into Jordy's cash stash," I say cheerfully, winking at him. He raises a brow, and I shake my head.

"Can I come?" he asks.

"Okay," Jordy says. "But no questions."

Man, this kid. Have I said that already? It bears repeating.

Luke mimes zipping his lips and obediently follows us back upstairs and down the hall to Jordy's room. A huge piggy bank—shaped like a pig, but oddly, painted in a tie-dye pattern that will give me a migraine if I look at it for too long—is lying on its side in the middle of the open floor space. I lower myself to sit beside it and heft it into my lap. It's heavy, evidence that either Jordy has a heap of money saved or that he has a heap of pennies saved.

"Well?" he asks impatiently.

"I'm looking." I inspect the monstrosity carefully. There's actually a hatch underneath that seems to indicate it's meant to be opened and closed rather than broken open to retrieve the contents, but I can't work out how to open it.

Frustrated, I finally set the damn thing on the floor and stare into the beady black eyes. Jordy sits beside me and does the same.

There's a muffled chuckle from the doorway, and Jordy and I look up at a grinning Luke.

"May I speak?" he asks politely.

"Is it going to be helpful?" I counter.

He grabs a pencil off Jordy's desk and comes to sit with us. "I don't know if you remember, Jordy, but this piggy used to have a tail."

I close my eyes as his meaning sinks in. When I open them, he has the pig in his lap, ass up, and is probing in a small hole with the pencil.

Don't judge me, but I find it weirdly hot, and my dick twitches.

I clear my throat.

Luke looks up, and my face must show what I'm thinking, because he freezes and his eyes go wide. Heat creeps up my neck, and I shrug.

He shakes his head and turns his attention back to the pig. Thankfully, Jordy didn't notice our little exchange.

"There!" Luke declares with satisfaction as something clicks inside the pig. In the next moment, the hatch springs open and coins pour out. Jordy cheers.

Luke and I get up off the floor. "We'll leave you to count your cash," he declares. Jordy barely notices we're leaving.

As we head back toward the stairs, Luke asks, "What's he need the money for?"

"I can't tell you," I say. "It's a secret. But it's important to him, and I think you need to let him do it."

Indecision wars with frustration on his face as we go downstairs, but by the time we get to the kitchen, he sighs, seeming resigned.

"If you think so. I trust you."

I swear, my heart nearly bursts. I knew Luke trusted me with the kids, but this is different. He trusts me to make decisions that may affect their welfare, and that's the best damn gift I've ever been given.

I grab his wrist, swing him around, and kiss him, loving the way his sound of surprise fades into an appreciative moan.

"Love you," I murmur, and he smiles against my mouth before he pulls back.

"What was that about upstairs?" He wiggles his brows, and I snort, letting him go and returning to my chair at the table.

"What, you wouldn't be turned on by the sight of me giving a ceramic pig a prostate massage?"

He rolls his eyes. "Of course I would, but then you

know how much I love that kind of massage. I didn't realize you did as well."

Here's the thing: Luke loves to bottom. Like... really loves it. And since I like it either way, I have no problem with topping him, especially since it makes him very, *very* happy. Plus, he's really good at it; wring-the-last-drop-of-fluid-from-stone kind of good. So we never really talked about anything else.

I shrug. "I don't mind a good prostate massage every now and then."

"Maybe that's something we should try, then."

I raise a brow, a little surprised. "Is that something you'd want to do?" I can't deny feeling some definite interest.

His smile is soft. "I want to do everything with you."

EIGHTEEN

Luke
———

I have never felt so ambivalent about a holiday weekend in my life. As I slip my laptop into the bag and grab my phone, I have to wonder if maybe it would be better to just claim that work has exploded and spend the weekend hiding at the office.

Wishful thinking.

I meet Grant at the second-floor stairway landing. We came in together this morning, and I have to say, I really like how couple-y that feels. He drops a kiss on my cheek when I stop beside him, and one of our passing colleagues makes an "aww" sound.

"Ready to go?" he asks, studying me, and I make a face.

"I guess."

He slings an arm around me and turns me to the stairs. "It won't be that bad. He's going to be on his best behavior, I'm sure."

That's right… Matt arrives tonight. He took a half day from work so he'd get here before midnight but agreed that it would be best to wait until tomorrow to come over. He's got a room at a B&B not too far from our place.

The kids are... well, Jordy's cautiously excited to see his uncle again. They've been talking two or three times a week since this visit was arranged, and I think Jordy really likes having another connection to his parents. Mila, on the other hand, is still just cautious. She's spoken to Matt one more time, and although it seemed to go well, she's been a bit quieter than usual. More like she used to be and less the vivacious teenager we've seen lately. I'm flat-out worried, although Ginger assures me she's just processing and that I should give her time.

I sigh. "I just want it over with. I think it's the anticipation that's the worst. There's also a tiny part of me that's convinced he's just not going to turn up and I'll have to help Jordy get over another broken heart."

Grant's silent, and I glance across at him as we reach the bottom of the stairs and start through the lobby.

"You're thinking the same thing, aren't you?"

He nods reluctantly. "I'm also worried that he'll turn up this time, but then decide he was right to leave the first time and we'll never hear from him again. I think that would hurt Jordy even more."

It really would. "I guess we'll find out."

By the time Friday morning rolls around, I'm not just apprehensive, I'm actively wishing Matt to perdition. Jordy barely slept all night—first because he was excited and couldn't get to sleep, and then because of the nightmares. He still occasionally gets them when he's stressed, and I suppose the idea of seeing his uncle in just a few hours triggered them. The first time he woke up screaming,

Grant swapped rooms with him, and Jordy was able to drift back off once he was in bed with me, but it didn't stop him from waking another three times.

As a result, we're all a little sandy-eyed and exhausted this morning. Grant's walking a little stiffly, too, probably because Jordy's twin bed is too small for him. What I really want right now is to pack up Grant and the kids and go stay in a fancy suite at a resort for a few days. Jordy can go nuts with the kids' club, Mila can sunbathe by the pool and talk on the phone with her friends, and Grant and I can sleep for ten straight hours and then have wild monkey sex and order room service. Maybe later this summer, after the new director is settled in, we can wrangle a long weekend and get away. I'll have to mention it to Grant.

Not now, though, because Matt is due any second.

With impeccable timing, the doorbell rings. I expect Jordy to go racing for the door, but he stays at the kitchen table, his gaze locked on the sliced apple he's been eating.

Uh-oh.

Grant and I exchange glances.

"Why don't you go get that?" he asks casually. "I'll finish up in here." He takes the dishtowel from me and begins to dry the last of the breakfast dishes.

"Thank you," I mouth. "Come on, Jordy, let's get the door."

Thankfully, Jordy gets up—he even precedes me down the hall. I guess he just wanted company?

I debate whether to call Mila down now or wait until Matt's in the house. She'll have heard the bell, so she's obviously making a point of some kind. Teenagers are so complicated.

Jordy opens the front door, and even though I could have sworn I was prepared, the sight of Matt is like a brick to my stomach.

He meets my gaze. "Hi."

My throat is too dry to respond. I swallow. "Hey. Uh, come in."

He steps over the threshold and smiles at Jordy. There are a few lines around his eyes that I didn't notice via video chat. Other than that, he looks exactly the same—right down to his haircut. "Hey, Jordy. I brought this for you." He hands over a gift bag that I hadn't even noticed—one of two. I'm guessing the other, much smaller one is for Mila.

Jordy, suddenly shy—or nervous?—says "Thank you," and takes the bag but makes no move to open it.

I close the front door. "Why don't you take Uncle Matt into the living room and see what he brought you while I go get Mila?" I suggest, but from the look on Jordy's face, it's not going to happen. "Or I'll take Uncle Matt into the living room while you go get Mila," I amend hurriedly.

"Nobody needs to come and get me; I'm here," Mila announces from halfway up the stairs, and I thank any deity that might be listening. She's wearing a faintly challenging expression, but she's here, she's talking, and I'm not going to ask for more.

"Great!" I chirp. "Living room." Because suddenly full sentences are too hard.

Jordy leads the way, his confidence somewhat restored with both me and Mila here to support him. I wave Mila forward and bring up the rear. I'll just get them settled, then slip away to the kitchen on some excuse and give them time to chat.

"Sit next to me, Uncle Luke," Jordy demands, and my mental plan undergoes a rapid change. Guess he's still feeling insecure.

"Sure thing, pal." I follow him over to the couch.

"It's good to see you, Mila," Matt says, and he sounds

genuinely sincere. "This is for you." He offers her the gift bag. She looks completely unimpressed, but to her credit thanks him politely as she takes it and pulls out several gift cards.

"These are great. Thank you," she says again, but with no real change in tone. I catch a glimpse of the store logos on the cards, and they're all for stores she likes, so I suppose it's more about Matt than the gift itself.

Jordy's ripped into his too and pulls out a Dodgers jersey in approximately his size. It looks like it might be a tiny bit too big, but he likes that, so it works out.

I mentally give Matt points for his choice of gifts as Jordy thanks him again with somewhat more enthusiasm than Mila.

And then the room lapses into silence.

"How was your flight?" I ask, desperate.

He shoots me a grateful look. "Smooth. Kind of boring, really. The time difference always surprises me."

I nod understandingly. "Yeah. We drove, so it didn't hit us quite so hard. Uh, is the B&B nice?" Oh, hell.

Matt opens his mouth to answer but is cut off by Mila. "Where's Grant?"

I cast an apologetic look at Matt. "He's in the kitchen."

"Why isn't he here?"

Starting to lose patience, I ask, "Does he need to be?"

She shrugs. "I just thought he'd be here to greet our guest."

Clearly, I've underestimated my niece. I stare at her wordlessly. With one sentence, she's established Grant as a part of our family and Matt as the outsider, and I literally don't know what to say.

"Uncle Matt should meet Grant," Jordy agrees, then looks at Matt. "I told you about him, remember? He works with Uncle Luke and plays ball with me."

"He's Uncle Luke's boyfriend," Mila adds, and honestly, I am seriously considering strangling her.

"I know," Matt says calmly. "Jordy's told me about Grant."

Point for him.

"I'll go get him," Jordy volunteers, and he's gone before I can think of anything to say.

I force a smile.

And we sit in awkward silence.

"Uh, Mila," Matt begins, "how's work? It must be fun working at a summer camp."

She shrugs. "I guess."

Wow, she can really hold a grudge.

"And you have a boyfriend." Matt tries again. "That was a real surprise."

"Why?" She tilts her head and looks him square in the eye. "Years have passed. I've grown up."

Matt takes a deep breath.

"Mila, if you'd really rather not be here, you can go upstairs," I announce. She's pissed, and hey, she's allowed to be. Entitled to be, even. But… "Or you can tell your uncle that you're angry and let him apologize. But maybe don't make this hard for Jordy."

"He's not my uncle," she declares. "Or at least, I prefer not to acknowledge the accident of birth that made him so. My real uncle never abandoned me just because things were tough. I'm not ready to let go of my anger yet, Uncle Luke."

Matt's jaw drops, and I'm completely at a loss for words (even as my heart sings with love for her), so of course that's the moment when Jordy walks back in with Grant in tow.

Grant reads the room in a heartbeat. "Jordy, we should have brought some drinks. Let's go grab them."

Jordy frowns. "In a minute. I want you to meet Uncle Matt."

"Grant Davis?" Matt sounds stunned, and it hits me that Jordy must never have mentioned that my boyfriend Grant is the same Grant we went to college with. I don't know why I assumed that he would have, but I did. And now Matt's being blindsided.

A tiny part of me feels smugly satisfied.

"Hey, Matt." Grant steps forward, hand outstretched. "Good to see you again."

Mila snorts, and I shoot her a warning look as Matt gets up to shake Grant's hand.

"Uh, yeah, wow. I didn't realize…. So you two hooked up again after all these years."

Something about his tone makes me uncomfortable, and I can tell Grant feels the same by the way his smile sets.

"Yep. It was a lucky day for me when Luke showed up at the office."

"And now you're living here."

"Yes," Mila says.

Grant raises an eyebrow at her. "Well, technically I live about ten blocks away. But the company is better here."

"And you really should just move in officially," my devil niece insists, although I can't say I disagree with her in this case.

"Thanks, honey. We'll talk about that another time. Come and help me get some soda and glasses."

She scowls, but she's obviously not ready to let Matt think she might ever disagree with anything Grant says, so she gets up and heads out the door with Grant following.

Jordy looks confused. "Is Mila okay?"

Smiling brightly, I stretch out an arm and he comes to sit beside me. "She's fine."

"Okay. Is Grant going to move in for real instead of just staying over? 'Cause that would be cool."

"We haven't talked about it yet. I'm glad you like the idea, though."

"Grant's a great guy," Matt interjects smoothly. "I'm glad he could be here for you when I couldn't."

Couldn't? What an interesting word choice.

"Jordy, do you want to show Uncle Matt your room?" I really need a second to regroup.

"Yeah!" Jordy leaps up. "I've got some awesome limited edition souvenirs from the parks, Uncle Matt. Grant got them for me before they even went on sale in the shops."

Something indecipherable flashes across Matt's face, then he smiles and gets up to follow Jordy out of the room.

As soon as they're gone, I sag back against the couch. Holy fucking hell.

"You okay?"

I look up to see Grant leaning in the doorway, and I huff. "Not really."

He comes to sit, wrapping his arm around me, and I turn into him with relief.

"I hope you don't mind," he says, "but Mila told me what happened, and I said she could go spend the morning at Anita's house." Anita is one of her friends who lives a block away. "She'll be back for lunch and promised no more sniping."

I close my eyes. "Thank you. That's perfect."

He drops a kiss on the top of my head. "It's the first time she's seen him in years, and she was barely ready to even talk to him again. It'll get better."

"I know." I sigh. "I wish she hadn't been rushed into it, but Jordy wanted to see him, and…" I trail off and sigh again. "I hate when I have to try and balance what they need."

"Jordy seems pretty excited," he reminds me. "Now that he's past being nervous, anyway. That's good."

I straighten and smile at him. "I really love you when you show me how much you care about my kids."

His laugh turns my smile to a grin. "Jordy thinks you should move in 'for real.'" I make air quotes with my fingers. "And Mila would likely agree, if only because she thinks it might spite Matt."

He snorts. "Yeah, I noticed. Next time she wants to stay out late with her friends, you should tell her that Matt always loved to party, too. I bet she'll be in her pj's and curled up in bed before you finish the sentence."

It's my turn to laugh. "Probably. But hey, no avoiding the question."

"You didn't ask a question."

I huff. "Semantics. You wanna move in with us?"

That soft look I love so much comes into his eyes. "Yeah. But you have to—"

"Make sure the kids are okay with it. Yeah, I will, but I really don't think it's going to be a problem."

My phone buzzes with a text, and I pull it from my pocket. It's from Mila.

I'm sorry I upset you.

I show it to Grant. "I really feel like I'm failing this parenting gig sometimes." I text her back.

I love you anyway. I'm sorry you had to do this when you weren't ready.

Grant kisses my cheek. "You're really not failing."

Three dots dance on my screen, and then Mila's next message pops up.

It makes Jordy happy, so it's ok. Luv u 2, Uncle Luke.

Maybe I'm not failing after all.

NINETEEN

Grant

"I can't believe Matt's actually here," Stu says quietly beside me at the grill, his gaze fixed on Matt across the yard where he's talking to Dimi, Trav, and a couple of the parents who've joined us today.

"Yep." I don't say anything more, because really, what's there to say? I'm worn thin from dealing with Matt and all the drama he's brought with him over the past thirty hours or so. Not that he's done anything overt to cause it—well, other than leaving in the first place—but the kids are both tense and that means so is Luke.

I bet you're surprised that I said "kids" instead of just "Mila," right? Yeah, me too—and Luke. We thought that once Jordy got over his initial apprehension, he'd be fine, but he was really upset when he realized Mila had gone to Anita's, and after she got back, he basically would not be in a room if Mila, Luke, nor I weren't in it. Plus there were more nightmares last night.

The original plan had been for Matt to come over early this morning and help us set up. Luke thought that having him here while we were all working would be better for the kids than the more "formal visit" setting we had yesterday. But after last night, he decided that a break from one-on-one time with Matt was needed. The kids both looked a little relieved when he told them, which just made Luke worry even more that he's been doing things wrong.

Matt was not thrilled when Luke called to tell him to come later, but he agreed. He's been very agreeable, really —I can't say what it is exactly that's making me so irritable about him. He's been perfectly friendly to me, although I don't think he's entirely over his shock at my presence and there have been a few moments when I got the distinct impression he wished I'd just go home.

So we're all tired today, and although it's been good to meet and talk with the kids' friends' parents and chill with our friends, I probably wouldn't mind if it started to rain and everyone went home.

I look up at the clear, endless blue sky.

Not happening.

"You want to be careful," Stu warns in that same quiet tone, and I give him my full attention.

"What? What's happened?" My gaze flicks around the yard, clocking the locations of the kids and then Luke before returning to Stu's unsmiling face. I don't know him all that well socially, but we've worked together for a few months now, and I know Luke considers him a good friend. I like him. I also trust his judgment, which means I'm now on high alert.

"Nothing's happened. I'm sorry, I didn't mean to freak you out. But I think you should keep an eye on him. He's got something in mind."

I bite my lip. "Did he say something?"

"Not really. Look, I know this sounds weird and conspiracy theorist-y. He just…. The way he looks at Luke and talks about him… He's got a lot of feelings there, and

I don't think he's ready to let go. Obviously Luke's not interested, but that doesn't mean Matt can't cause trouble."

"Fuck." I sigh. "Honestly, I'm not thrilled that he's here, and it's added a lot of stress for all of us. But Luke really wants the kids to have this tie to their parents, and as long as he's not causing trouble…" I shrug and turn the hot dogs Jordy requested for him and his friends.

"Are we talking about Matt?"

I jump and whip around to brandish my tongs at Derek. "Don't fucking do that!" I hiss. "You scared the crap out of me."

He grins his "you've gotta love me" smile. "Sorry. Not my intention. It was fun to watch you leap out of your skin, though."

"I could learn to hate you," I warn, but I'm smiling as I turn back to the grill.

"So… Matt?" he asks, and Stu murmurs agreement. "There's something about that guy. He's got an agenda."

Oh, fuck. Derek's got great instincts, so this is a big, fat, red flag I can't ignore.

"Guys, I really appreciate the warnings, but I need something concrete."

Derek spreads his hands, nearly dropping his bottle of beer. "There's nothing concrete. And hey, maybe his agenda is about reconnecting with the kids and rebuilding their relationship."

"But you don't think so." I look across the yard again.

"I don't think so," Derek affirms. "Trav doesn't like him at all. I don't get that vibe—he seems perfectly affable to me—but I can tell he's set himself a target and he's working toward it, and I can tell he doesn't like you."

I'm surprised by how much that surprises me. "I guess it can't be easy for him to see me all but shacked up with his ex-husband," I concede. "We used to be friends, though."

"Good friends?" Stu asks. "Or just part of the same broader friendship group? Because I've seen Matt with his friends, and I agree with Derek. He doesn't like you, and I feel like if he'd ever really been your friend, some of that would bleed through now."

I think about it. I feel a little bad bashing Matt this way —he really hasn't done anything awful since he arrived. He's been trying hard, and it doesn't seem fair to not appreciate that effort. But… "Well, we weren't really close. I guess it was more of a group thing. I can't remember ever hanging out with just him."

"And I don't think he'll invite you to do so anytime soon," Derek warns.

"This sucks," I declare. "It's already hard enough without adding personality clashes."

Stu laughs. "Personality clashes? That's such a diplomatic way to put it."

"Grant!"

We all look up to see Jordy racing over with the three friends he invited today. The four of them have been in the pool, and they're still dripping and barefoot as they come to an abrupt halt at the edge of the designated "no running" zone, something I came up with last time we used the grill and I noticed them running helter-skelter way too close. The rules are no running on the pool deck or in the area around the grill if it's on, and failure to abide by this results in suspension of pool privileges for either a week or until I decide otherwise. Jordy moaned and groaned about it, but he's been following the rules and there have been no horrific burns accidents. Luke told me it's super hot when I get all "responsible adult." Either way, I see it as a win.

"We're *starving*," Jordy announces now. "Is lunch nearly ready?" He comes closer, peering at the grill.

"Hot dogs in two minutes," I promise. "You've got time to dry off and get a plate and some buns and salad." I say that with the hope that it will inspire Jordy to have some salad, but I'm not really expecting it. He might go for the potato salad later, or have some corn when it's ready, but the green, leafy stuff is not high on his priority list, and it's a holiday, so…

"Thanks!" The boys race off toward their pile of towels, and Derek chuckles.

"That was such a dad thing to say," he teases, and heat creeps up my neck.

"Shut up." I glance around anxiously. The last thing this powder keg situation needs is Mila or Matt thinking I'm trying to be a dad to the kids.

I'm not. I care about these kids, but Luke is their parent, not me.

"It's great," Derek says seriously, the amused tone gone. "And Jordy obviously responds to it."

"I don't think you need to worry about overstepping," Stu interjects, clearly reading my mind. "Mila, for one, would have said something if she wasn't comfortable with the role you've taken on in their lives. And as Luke's boyfriend, it's natural that you should take on some of the responsibilities of adulthood in the house."

I bend down and pull the packages of steak out of the cooler, ready to put on the grill when the hot dogs come off. "It's all just complicated now—today especially. But I'm probably moving in soon."

Derek raises a brow. "Probably?"

I shrug, trying to be casual when I feel anything but. "We need to be sure the kids are okay with it. They've said stuff that indicates we're good, but we want to double-check. And this weekend isn't the best time for that."

"Congratulations," Stu says. "I think the kids are going to be thrilled to have you move in officially, and I'm happy for you all." He claps me on the shoulder, and I grin over at him. It feels good to have validation from someone who's been in Luke's life for a while.

"Thanks."

"Do you want another beer?" He tips his head toward the empty bottle sitting beside the grill, and I nod.

"Yeah, that'd be great."

As he wanders off to get it, Derek says, "I'm happy for you, Grant. If anyone had asked me a year ago what you would need to be happy, this isn't what I would have described, but it's perfect for you. I'm thrilled to be proved wrong, because you really fit here, with Luke, as stepdad to these kids." He lowers his voice a little. "I've got your back if anything happens with Matt. Luke's got legal papers, yeah?"

There's a little clutch in my gut at the thought. It's never been a real concern, because I've known since before Matt came back into the picture that Luke has sole custody of the kids, but even the thought of someone trying to take them makes me go cold all over.

"Yeah," I manage. "There's no issue there. It's the emotional damage we're worried about."

"Anything we can do, just reach out," he promises, and then the opportunity to say more is gone as we're swarmed by preteen boys bearing hot dog buns and clamoring for food.

Lunch is mostly cleared away the next time I have a

moment to observe Matt. There's still fruit and cheese and some other snacks out, and I'm sprawled out in a deck chair beside Luke, half listening to the conversation he's having with Anita's mother and Jamie's dad about college prep (college prep!), my gaze drifting around the yard. The teenagers have gone back to the pool, but Jordy and his friends are tossing a ball around. The adults are in various stages of food coma, scattered around the yard in small clumps, enjoying the sunshine and the utter luxury of a Saturday without household chores.

Across the deck, Matt is in a group with some of Jordy's friends' parents, and they seem to be chatting… but Matt's attention is firmly fixed on Luke.

And I really don't like the look on his face.

He's not even trying to hide it.

I mean, I get it. Luke's amazing. Sweet, smart, funny, sexy… I'm totally in love with him, so I don't blame Matt for still feeling that way. Especially since I'm pretty sure he wouldn't have left Luke if it weren't for the kids. But that's the thing—eventually, they would have split up anyway, because Luke's the kind of man who could never walk away from people who need him, and Matt's not. I don't want to diminish his right to choose his life direction. He didn't want to raise kids, he tried, and he couldn't handle it. Forcing himself to stay wasn't going to help anyone… but there were better ways for him to do it than just walking out and not getting in touch for years. Luke says he was always a great uncle to the kids—why didn't he try stepping back into that role? Weekend visits. Occasional babysitting. Staying a part of their lives, at least, and giving them and Luke some support. Totally disappearing and only making contact through friends? Not okay.

What he's doing now, trying to reestablish contact with the kids and be a part of their lives, that's great. I know

Mila is struggling, but I agree with Luke that she'll one day be glad of this connection to her mom's family. And Jordy has been happy enough to be in touch with his uncle again that I believe the biggest issue is just nerves, which he's probably picking up from all our tension. Matt's been trying hard, and I respect that, because it can't be easy.

But that doesn't mean I have to like the way he's looking at my guy.

"Hey."

I tear my gaze away from Matt and smile at Jas as she drops into a chair beside me. "Hey, yourself. I'm glad you made it, but you just missed lunch." Jus turned up right before the meat was done cooking, but Jas went to a friend's place first.

She shrugs. "Looks like there's still plenty to graze on. I'm stuffed, anyway. Brunch is always a good idea, but it throws off mealtimes for the whole day." She tips her chin across the yard. "Is that him? The kids' uncle?"

So much for thinking I'm subtle. Although, she does know most of the other people here. "Yeah, that's Matt." I'm pretty sure I'm about to have yet another conversation about him. At least Jas hasn't spoken to him yet and can't tell me how much he dislikes me.

She hesitates. "Luke traded up."

A surprised laugh explodes from me. "Uh, thanks? That's not what I expected you to say."

She shrugs. "There's not much else I can say." She hesitates again. "Jus texted me before. He thinks Luke traded up, too, and not just because you're better-looking."

I sigh, checking to see if Luke's paying attention. "Jus is not the only person here today who feels that way," I tell her quietly. "So far, he's been trying really hard with the kids. Is there anything Jus thinks we need to know?" I look around, trying to find Jus in the crowd. He's over by the pool with Dimi and Trav and some of Luke's team, laughing about something.

Jas shakes her head. "Nothing specific. He said Matt made some comments about whether we'd move with Luke and the kids when they go back to LA and... Look, Jus only mentioned it because it seemed like a weird thing to say. He thinks it was nothing, which is why I'm the one here telling you and not him."

"You're not making me feel better," I advise her. "Just tell me."

"He—Matt—said that from what Jordy's told him about us, we'd be welcome to look after any house he lives in."

I consider it. "It's weird," I concede finally. "But it really could be nothing. I mean... what else would it mean? That he thinks when Luke and the kids go back to LA, he'll be living with them? It was probably just a throwaway compliment that came out wrong."

She shrugs. "Probably. To be honest, my opinion of him is biased by the fact that he left the kids and the way they've been feeling since he got back in touch. Jordy's kind of excited, but he's always... nervy now. Like he can't relax. And Mila's just tense about it. I don't like that."

"Me either." My gaze flitters around the yard. Mila's in the pool, whispering with Jamie. If it weren't for the fact that there're about forty other people here, I'd say they were too close. Jordy's got this look of utter determination on his face as he winds up to pitch to his friend, and I can't help but smile. "We'll see how they feel after this weekend. I know Luke's worried."

"Jus and I are here if you need anything. And just in case you were wondering, yeah, we'd move to LA with you guys."

I whip my head around. She's watching me with a steady gaze, and I force myself to clear my throat.

"So you'd be okay with it if I officially moved in and you had another person to look after?"

Jas grins and leans over to drop a sisterly kiss on my cheek. "Grant, Jus and I have been wondering what the hell you've been waiting for." She stands and wanders off in the direction of her brother, and I blow out a long breath.

Luke and I haven't talked about him moving back to LA, but we both know it has to happen eventually. Once the audit has been completed, there isn't a job for him here. It likely won't be until next year, but when the time comes, I already know I'll go with them. If I can wrangle some kind of transfer to Joy Inc.'s head office, great, but even if I can't, there are a million job opportunities for someone with my background and experience in the greater LA area. I love working for JU, but I love Luke and the kids more.

And hey, the move will definitely be easier if we've got Jas and Jus with us.

LATE AFTERNOON HAS GIVEN way to twilight, and Luke and I are bringing out the next round of food—leftovers and sandwich fixings, chips, popcorn, fruit, cheese. Our huge late lunch means that most of the people who are still here aren't really hungry, but it'll be a couple hours yet before the last of our guests clear out. We talked about moving the party to JU or even to the town center for one of the fireworks shows but decided against it. That was the right call—it's been a long day and we're all worn out. Jordy succumbed to his exhaustion shortly after his friends left, about thirty minutes ago, and is curled up asleep on a pool lounger. That's a real nuisance, because he'll wake up in a couple hours and not be able to sleep properly tonight, but he's slept so badly the last few nights that neither Luke nor I could bear to wake him.

"I'll take this out," I say, hefting a platter, "and be back for the rest."

Luke makes an absent noise. He's studying the contents of the pantry like they hold the answer to the meaning of life. "Do you know where the fancy crackers are?"

I laugh. "I'll ask one of the twins while I'm out there," I promise, because if anyone would know, it's them.

The screen door bangs behind me, and I carry the platter of savory pastries over to the table and set it down. Di, who I've gotten to know pretty well, gazes at it wistfully.

"Grant, you're killing me. If I eat another bite, I'll explode."

Winking, I say, "But what a way to go. The twins have to be the best cooks on the planet." I look around. "Have you seen them?"

She waves dismissively, reaching for a pastry with her other hand. "They're somewhere. Hey, do you think I could get them to cook for me?"

I stop, turn, and glare at her. "Any attempt to poach the twins will result in the immediate end of our friendship, and I'm pretty sure Luke will stick you with the worst jobs he can think of until the end of time."

She huffs around a mouthful of food, and I consider my point made.

Spotting Jus with Mila and Jamie, I head in that direction. They're talking about college when I reach them—more specifically, the benefits of going away for college versus staying in your hometown. Staying wasn't an option for Jus and won't be for Jamie, since the local campus of the University of Georgia won't be built and open for at least three years, but if Mila's back in LA within the year, it will be for her.

I wait for a lull in their discussion before speaking up. "Sorry to interrupt. Jus, do you know where the fancy crackers are?"

He nods. "Yeah, I put them— You know what, I'll come and show you. It'll be quicker than describing where I put them."

"I'll come with," Mila says. "I want to grab a cardigan now that it's cooling down."

"And I need the bathroom, so you're three for three," Jamie adds dryly. "Hey, when you were looking at colleges, did you consider the ball program?"

I answer his questions as we cross the yard to the deck. It's nice to see him taking this so seriously, and we've slowed down a little as we discuss the pros and cons of playing a sport while working toward a degree. I'm not really paying attention as I open the screen door and enter the house, so I nearly run into Mila, who's standing frozen in the hallway outside the kitchen.

"M—"

Jus shakes his head sharply, cutting me off. Behind me, Jamie eases the screen door closed.

What the hell—

Then I hear it—Matt's in the kitchen, talking earnestly, presumably to Luke.

"...just saying I'd like you to think about it. I know things have been hard for you the past couple years, and that's all my fault. I made a mistake. I can't begin to say how sorry I am. It was the dumbest thing I've ever done. I love you, and leaving you was stupid. But I have a better perspective now, and you were right. There's no way we ever could have let the kids go. I'm ready now to be a parent like I should have been then. It would give them the support and stability they need—we would be a family the way we always should have been."

I blink away the red film of rage that's obscuring my vision.

"Matt, I... You've blindsided me with this." Luke's using the careful, blank tone of voice he only brings out when he needs to process and doesn't have time. I can only imagine what's going through his head—he'll be worried about the impact this will have on the kids; how Matt will react to being told no. How the kids will handle it if Matt suddenly disappears again.

"I know, and I'm sorry." Christ, has Matt always sounded like a smarmy bastard? "Like I said, you should take some time to think about it. I know you have... entanglements you'd need to deal with." Wait, does he mean me? Really? He's calling me an *entanglement*? I suck in a deep breath, and Jamie's hand lands on my forearm, gripping tight. "And I'm living in LA right now, but if you need to be here for a while longer, I can make arrangements. Maybe take a sabbatical for the rest of the year. Whatever it takes for us to be together."

There's a long pause, then I hear... Is he *kissing Luke*? The red film of rage is back.

"Stop, Matt. You've... given me a lot to think about."
What?
What the fuck?
Mila flashes a look over her shoulder at me, and her face is devastated, tears tracking down her cheeks. She shoves past Jus, racing down the hall and slamming out the front door.

"Fuck." I start after her, but Jamie pushes past me.

"I'll go. Sort things out here." He follows Mila, leaving

me and Jus in the hallway as Luke and Matt come to the kitchen door to see what the noise is all about. Luke's pale, his eyes big and standing out in his face.

"What…?"

"Mila's upset," Jus says, saving me from having to speak. I don't know that I could say anything rational right now. "Jamie's gone to check on her."

Luke's gaze flicks from him to me. I don't know what my expression says right now, but I'm pretty sure it's not good.

"Why is Mila upset?" Matt asks, and Jus's arm shoots out to block me just in time, because *I'm going to rip his motherfucking head off*.

"Teenage thing," Jus says, although anyone with half a brain would realize Mila is upset because she overheard their conversation, and Matt's the world's biggest douchemonkey for even asking with that stupid smug expression on his face as he looks right at me.

It's only my respect for Jus that keeps me from shoving him out of my way so I can beat the living fuck out of Matt.

"We have guests," I say through clenched teeth. I hate the shock and emotional exhaustion on Luke's face, but more than that, I hate that he didn't tell Matt to fuck right off.

The front door opens, and a moment later, Jamie appears in the hallway. He takes us in cautiously. "Mila and I are going for a walk."

"I… Okay," Luke says. "Is she…?"

"She needs a minute."

Luke looks like he's been punched in the gut, but I can't think about that now. I dig in my pocket and pull out my phone. "Here." He's still in swim trunks and a T-shirt, and Mila was wearing her swimsuit and a cover-up. They can't go wandering around after dark without a phone, and I don't want him to take the time to go get his while Mila's standing in the street. I unlock it and disable the auto lock. "Call if you need anything."

He takes it. "Thanks, Grant."

None of us say a word as he walks back up the hall and we hear the front door close. I count to ten in the heavy silence, then look at Matt.

"It might be best if you went back to your hotel."

He smirks at me. "That's not your decision to make. This is Luke's house."

This time, Jus turns and full-on body blocks me. The kid has good instincts. Matt takes a nervous step back, and I force myself to inhale deeply and relax. Jus eases his grip slowly, ready to stop me again if necessary.

"Go, Matt," Luke says. "There's a yard full of people here and now isn't the time for this."

Matt wavers, clearly caught between wanting to stay and wanting to make Luke happy. In the end, he pats his pocket and then pulls out a car key.

"Call me later?" His voice is pitched low, intended for Luke only, and Jus tenses.

Luke gives a single, sharp nod, and Matt retreats up the hallway. A minute later, the front door opens and closes.

Jus looks past Luke into the kitchen. "I'll just get some of this food out," he mutters, turning sideways to sidle into the room. I follow him, passing Luke without making eye contact.

I'm so angry.

I'm so hurt.

I'm so... I don't even know. I feel as though my insides are being shredded.

I grab a platter and walk back out, through the back

door, only to stand on the deck like an idiot, not sure what to do.

"Grant?"

I turn my head and meet Derek's gaze.

"Fuck," he whispers. "What happened?" Then he shakes his head. "Wait." He takes the platter from me, deposits it on the table, then detours to the cooler and grabs two bottles of beer. "Here you go," he announces cheerfully, coming over and handing me one. "Now, I know we're not supposed to be working today, but I wanted to ask about that marketing promotion you mentioned." He grabs my arm and steers me off the deck and into the yard, over to where Dimi and Jason are sitting by the abandoned pool.

Why is the pool abandoned? It was full of teenagers a few minutes ago.

Has it really only been a few minutes since I was last out here?

I blink and look around the yard. Mila's friends are huddled around a table we set up to allow for extra seating. They have their phones out and are chatting quietly. Anita looks up at that very moment, smiles at me, and calls, "Hey, Grant! Have you seen Mila?"

I make myself smile back. "She and Jamie went for a walk. They shouldn't be long."

She looks a little puzzled, but one of the boys cackles lecherously, and her attention is immediately taken up with elbowing him in the stomach.

Derek pushes me down into a chair and takes the one beside me as Dimi sits up and Jason frowns.

"What's wrong?" Dimi asks, scanning the yard. "Is Mila o—?" He stops suddenly and his gaze swings to me. "Did that jackhole upset her?"

I sigh, realize I'm holding a perfectly good beer, and

chug. It might not be the tequila I'm suddenly craving, but it'll do the trick.

I wipe my mouth. "Not directly," I answer finally. "He didn't know she was listening when he told Luke they should be a family again."

Derek chokes on his beer.

Like… literally. Beer sprays everywhere, and he's hacking and coughing and gasping for breath.

"He… said… what?" he wheezes, waving Jason away when he pounds on his back.

Trav comes to join us. "Jeez, Derek, are you okay?"

"Shh," Dimi says, his gaze pinned on me. "What exactly did he say?"

So I tell them. The words are burned on my brain, and I recite them in a monotone. It all seems so surreal.

Is Luke really thinking of going back to him?

How can he?

I just don't understand. My brain can't process it.

My words stumble to a halt right around when Jamie went running after Mila.

My friends look shocked. And angry.

"That fucking asswipe," Derek seethes. "Is he still here?"

I shake my head. "Luke told him to go."

"Good for Luke!" Trav declares, but I shake my head again.

"He said he'd call him later."

"What?"

"Wait, what did Luke say, exactly?"

Derek and Jason speak at the same time, and I pick up the story around where I left it. When I'm done, they all just look at each other, seemingly at a loss for words.

"Grant?"

I turn to look at Jus as he approaches. He's got his phone in his hand and his face is worried.

"It's Mila."

I reach out and take the phone.

"Are you okay?"

Air bursts from her in a sob, then she says, her voice shaking, "Yes. I'm okay. I want to come home."

"Do you need me to come and pick you up? Where are you?" I look around. Where are my keys?

"No, we're not far. We don't need a ride. I... Is he still there? I don't want to be there while he's there."

I shake my head, then realize she can't see me. "He's gone. Mila, are—"

"And I don't want to talk to Uncle Luke," she bursts out, then sobs again. "I can't... How could he... Grant, please don't go. He didn't mean it."

My head clears in an almost painful rush and I straighten. "Mila, I will be right here when you get back. I'm going to wait at the front door for you, okay? Just come back now. Yeah?"

There's a moment of unsteady breathing, then she says, "Yeah."

I stand and begin walking across the yard. "Give the phone to Jamie."

There's a muffled exchange of words, then Jamie's voice says, "Grant?"

"Is she really okay, or should I come and pick you up?"

"She's okay. We're just at the park down the street—we'll be there in a few minutes."

"Okay, I'll be waiting." I end the call and hand the phone back to Jus, reaching for the back screen door with the other hand.

"She okay?" he asks, following me inside.

"Yeah. She—" I break off as Luke comes out of the kitchen.

"Grant," he begins, but I shake my head.

"Mila's on her way back." I lead the way to the front door, open it, and step out onto the front porch. Luke and Jus follow.

I look down the street, and sure enough, I can see Mila and Jamie walking toward us from the direction of the park. They're still a few houses away. Jamie has his arm around Mila's shoulders and she has her head down, but that's all I can really see in the deepening gloom of twilight.

We wait in silence. I hear footsteps inside the house, and a glance over my shoulder shows Jas coming out to join us. That's good. Mila will need someone to help her get settled.

They get to the path leading up from the street, and Mila looks up and stops dead. She says something to Jamie. He looks in our direction and answers her, and even in the poor light I can tell he's not happy. She shakes her head vehemently. His shoulders sag, and he turns and walks up the path toward us, his face set, and stops at the base of the steps up to the porch.

"Mila says…" He stops, swallows, and fixes his gaze on the steps. "Mila wanted me to tell you that she doesn't want to speak to you tonight, Luke."

Fuck.

Poor kid. Imagine having to tell your girlfriend's uncle that.

I don't look at Luke.

Nobody says anything for a long moment.

"Thank you for looking after her tonight," Luke finally replies in a quiet voice. "Please tell her we'll talk in the morning. Jas, would you mind…?" He trails off, and Jas hurries to reply.

"Of course. I'll stay with her until she's asleep."

Another silence, then Luke says, "Fine," and goes back into the house.

My heart hurts for him.

I stay on the porch.

Jamie turns to look down the path, and Mila walks up to join us. Her face is tear-streaked, her eyes red and puffy, and she comes up the steps without stopping and wraps her arms around my waist, pressing her face into my chest.

I hold her tight. "It's okay."

"Don't leave," she mutters, her voice muffled.

I hesitate, and her head snaps up.

"No! You can't go." Fresh tears well up in her eyes.

"Mila, it's not that simple. Your uncle gets a say in this too."

She shakes her head hard. "He's being an idiot. Please, he'll come to his senses."

I swallow. "Look, nothing needs to be decided tonight. Go on up to bed and we'll see how things look in the morning."

Her watery gaze meets mine. "You'll be here? You'll stay tonight?"

I bite my lip. "That might be awkward, honey. But you know I don't live far, and… and I'll come over tomorrow." Honestly, I'm a bit confused by her attachment to me. We get along well, and she's never indicated that she doesn't like me in Luke's life, but I wouldn't have said we were besties.

She hesitates, then nods. I let her go and step back, and Jas comes forward and puts an arm around her. "Come on, I'll bet you'd like a shower after being in the pool most of the day." She steers Mila inside, leaving me on the porch with Jus and Jamie.

We look at each other.

"That sucked balls," Jamie says bluntly, and a startled laugh bursts from Jus.

"Thanks for stepping up," I tell him. "I'm sorry you got dragged in."

He just shrugs and hands me my phone. "Mila's my girlfriend. Her drama is my drama." He hesitates. "It's not my business, but I think she's right. Luke would be an idiot to go for that other guy. He's just… Well, you know him better than me, but he worries about Mila and Jordy so much. I think…" He hesitates again. "Maybe it's stupid, but I think he got hung up on the idea of family. He'll realize that he's already given them a family without *him.*"

I rub the bridge of my nose. There's a headache forming behind my eyes. "You're a smart kid," I say tiredly. "And I appreciate the vote of confidence." I don't bother to tell him what I'm up against: a loving relationship that lasted fifteen years. A history. Blood ties with the kids.

And really, if Luke's still invested in that, if it's something he wants… do I really want to try to convince him he'd be better off with me? Can I handle knowing for the rest of my life—or the duration of our relationship—that he wanted to pick Matt and I persuaded him not to?

Jamie's right. This sucks balls. And not in a good way.

"Come on." I wave them toward the door. "Let's go tactfully convince people they want to go home."

We troop through the house. The downstairs is empty. Out on the back deck, I can tell that people know something is going on. Luke, his face set and pale, is trying to get a zombie-esque Jordy upright, coaxing him to go to bed.

I see my friends across the yard, their attention focused on me, and head in that direction.

"It's fine," I say before they can ask anything. "But if you could make noises about how it's getting late and help me clear everyone out, I'd appreciate it."

Dimi claps me on the shoulder. "Consider it done."

As the others move out, picking up their empties and exclaiming what a long day it's been—Jason has the worst fake yawn ever—Derek steps up beside me.

"What do you need?"

I shrug. "A time machine would be nice. Honestly, I want to get everyone out so I can clean up and go home to wallow in my misery."

He huffs. "You know, when you and your boyfriend… uh, fight and you plan to sleep elsewhere, you don't have to stick around to clean up first. Go."

I want to. My whole body just yearns to *leave*. But when I glance around the yard, I know I can't. We've been tidying as we go, but there's still a lot to do, and I just can't stick Luke with all the cleanup.

I shake my head. "No, it's fine. I'll—"

"You'll go," Derek says, taking my arm and steering me toward the back deck. "We'll stick around and tidy up. I swear, we won't leave it like this."

Oh, man. I'm so tempted.

"Do you need anything? Where are your keys?"

"Inside." Oh, fuck it. "You'll clean up?"

"Absolutely," he assures me. "We've got it. Go."

So I go. I ignore everyone, go into the house, get my keys from the top of the fridge, and walk right out the front door. My laptop is in the study, but I won't need that tonight. It can wait.

I get in the car. By some miracle, nobody's blocking me in.

I don't remember driving home. I just suddenly realize that I'm in my garage. So I get out of the car and go inside. My house is a bit stuffy—it's been days since I've even been here. Nearly a week. I open some windows, even though it's still a warm night. Fresh air is fresh air, right? I check the fridge, but there's nothing there—a couple of beers, a few bottles of water, some condiments. The cupboards are similarly sparse.

So I go have a shower.

It's been a long day, and the water beating down on me feels good. I block out everything else and just focus on the water hitting my skin, until eventually it turns cool and then cold and I start shivering.

In an old pair of gym shorts and a holey T-shirt, I wander back to the kitchen and get a beer from the fridge. I don't have any hard liquor in the house. I'm not usually one to have more than a beer at home. Right now, I wish that wasn't the case. Two beers aren't going to be enough to drown out the cacophony of thoughts cycling through my head.

I'm about to take my beer out to my deck, which isn't as nice as the one at Luke's place, and stare at the back yard, which also isn't as nice as Luke's, when the doorbell rings.

Fuck.

I'm frozen to the spot.

It rings again, and I force myself to move in the direction of the front door.

Please don't let it be Luke.

I just… don't think I can handle any more tonight.

My stomach sinks as I realize what I've just admitted to myself. In my gut, I believe Luke's going to choose Matt.

I stop with my hand on the door handle. I can't. I just can't open the door and have him tell me that tonight.

The bell rings again.

"Grant?" The muffled yell is like music to my ears… because that's not Luke. Without stopping to wonder why he's here, I yank the door open.

Derek pushes past me, a paper bag in one arm. "Finally!"

Trav gives me an apologetic look. "Sorry. He was worried. Uh, Dimi and Jase should be right behind us. They stopped at the gas station for snacks."

I look out toward the street, and sure enough, Dimi's car is pulling up to the curb.

"What are you doing here?"

No one answers. I'm talking to an empty room. From the direction of the kitchen, I hear cupboards being opened and Derek saying, "Check the freezer for ice, babe." He raises his voice. "Grant! What do you want, tequila or bourbon?"

Tears sting the back of my eyes, and I blink them back. "Bourbon," I call, then clear my throat. I'm a bit croaky.

Dimi and Jason reach me, arms full of bags. "Good, you've started. But let's skip the warmup." Dimi plucks the beer bottle I'd forgotten about from my hand. "We brought every heart-attack-inducing snack food we could find. My sisters swear that junk food makes everything better, so we're testing that theory."

I close the front door and follow them back to the kitchen, relief and gratitude battling for supremacy inside me. Getting drunk and eating myself sick isn't going to solve my problems, but I'm willing to give it a shot.

And with my friends here, I don't need to be alone with my thoughts.

TWENTY

Luke
———

I didn't sleep Saturday night.
Not at all.

My brain wouldn't switch off, but I couldn't think clearly either. I lay on top of the covers, unable to get into the bed Grant and I sleep in together, staring at the ceiling through the gloom of the dark room.

How did it all go so wrong?

I try to do the right thing. Always. Especially the right thing for the kids. So why is it always so hard?

Was I wrong to just let Matt go without a fight when he left? Should I have insisted he maintain contact with the kids?

Should I have talked about him more in the last couple of years, reminded the kids of the good times instead of letting them (Mila) pretend he never existed?

Was I wrong to let him reconnect with them? Was I wrong to encourage them to talk to him? Should I have never let him visit?

Or should I have pushed harder? If I'd made Mila talk

to him sooner, she might have made peace with her feelings by now. Should I have made her stay on Friday, forced her to interact with him instead of letting her hide at Anita's?

Should I have smacked Matt in the face when he suggested I go back to him? Laughed at him for thinking he ever had a chance with me now?

Or is going back to him the right thing to do?

I love Grant.

But I loved Matt too.

I loved him for years.

And don't the kids deserve to have their uncle in their lives? To know that there is an indisputable link to their parents, always there, day in and out?

I don't know what to do.

And Mila…

I will never forget the way she looked at me.

That she wouldn't even talk to me.

My whole body aches, but it's nothing compared to the agony of my emotions.

I wait until five o'clock rolls around, then get up, shower, and dress. I go downstairs and make coffee. I sit at the table and look around the kitchen.

It's clean.

Grant left last night while I was putting Jordy to bed. I came downstairs and he was gone, along with most of our guests. Di and Stu were still here, arguing with Derek, who was trying to convince them to leave.

They knew something was wrong. They asked questions. Where was Grant? What happened?

I told them not to worry, we'd talk about it later, then ushered them out. Di almost refused to go, but then I said "Please" and my voice cracked, and I think she realized I was hanging on by a thread.

Which left me with Jas and Jus, witnesses to my failure as a parent, and Derek, Trav, Jason, and Dimi.

Grant's friends.

I'd started to think of them as my friends too, but let's be serious—in moments like this, they'll always be his friends first. As evidenced by the fact that they could barely look at me as they put things away and cleaned.

I asked them to go. Derek looked me right in the eye and said, "I promised Grant we'd clean up. He always faces up to his responsibilities, and I won't let him down."

I wish he'd just hit me instead.

Then they left.

Jus and Jas hung around for a while. They both offered to stay. I sent them home.

What do I do?

What's the best option for everyone?

What's best for the kids?

What do I do?

"Uncle Luke?"

I look up. Jordy's in the doorway, rubbing his eyes. Outside, the sun is rising—I guess I've been sitting here for a while.

"Hey, pal. You're up early." It's not unexpected, given how early he crashed last night. I'm a little surprised he wasn't up earlier. At least there were no nightmares last night.

"Yeah. Is everything okay? You look… sad." He ventures in cautiously.

I force myself to smile. "Everything's fine. I was just thinking."

He doesn't look convinced. "Is Grant still sleeping?"

It's like a body blow, but I say, "Grant went back to his house last night," and I almost sound normal.

Jordy stills. "Why?"

I shrug. Words won't come.

"Is it because of Uncle Matt?"

Fuck. I really don't want to lie to him, especially because the truth is very likely to come out. "Sort of. It's… been a very busy few days here," I prevaricate.

He just looks at me, and I hope my face doesn't show what I'm feeling.

"Wait here." He dashes out, and a minute later, I hear him on the stairs. I want to call out for him to be quieter so he doesn't wake his sister, but yelling that would defeat the purpose of the words, right?

So I just sit with my cold coffee and wait.

He's back a minute later, thundering down the stairs and skidding into the kitchen, a small wrapped box in his hands.

"Here," he says breathlessly, thrusting it at me. "This is for you. Because you're the best and I love you."

Oh.

Speechless, I take it and stare at it, blinking.

"Open it," he demands impatiently, shifting from foot to foot. I shake my head to clear it and begin peeling away the red-and-white striped wrapping paper. Inside is a cardboard box, plain black. I turn it over and find where the lid is tucked in.

It's tight, and I need to wriggle my thumb in to get it open. I set it on the table and peer inside. It's a mug.

"Take it out." He sounds less confident now, and I smile at him—the first thing I've done since I got up that feels natural.

"You didn't have to buy me anything. Wait—is this why you wanted to open your piggy bank?" I hate the idea of him spending his savings on a gift for me.

"Yes. You deserve a present just because. You buy us

stuff when we've been good and when you think we deserve it, so how come I can't buy you something?"

I clear my throat. "I guess you can. Thank you, Jordy. I can't tell you how much this means."

He swallows. "You haven't looked at it yet."

It won't matter if it's the ugliest mug on the planet, I'll still love it, but I obediently slip my fingers into the box and slide the mug out.

And nearly drop it.

World's Best Dad, it proclaims in multicolored bubble writing on a white background.

I can't speak.

"I know you're not really my dad, but you still are. I remember my dad—well, a little bit—and he used to play with me and make me eat vegetables and ask me how school was. He yelled at me when I did stupid stuff, and he let me sleep with him and Mom when I had bad dreams. You do all that stuff too, and I know you worry about us and love us. So, you're my dad." He stops, and I think he might be done, but then he says, his voice wavering, "Is that okay?"

"Yes." The word bursts from me. "Of course. I—I'm so honored. Your dad… he and your mom loved you so much, and I was so… honored that they trusted me to look after you. Even before we lost them, when you'd sleep over or we'd go out for the afternoon, they trusted me and that mattered. Thank you, Jordy. This is the best present I've ever gotten." I hope he knows I mean more than just the mug.

He lurches awkwardly forward to hug me, and I hold him tight. He's growing up so fast, and again I wonder if I'm doing this parenting thing right. What would Mandy say if she were here?

When he finally pulls back, he's smiling. "Can I play Fortnite?"

"Uh…" I blink. "Get dressed and have breakfast first. And have a shower. You were swimming yesterday."

"Okay!" He turns to go, then swings back around. "Uncle Luke?"

"Yeah?" I brace myself for whatever's coming. It could be another life-shaking declaration, or it could be a request for pancakes.

"I just want you to know that I really like Grant and it would be okay with me if you and him got married one day and he was my uncle too."

My lips stretch in a semblance of a smile. "Marriage is a big step." It's completely inane, but it's the only thing that came to mind.

He nods solemnly. "Yep." And then he races out.

I sit at the table, trying to get my breath, trying to make sense of everything, staring at the mug, the beautiful, amazing, unbelievable, heartbreaking mug Jordy bought me.

What do I do?

"I thought you'd like it."

My head snaps up. Mila is standing in the doorway, pale, looking tired, her eyes a little red.

I did that to her, and it kills me.

I open my mouth—to say what, I don't know—but she shakes her head and walks in, passing me on her way to the fridge.

"Jamie and I took him to that store in town that sells tourist crap. Grant convinced him not to spend all his money, so he only had ten bucks. He spent nearly an hour trying to decide what the best present would be to show you how much he loves you." She shuts the fridge door without taking anything out. "I am so angry with you right now."

"I know. I'm sorry." My voice cracks.

"How could you let him talk to you like that? Like you need him to make us a family? Like you haven't been good enough, worked hard enough these past years? Like he deserves another chance? How could you even listen to him when he was telling you to shake Grant off like he means nothing?" A tear runs down her face. "You can't just *leave* someone because it might make things easier or better or… I don't even know!"

I stand, because I can't stay seated, but I don't move toward her. "Mila—"

"No! It's my turn to talk. He *left* us. Just left. Walked out like we meant nothing, like Mom hadn't trusted him with us and expected him to love us forever. Like he hadn't promised to love *you* forever, even if things got hard. I was at your wedding, Uncle Luke. I was only little, but I remember your vows. I thought they were the most beautiful thing I'd ever heard. I know people change and sometimes divorce is the best option, but that doesn't mean just walking out and not coming back!" She sucks in a deep breath. "And even before he left, he wasn't a very good parent. You were the one who made sure we ate properly and got to school on time and had new clothes and did our homework. He was a fun uncle, but he sucked at all the everyday stuff. I felt… I felt like Jordy and I were just a burden to him, and that sucked. I mean… I know that you and he probably didn't want kids, but it was still crap to feel like he didn't want us."

I don't know what to say. I can't tell her he did want them, because… it's not true. Matt never wanted kids. He was completely freaked out when he realized Mandy and Bill had left guardianship to us.

"He loves you. He always loved you."

She sniffles. "Yeah, as long as he could be the fun uncle who gave us back at the end of the day. His love didn't mean a whole lot when he decided he'd rather give up his home and his husband than be a parent to us." She slumps into a chair and stares at the table. "I just... I get that you loved him. I loved him too. Part of me still does, because he was a pretty cool uncle and I have a lot of great memories. Maybe you still love him. I don't know. But the fact that he thinks he can just walk in after more than two years and you'll dump your boyfriend and go back to him... that's not respectful of you. That's not considering your life and your feelings. He's being the same selfish person he was when he left."

I take a deep, shaky breath. She's right about that. Matt and I haven't had more than a handful of short conversations since he first called, and they've been about the kids. He hasn't made any effort to actually talk to me. Two years is a long time, and if he expects me to believe that he's changed, surely he can see that I might have changed too... so why not want to get to know the person I am now?

"You're making some excellent points," I say quietly. "But it's not that easy, Mila. I know you're angry with him, and I am too. I can't lie about that. But he's your uncle. Your mom's brother. Your mom was... You know I don't have any contact with my parents. Your mom was like a sister to me—more. She was my family when I didn't have anyone, even more than Matt was. And she never gave up on Matt, not when he was a delinquent teenager, not when he barely ever called her in college, not ever. She believed in the bonds of family, and I would be doing her a grave disservice if I didn't do everything I could to keep her family together."

Mila stares at me.

Then she bangs her head on the table.

"Mila!" I leap forward, but she's already upright again and talking.

"That's the stupidest thing ever. Mom *loved* you. She loved you just as much as him, maybe more, because the two of you were friends, not just siblings. And even if she did want you to do everything you could to keep the family together, that doesn't mean she'd want you to be unhappy. *He* made the choice to leave. If he really wants to stay in touch with us, he'll do that even if you don't go back to him. If this is just because he's suddenly decided he wants you back, do you really think he'll stick it out? Jordy and I are still here. Nothing's changed." She shakes her head. "Two days ago, we were talking about Grant moving in… was that, like, just bullshit? I thought it meant you and Grant were committed to each other. That you love him and want him to be a part of our family. Mom would never have expected you to give that up just to keep Uncle Matt in our lives."

Jesus, when did she grow up and get this insightful?

"Okay. Okay. I can't disagree with you, because you're right. I hope you can see why I'm conflicted right now, though. This is a really difficult decision."

"Why? I don't get it. I mean, I get why you're feeling all conflicted. You and Uncle Matt were together for a long time, and you feel an obligation to Mom, and you want the right thing for us. Yeah?"

I nod.

"Sure. But I still don't get why it's a difficult decision, because on the other side of the scale, Uncle Matt had no problem just abandoning you with two kids to raise after all that time together. Mom loved you. She used to joke that if you ever broke up with him, you'd still have to meet her for lunch every week, remember? We talked about this just the other week. She'd want you to be happy, and she would be so—so—" Her voice breaks, and fresh tears stream down her cheeks. "She'd be so happy with the way you look after us and love us." Swiping the back of her hand across her face, she meets my gaze. "If you don't actually love Grant and don't want to be with him, that's okay. But it's not okay if you're seriously thinking about going back to Uncle Matt just because he fed you some bullshit line about family. 'Cause if it comes down to it, Grant's been a better parent to us in the last few months than Uncle Matt ever was, and he volunteered for it all. You never expected him to play ball with Jordy or drive me to meet my friends, did you? I didn't. He does all that because he loves you and wants to make your life easier and he likes us and likes hanging out with us. He remembers when we have school projects and asks us how we went on tests. He gives Jamie the stink eye every time we go out. And-and when I was being a bitch the other week because I had my period, he went and got me ice cream without me having to ask, and he even remembered my favorite flavor. Uncle Matt went to the drugstore to get me tampons when I got my first period and it was such a burden for him that he never came back!"

She breaks down in tears. It feels like the ceiling's just crashed in on me. I go sit next to her and put my arm around her, kissing the side of her head.

"Mila, Matt's decision to leave was *not* because you got your period." Fuck, has she talked to Ginger about this? Or has she been holding on to it for two years? "He had probably already decided to leave before then. I don't know if you remember, but we'd been arguing a lot that week."

She nods. "I know. Ginger and I have talked about it.

But do you see what I'm saying? He couldn't even bring home my tampons before he left—he never stopped to consider that it meant you had to go out and get them and I was upset and uncomfortable. Grant didn't even need to be *asked* to do something to help. He just steps up." She shakes her head. "Look, I didn't mean for this to be about making comparisons. I just mean that Grant fits with us. He looks after all of us. He loves us. He loves *you*. I thought you love him, but I don't understand how you could have… Last night… He was so hurt, Uncle Luke."

I sigh, resting my head against hers. "I know. And I do love him. So much, Mila, I can't even say. I fucked up."

It's so clear now. I'm thirty-seven years old, trained to think critically and analytically, and it took a fifteen-year-old's blunt talk to make me see clearly.

"I'm going to call Matt, and then I'll go see Grant. Can you check if your brother's had a shower or if he got distracted by something?" I try not to let my hands shake as I get up. What if Grant won't talk to me?

"Sure." She stands, then puts her arms around me and hugs me tight. "I love you, Uncle Luke."

I bury my face in her hair. When did she grow up? It feels like just yesterday that she was a shrieking, laughing toddler. "Love you too."

This is my family. It has nothing to do with blood ties and everything to do with love.

I just have to show Grant how essential to it he is.

TWENTY-ONE

Grant

It's still early when I stumble out of bed and into the bathroom. To say I drank myself into a stupor last night would be understating it, and I'd really like another few hours' sleep, but a side effect of drinking that much—and especially when you alternate shots of liquor with glasses of water; thanks, Trav—is that nature calls. Urgently.

Unfortunately, by the time I'm done draining my bladder, I've woken up enough to remember everything that happened last night, and I know I'm not going to be able to go back to sleep. I have a headache and my eyes feel sandy, but I've actually had much worse hangovers. I jump in the shower and let the hot water loosen things up a bit.

I'm pretty sure I have guests sacked out in the spare room and the living room, so I pull on a pair of shorts and a T-shirt before going to find coffee.

Jason's already up and in the kitchen, sipping a cup of my deepest desire and looking way too alert.

"You're up earlier than I thought you'd be," he says quietly, getting up and pouring me a cup of coffee.

"Thank you," I mutter, then after a gulp of hot liquid, "My brain is too busy to sleep more. How are you so functional?"

He shrugs. "I didn't drink that much. I figured someone would need to be able to make coffee and organize breakfast."

I freeze. "Breakfast?" A nice, greasy breakfast would be perfect right now. "No. There's no food in the house."

"I know." He holds up his phone. "But there's a grocery store in town that's on Uber Eats, so I placed an order. It should be here soon."

I take another big swallow of coffee. "If you weren't in love with Dimi, I would marry you." There's a sharp stab in my chest, but I ignore it.

He grins. "No marriage necessary." The grin fades slowly, and he asks, "How are you this morning?"

I shake my head and stare at my coffee. "I just don't understand." The words feel familiar. I must have said them a million times last night, although the memories are hazy. But I really don't understand. How could Luke do this—to me, to us? How can he even consider ending us to go back to Matt? I thought we were on the same page. I thought we felt the same way.

The doorbell rings, and Jason gets up.

"That'll be breakfast." He rests a hand on my shoulder. "I'm sorry, Grant."

He goes to answer the door, leaving me with my thoughts. I'm glad he didn't tell me it would get better. I'm not an idiot; I know that. But hearing it never made it happen faster.

The worst part? Everything is unresolved. Today or tomorrow or someday soon, I have to talk to Luke and hear him tell me it's over. And the kids... How can I just stop playing ball with Jordy? That's not fair. It's not his fault. But if I keep visiting to hang out with him and Mila… Talk about rubbing salt in an open wound. Plus, Matt might not want me around. It's awkward having your guy's ex in the picture—trust me, *I know*.

Jason comes back in with his hands full of shopping bags, and I jump up to help. It's a nice distraction, as is preparing breakfast, and he and I are sitting down to bacon, eggs, and toast when the others begin stumbling in. Dimi looks just as seedy as I feel, and Derek is definitely not his usual self, but Trav is fairly perky—he probably drank even more water last night than he made me drink.

We're mostly done eating when the doorbell rings again. I look at Jason, who shrugs.

Fuck.

There aren't many people it could be, and most of them are already here.

"Want me to go?" Trav asks softly, but I shake my head and drag myself off to get it, praying for a door-to-door salesman.

It's not.

He looks tired and stressed, and every molecule of my body wants to reach out and hold him. For the first time in months, I don't know if that would be welcome.

That hurts.

"Hey. Hi. Uh… can we talk?" He's hesitant and unsure, so unlike the Luke I know.

I don't want to say yes, don't want to hear him say we're done, but putting it off isn't going to change anything.

"Yes," I croak. "No." I have company. As much as I love my friends, this is not a conversation I want to have with an audience. "Um. The guys are here." Part of me sags with relief at being able to delay, but the responsible, intelligent part of me knows I need to get this done. "We could go for a walk."

He nods. "Whatever you want."

Oh, hell.

"Shoes." I turn and walk down the hall. I'm pretty sure I left a pair of running shoes by the back door. Luke doesn't follow me, which is a slap of its own. Doesn't he feel welcome in my house? We were practically living together—hell, just two days ago we were talking about living together.

In the kitchen, my friends are silent. They watch me cross the room to the little bench by the back door and fish around under it for shoes. They watch as I put them on. And they watch me stand up and take a deep breath.

"We can go," Derek offers quietly, but I shake my head.

"Please stay. Take your time. I… I probably won't be long."

Trav winces. I shut everything out and head back to the front door.

Luke is waiting on the front porch, looking out at the street. It's a nice street, I guess. I certainly liked it when I was looking for somewhere to live.

Silently, we walk down the steps and along the path to the street. I automatically turn in the direction I would go to get to his house, then freeze and pivot the other way.

"How's Mila today?" I don't want to be the first to speak, but I really need to know she's okay.

"Angry with me. It's weird, but it's such a relief when she gets angry with me. She never used to—not that she'd show, anyway. She's upset, but we talked." He clears his throat. "I talked to Jordy, too."

I cringe. Jordy, who would have woken up this morning with no idea of what happened after he conked out last night. "Is he…?"

"He's fine. They reminded me how incredibly smart they both are."

We lapse into silence again. Going for a walk was a good idea—it means I don't actually have to look at him. I think if I had to look at him, this would be too hard. This isn't too bad. It's a gorgeous day, and thanks to food and caffeine, my headache is almost gone. Fresh air and exercise are good, right? I can almost pretend—

"I'm sorry."

Reality crashes back.

There's a weight on my chest making it hard to speak, hard to breathe. I force words through my too-tight throat.

"Don't be sorry. You're allowed to feel how you feel." I congratulate myself on my maturity. Not that I really have a choice. Luke and I still have to work together—I can't really stop talking to him completely and pretend he no longer exists.

"Well, maybe, but I shouldn't have let my insecurities screw with us—with what we have. I should have gone with my instincts instead of letting all my issues instill doubt. I should have laughed in Matt's face and told him to fuck off."

Wait... what?

"What?" I grab his arm and bring him to a halt. "What?"

He looks at me questioningly. I suck in air.

"You're... not breaking up with me?" It's the hardest question I've ever had to ask.

"No. I'm so sorry, Grant. I... I can't lie. I did wonder if it would be best for the kids for me to go back to Matt, but that was stupid. I didn't want to, not really, even though part of me thought I could pretend these past couple years never happened, you know? But I don't want to pretend these years didn't happen. It's been hard, but there's been a lot of good things, really good things, even before I met you again." He stops and swallows hard. "I fucked up, and I'm sorry."

This is surreal. The world seems to slow down.

"You're... you're not...?" I croak, and he frowns.

"Grant? Are you okay?" He touches my face, and things snap back into focus.

I step back, and his hand drops.

"I'm sorry," he repeats. For the first time today, I look him in the eye. His sincerity shines from them, along with what looks like guilt. Typical Luke. He'll be beating himself up about this for years, no matter what I say.

I can't just forget, though. I can't just let it go as if it was nothing.

"You hurt me." The words weigh heavily in the air. "I know you've got hang-ups about family, and I know you want the kids to have as much family as possible, but I never thought you could just throw us away like that. Or even think about it. I supported you when you let Matt back into the kids' lives, even though I think he's a dickweed for ever leaving and doesn't deserve it. I didn't realize that while I was making long-term plans for us, you just considered me a placeholder."

He gasps. It's not true—I know it's not true. Luke may have ripped out my heart last night, but I still know he was invested in our relationship. Just not enough to drown out his insecurities, I guess.

"You were never a placeholder," he insists. "Never. I love you. I love you more than I ever loved Matt, and it actually *hurts* me to say that, because I spent fifteen years of my life with him and planned to be with him forever. Knowing that I could have had you instead if I'd just woken up to myself in college *kills* me. And then I think that if we'd gotten together back then, I wouldn't have the kids now, and I can't decide what would be worse—not having them, or if I'd never met you again." He stops and takes a deep breath, and it sounds a little strangled. "I wish more than anything that I could go back and change last night. I was tired. Most of the time, I feel like I suck at being a parent. And Matt knows my weak points and he hit them all. I want the kids to feel secure. I want to make Mandy proud, wherever she is, and she *never* gave up on Matt, so I felt like I shouldn't either. But as Mila pointed out this morning, Mandy loved me. She wouldn't have wanted me to be unhappy, and she wouldn't have expected me to sacrifice my life so Matt could get his way. And she would have loved you. You both have the same sense of humor, and you love me, and you love the kids. If she was here, she'd call me a fucking moron for ever even thinking of letting you go."

He looks so fierce and determined, and emotion swells in my chest.

"I love you," I whisper.

His smile is sad. "I know. I don't ever doubt that. You never make me doubt myself. I hate that I hurt you. I love you so much, I can't believe it."

We just stand there, staring at each other, until Luke looks away.

"I called Matt this morning and told him what I should have said last night. He's welcome to stay in contact with the kids, but there will never be anything between him and me again."

I start walking again. "How did he react to that?" Not well, I'll bet.

"He wasn't happy," Luke admits. "Told me I was making a mistake and tried to lay on a guilt trip. But when I said it wasn't up for discussion, he seemed to accept it. He wanted to see the kids again this afternoon as planned before he goes back to LA, but Mila isn't ready and Jordy decided he doesn't want to if Mila's not there. He's happy to keep video chatting, though, so Matt will just have to be happy with that for now."

He sounds worried, and I can guess why. "You think he's going to disappear on them again?"

I see him shrug from the corner of my eye. "Maybe. I really don't know. I hope not, for their sakes, but there's not a lot I can do—that I'm *willing* to do—if he does. He's responsible for his own decisions. My priorities need to be the kids, me… and you. If you want that."

I stop again, turn to face him. He's nervous, his gaze flicking away and back, squeezing his hands together.

He fucked up last night.

He really hurt me.

But he loves me.

And he's sorry.

Most important… I love him.

I grab his T-shirt and yank him forward. Our mouths crash together painfully, but I don't care. One night apart, one night thinking I might never have this again, was too much, and all I want right now is the taste of him, the feel of him against me. Even when a need for oxygen forces me to break the kiss, I rest my forehead against his, unwilling to have any more space between us. One of his hands is at the back of my neck, the other gripping my shoulder, and the heat of them, the hold he has on me, is comforting.

"I'm never going to be that stupid again," he mutters. "I love you. I'm not ever letting you go."

The last of the heavy weight that's been dragging me down for the past twelve hours lifts, and I smile.

Epilogue

GRANT

"You're so unreasonable!" Mila screeches, her voice pitched high enough to make me wince even though I'm not in the same room. "Everyone else is going! It's bad enough that they all know my uncle won't let me *get in my boyfriend's car*, now they're going to see that you *treat me like a baby*!"

Luke says something I can't quite make out, because he's speaking at a regular noise level, but obviously whatever it is doesn't make Mila happy.

"You're the worst and I hate you!" she shrieks, and then races upstairs and slams her bedroom door.

"Wow," Jas says from where she's peeling potatoes for dinner. "I've never heard Mila let go like that."

"Me either. It's normal, though, right?" Teenagers are supposed to hate their parents, aren't they? I frown at the mail I'm supposed to be opening.

"Yeah, sure. There was something seriously wrong at our house if a week went by without either me or Jus having a shit fit. She'll get over it."

Luke comes in, meets my gaze, and sighs, rolling his

eyes. "Sometimes I wish she'd go back to never showing her anger."

"No, you don't."

"No, I don't," he agrees. "Did you hear? She *hates* me." He sounds almost... delighted? "She never would have said that before."

"I guess she feels all secure now."

He grins.

"So where's she not allowed to go?"

The grin fades. "A party at the beach."

I blink. "The beach?" The nearest beach is a two-hour drive away. "Other parents are letting their kids go to a beach party at night?" That can't be right. I know a lot of Mila's friends are older, thanks to Jamie, but there are still several in the group that are her age. Who'd let a fifteen-year-old make a four-hour round trip for a party after dark? "Is it supervised? Are the parents hiring a bus or something?"

He shakes his head. "It's not at night, it's during the day." I bite my lip, and his expression turns wary. "What?"

I'm hesitant, because when it comes down to it, Mila's not my kid. I mean, Luke's been pretty clear since I moved in that I have parental status in the day-to-day running of the house, and the kids ask me for permission to do stuff all the time, but I would never presume to make a decision like this or to contradict him. But he asked, right?

"You're maybe being just a little bit overprotective. How were they planning to get there? Carpool?"

He nods.

"On a weekend or during the week? Maybe we can drive her, take Jordy to the beach—a different one—and get lunch somewhere. You guys haven't left Joyville since you got here. I bet Jordy would love to see the Atlantic Ocean."

His expression goes all soft. "You're so amazing." Then he sighs again. "What do you think, Jas? Am I being unreasonable?"

Jas puts down the knife and turns to face him, a thoughtful look on her face. "I don't think you're going to like what I think."

He laughs. "Tell me anyway."

She shrugs. "I think you should let Mila go to this party—as long as she's home before dark—and I think you should let her go in Jamie's car with her friends."

Ooooh. Jas is pushing boundaries.

Luke looks at me and raises an eyebrow. "Do you agree?"

"Honestly? Yes. Jamie's showed us he's solid. He's been nothing but respectful and reliable. Mila hasn't broken the rules or gotten in trouble all summer. She's going back to school next week, and she seems focused and ready. The rules still need to apply, but I think it's fair for him to drive her when they go out. And I think a daytime beach party that all her friends will be at is reasonable." I almost hold my breath waiting for his response.

He makes a face. "She's growing up."

I nod. "Kids do that, I'm told." Last week, Jordy sat us all down and said that since he was starting middle school soon, he wanted us to start calling him Jordan. I thought Luke was going to cry, and I have to admit, it hit me hard too. We still slip up all the time, but we're trying to respect his wishes. I still think of him as Jordy, though.

"I'll go talk to her."

Jas looks over at me as he leaves the room. "You're really okay with Jamie driving her around?"

I shrug again. "I'm going to talk to him first, make sure he remembers the rules."

She laughs. "You guys are so overprotective."

When we get to the office the next morning, it's in total upheaval. Stu grabs Luke before we even get to the stairs.

"Finally! We thought you'd never get here."

Luke and I exchange glances. "It's not even eight yet," he says. "What are you doing here? You don't normally get in this early."

"I came in to check some reports without distractions. But Malcolm and Seth are making a surprise visit."

"When?" I ask, thinking they called to let the audit team know ahead of time.

Stu glares at me. "*Now*, you idiot. They're here, in with Dominic."

Dominic Hurst is our new director. He's younger than any director we've had before, in his late forties, but he's got an exceptional business reputation, and so far, he's fit in well and is doing great things. He and I see eye to eye on my plans for my district, and with his support, I'm on track to challenge Derek's number-one status this quarter.

Luke swears he gets a vibe from Dominic, but there's not a lot of information available about his private life, so I can't say if that's right or not. I know he's divorced from a woman, but that doesn't mean he's straight. It doesn't matter anyway—all that matters to me is that he's a good director and his arrival meant that Luke could hand over all those duties and focus on only his job.

"Did you find out why they're here?" Luke asks calmly, and Stu shakes his head.

"All I know is that nobody knew they were coming and they want a meeting with us this morning and then a full management meeting this afternoon."

I groan. That fucks up my day but good. "I'll talk to you later. I need to go shuffle some things around."

Sure enough, by the time I make it to my office, there's a memo in the JU app advising me that a full management meeting has been called for noon, lunch provided—which means we'll be there for a while. There's another memo, though, advising me that Malcolm and Seth want a meeting at eleven.

Hopefully that's not bad news.

"Come in, Grant." Seth smiles at me from where he's sitting at the table in the boardroom. Malcolm is over by the window, chugging down coffee. He moves toward the table as I do, and I try not to be nervous as I sit.

"We're just waiting for… Here he is."

I look over my shoulder as the door opens and my boyfriend walks in. He looks as surprised to see me as I am to see him.

Dread sets in. Maybe this isn't about my work performance. Maybe someone's complained about our relationship.

"Okay," Malcolm says as Luke joins us at the table. "We'll keep this short, because we're taking up enough of your time today. Grant, we want to officially thank you for coming to us in March and asking for the audit. We trusted you on that, and it was the best thing we could have done. Aside from cleaning up your district—and congratulations on the amazing progress you're making—it's let us clean up the company. It's too early to be certain, but all signs indicate that things are going to improve across JU going forward."

"Thank you," I say, a little uncomfortable. "I just wanted to be able to do my job to the best of my ability."

Seth smiles. "And it looks like you are. Your numbers are great, and they've just been getting better."

Luke's hand lands on my thigh under the table, and he squeezes—right as Seth and Malcolm turn their attention to him.

He doesn't move his hand. I'm okay with that.

"Luke… as usual, you've delivered. I know the audit is far from complete, but as Mal just said, we're already seeing benefits from it. It's opened our eyes to how much we were neglecting this arm of the business, and that's something we want to avoid in future. We'd like you to work with Dominic to create a business consulting and internal audit sub-department here at JU once this audit is complete. He agrees that there's a need for internal control points, and we think having a small team onsite is probably the best option. The head of the team would report directly to you in LA."

My stomach sinks a little at the reminder that Luke's job here is only temporary. We've talked about it, and of course I plan to move to LA with him and the kids when they go next year, but part of me is a little disappointed that after all the work I'm putting in to get my district turned around, I'll have to leave when things start to shine. Plus, I like working in the same building as Luke, and there's just no guarantee I'll be able to transfer to head office. Exec job openings there are rare, because Malcolm and Seth run a tight ship and people enjoy working at Joy Inc.

"Actually," Luke says, "would you be open to the idea of me heading that team up myself?"

Malcolm blinks. He and Seth exchange glances. "Well… it would be a demotion for you. And we really need you in LA, running the department."

"What if I run the department from here? We're a

technologically advanced company. I've been overseeing the department from here for the last five months, and once the audit's complete, I'd actually have more time to devote to those duties. I'll be able to fly out if necessary, but honestly, I doubt it will be needed more than once or twice a year." He spreads his hands. "There's no need to make a decision now. I'll discuss it with Dominic, put together a plan and proposal for the new team and for a restructure of the department, and you can review that and see what you think."

Seth smirks. "I will take that option. Someone once told me never to argue with a business consultant unless they were unconscious."

I laugh, because Luke's said the same thing to me after he won an argument.

Shaking his head, Malcolm adds, "I'm not convinced it's the best idea, but I'm willing to give you the chance to change my mind." He looks between us. "I know it's none of our business, but are things good? The kids happy?"

"Yes. They've really settled here, and I'm reluctant to uproot them." Luke smiles. "I've settled here too."

Malcolm sighs, but he's grinning. "I guess you'll just have to convince me, then. Okay, well if neither of you has any questions…?"

I shake my head, and Luke says, "Not right now."

"Then we'll see you at the meeting later."

We get up, say our thanks and goodbyes, and leave the boardroom. Outside, I grab Luke's arm. "My office."

Once we're safely behind closed doors, I push him up against the wall and kiss him until we're both panting and mindless. When I feel him start to go pliant like he does when he's so turned on he'll do anything, I pull back and go to my knees.

He looks down at me in dazed confusion, but when I

open his pants and pull his cock out of his boxers, he lets his head fall back against the wall with a thud.

I lick the head of his cock, tonguing the slit in the way he loves, and he moans so loudly I stop and shush him. My assistant is right outside the door, after all.

Then I swallow him down.

Deep throating is a skill I'm particularly proud of, and one Luke admires. He expresses his admiration now by digging the fingers of one hand into my shoulder and grabbing my hair with the other.

I alternate taking him deep and sucking and licking, pausing once to blow on his wet skin, making him shudder from head to toe, and when I'm sure he's on the verge of blowing, I bring my hand into play and tease the sensitive skin of his sac.

He goes off like a rocket.

Once I've licked him clean and tucked him back in his pants, I stand and pull him into my arms.

"Wow," he gasps. "What's that about?"

"Incentive to convince Malcolm," I say, my face buried against his neck.

He laughs breathlessly and takes my face in his hands, raising it so I'm looking him in the eyes.

"I have all the incentive I need. I'm staying. We're staying. This will happen. We're going to have our happy ever after."

And we do.

Hi from Louisa!

Hey folks! Thanks so much for reading *In Your Hands*. I hope you enjoyed this latest installment in the Joy Universe series!

Huge thanks go to Ginger Connatser, whose name I borrowed for therapist Ginger, and to Sharon Heffernan, who named Matt.

If you want more from JU, Derek and Trav's book, *I've Got This*, and Dimi and Jason's book, *Follow My Lead*, are available now for sale and in Kindle Unlimited. I also have a sneaky little free novella set in JU—you can download it now by subscribing to my newsletter at https://claims.prolificwords.com/free/RplOchBm. You can unsubscribe anytime—or stick around for regular freebies and bonus content.

Or if you're looking for something different, give my Met His Match series a shot—charming European billionaires and hapless tourists are a lot of fun!

All my books can be read as standalone, but you'll meet recurring characters and can follow their journeys through the series.

Please take a moment if you're so inclined to leave a review for *Follow My Lead*. Reviews can make a huge difference to a book's visibility. And to find out more about me and my books, check out my website or visit my author group, Seymour Books with Masterful Men.

Hugs!

Louisa xx

Also by Louisa Masters

M/M:

Met His Match

Charming Him

Offside Rules

Joy Universe

I've Got This

Follow My Lead

Novellas

Fake It 'Til You Make It

Out of the Office

M/F:

An Irish Flirtation (Emerald Isle Enchantment)

An Irish Attraction (Emerald Isle Enchantment)

Writing as Olivia Ventura

Miss Fix-It

Catch a Shooting Star

About the Author

Louisa Masters started reading romance much earlier than her mother thought she should. While other teenagers were sneaking out of the house, Louisa was sneaking romance novels in and working out how to read them without being discovered. As an adult, she feeds her addiction in every spare second. She spent years trying to build a "sensible" career, working in bookstores, recruitment, resource management, administration, and as a travel agent, before finally conceding defeat and devoting herself to the world of romance novels.

Louisa has a long list of places first discovered in books that she wants to visit, and every so often she overcomes her loathing of jet lag and takes a trip that charges her imagination. She lives in Melbourne, Australia, where she whines about the weather for most of the year while secretly admitting she'll probably never move.

http://www.louisamasters.com

Printed in the USA
CPSIA information can be obtained
at www.ICGtesting.com
CBHW030959040524
8055CB00024B/182